Olive Oil & White Bread

Georgia Beers

Ann Arbor
2014

Bywater Books

Copyright © 2014 Georgia Beers

Bywater Books First Edition: June 2014

Printed in the United States of America on acid-free paper.

Cover designer: Bonnie Liss (Phoenix Graphics)

Bywater Books
PO Box 3671
Ann Arbor MI 48106-3671
www.bywaterbooks.com

ISBN: 978-1-61294-049-6

Olive Oil & White Bread

1988

The Way You Make Me Feel

One

Jillian Clark stood in the on-deck circle, waiting for her turn at bat and reflecting on what her friend Tinny had told her.

Left center's got a weak arm. If you get the chance to go home, take it.

It was her Thursday night softball league—the third time this week she'd played—and she felt strong. Content. It was mid-August. Summer was almost over; she was fresh out of college and ready to start her first real, full-time job. Life was good.

She took a couple of practice swings then squatted down to tighten the laces on her cleats when her peripheral vision caught movement and she stood up straight to look around. Two women walked together, chatting animatedly. One of them was Laura, a woman Jillian had met in passing. The other—took Jillian's breath away. All movement became sluggish, until Laura and the most gorgeous brunette Jillian had ever seen were moving in slow motion, like a scene from a romantic comedy. For Jillian in that moment, nothing existed except that beautiful woman. Body moving fluidly as she walked, she was tall and curvy—and completely out of Jillian's league. She wore cut-off jeans and a clingy chocolate brown T-shirt with a V-neck that showed a teasing peek of cleavage. The color of the shirt accentuated her large brown eyes and what had to be ten pounds of thick, wavy, dark hair. Her skin was tanner than Jillian would ever be in her lifetime, even if she spent every day in a tanning bed, and she smelled like a combination of scents that Jillian couldn't quite pinpoint, but was immediately drawn to: sandalwood, something tangy, musky, something spicy. The woman looked directly at Jillian as she sauntered by, still talking with Laura, and their eyes held for a beat longer than necessary. She gave Jillian a lazy, sexy smile and arched one dark eyebrow as she did it. It nearly melted Jillian into a puddle where she stood.

Then the moment was over.

Wow.

Jillian stared after the woman whose scent still lingered in Jillian's nostrils, her eyes locked so obviously on the retreating form that some of her teammates began to laugh.

"Batter?" she heard a male voice say. He sounded far away.

"Jillian." This time it was Tinny, and Jillian blinked rapidly, looked around, felt weirdly confused. She saw Tinny's face as she gestured madly toward home plate. "You're up, Romeo."

A quick glimpse into the bleachers told her that Laura and her beautiful friend had taken seats and were watching the game. *Now is the time to be impressive. Now or never.* "No pressure or anything," she muttered under her breath and stepped into the batter's box. Holding up a hand to the ump, she dug her back foot into the dirt, twisted it left and right until it felt even and sure in the spot. She glanced at her teammate preparing to lead off from first, then gripped the bat, took one practice swing, and crouched into her stance.

The softball gods smiled on her. She waited for the second pitch—following her cousin's advice to never, ever swing at the first one—and the second the ball hit the bat, solid and direct, Jillian knew it was a base hit. As the ball flew into deep right field, she ran hard, stopping easily on second base and bringing in an RBI to the cheering and applause of her teammates. It was hard to tell from where she stood, but she was pretty sure Laura and—more importantly—the gorgeous brunette were watching. *How about that stunning display of athletic prowess, huh? Interested yet?* She shook her head at her own cocky thoughts.

And the smiling of the softball gods pretty much stopped there.

The next batter popped out to the short stop, so Jillian stayed on second. With two outs, Tinny came up to bat. She was a big woman, broad-shouldered and thick-legged, and Jillian watched with a grin as the outfielders took a few steps back, intelligently so. True to form, Tinny crushed a pitch right down the middle toward the left center fielder. Jillian took off like a shot. As she approached third, Tinny's voice echoed in her head.

Left center's got a weak arm.

That was all she needed for her ego to take over, and she ignored the third base coach, who was giving her the "Stop Right Here" sign as clearly as she possibly could without jumping up and down screaming. Jillian blew past her, determined to make an impression on the beautiful stranger sitting in the bleachers.

Turned out, Tinny was somehow mistaken. The left center fielder made a picture-perfect throw that Jillian heard whiz by her head. The catcher had the ball in her mitt well before Jillian had even made the decision to take her out. They collided in a billowing cloud of dust and sweat and body hitting body, an unstoppable force hitting an immovable object. The sound from the crowd was a collective wince.

As luck would have it, the catcher was roughly the size of a small mountain. The 5'4" Jillian didn't stand a chance, like a cartoon character hitting a brick wall and falling flat. That's certainly how it felt.

"Out!"

Jillian knew it before she heard it. Cheers went up from the opponents' bench. Jillian laid on her back in the dirt and groaned as the cloud of dust settled around her, certain she'd broken every bone in her body—or at least most of them—and wondered if she'd ever be able to breathe normally again.

"Batter? You okay?" the umpire asked, not unkindly.

Jillian glanced at the bleachers. Laura and her gorgeous friend were nowhere to be seen. "Nothing shattered but my pride," she muttered, not quite sure if that was true. She gingerly flexed fingers and toes, then legs and arms, to make sure everything still worked. Tinny came up next to her and grasped her arm.

"You okay, Jill? Jesus, that was a hard hit."

"Thanks for the news flash. I thought you said left center couldn't throw."

Tinny grimaced as she pulled her friend to her feet. "Yeah, I meant right center."

"Perfect. That's just perfect." Jillian limped off the field with Tinny's help, in dire need of an ice pack and a beer, and trying to ascertain just how big the black and blue bruise on her outer thigh was going to be. She shook her head, irritated by the whole event, sure that since she'd never seen the gorgeous brunette before, she'd probably never see her again. She'd blown it. Big time. She was sure of it.

She was wrong.

ও ও ও

Angelina Righetti looked around in awe. Never had she been in a straight bar that was so completely filled with lesbians. In fact, now that she was what her friend Laura liked to call "officially out," it seemed like she was seeing short-haired, athletic, slightly masculine women everywhere. This, she knew (from some lesson in her college econ class) was an example of the Law of Attraction. Start thinking about a certain product and suddenly you begin to see it everywhere you look. For Angie, this had been most true of cars, but lately, it was happening to her with gay women.

"Sweetie, close your mouth," Laura said, interrupting Angie's thoughts. "You're going to draw flies."

Angie spoke louder than she wanted to so she could be heard over Guns N' Roses belting "Sweet Child O' Mine" from the jukebox. "Is it just me or is this place crawling with dykes?"

Laura's beer dribbled down her chin as she tried to drink and laugh at the same time. She looked around as she wiped her face. "It's not just you. It's Thursday. This place sponsors, like, four softball teams on Thursday. Softball equals us."

Angie nodded, still not quite used to being part of the "us." Not quite used to it and not quite comfortable with it, if she was going to be honest. It still felt so new to her, even though Laura said she knew the second they'd met at college their freshman year. Laura had proven the existence of her impeccable gaydar to Angie more than once, so she couldn't really argue with her, but it had taken her three-and-a-half years to figure out what Laura knew immediately.

"You've got a pretty wide selection here," Laura commented with a waggle of eyebrows. "See anything worth trying out? Taking for a spin, perhaps?"

Angie knew that her answer was no, but she made a show of looking around anyway, scoping out the "merchandise." Laura was determined to find her a girlfriend, whether Angie was ready for one or not. And Angie felt like Laura had been so patient with her over the years that she owed her at least the pretense of trying. So she continued to scan, stopping here and there then moving her gaze along. To her surprise, her eyes settled on a very pretty woman sitting at the bar, sipping a wine cooler. She wore cut-off denim shorts, much like Angie's, and her auburn hair was French braided down the back of her head. One smooth leg was crossed over the other, and Angie's gaze slid up from ankle to very shapely thigh.

Clenching her straw in her teeth, Angie said quietly, "Wow. She's pretty."

Laura followed her line of sight then gave her eyes a dramatic roll. "Leave it to you to find the only straight girl in the place. That's Carly's sister," she said, referring to one of the girls on the team they'd watched. "She watches all Carly's games, then sometimes comes out for a drink. Straight as an arrow."

"Oh." The straight girl. *Figures.*

"What about that one?" Laura jerked her head toward the corner of the bar where three jersey-clad women chatted loudly. "The one with the glasses. That's Shirl. She's single."

Angie shrugged one shoulder and the sound she made was non-committal. Shirl didn't really float her boat.

"And that's Chris. She just broke up with somebody."

Angie followed Laura's gaze over her own shoulder. "Which one? Redhead or short blonde?"

"Short blonde."

She was sort of cute, Angie noted. Boyish. Like Laura. She pressed her lips together and looked around the bar again. She liked cute. She loved athletic. But she didn't want boyish. Or masculine. Or butch. She hesitated to say so to Laura because she was afraid her friend would take it as an insult, but she couldn't help it. She knew what she found attractive and it wasn't a little boy.

"You know who was cute?" she asked Laura, a memory suddenly hitting her. "That blonde at the game."

Laura furrowed her brows. "Which one?"

"Little with a pony tail. The one who tried to slide into home even though she was out by six miles."

Laura laughed and shook her head. "That was such a boneheaded move. Who the hell was she trying to impress?"

"I don't know, but I hope she's okay. *She* was cute." Angie thought back, remembering how attractive she'd immediately found the blonde. She couldn't recall ever having been so physically drawn to somebody she'd never met—and she certainly wasn't going to tell Laura about it and set herself up for teasing—but as they'd approached the game, the blonde was in the on-deck circle and bent over to adjust her cleat. She stood up and then Angie noticed the ponytail sticking out the back of the hat; it was adorable. As they got closer, the blonde turned to look at Angie and smiled. Blue eyes the color of a clear summer sky, and dimples. *Dimples, for crying out loud. That's what did it: the damn dimples; they made her swoon.* Angie smiled back at her because she couldn't help it. The entire time Laura was talking to her in the bleachers, she watched the blonde. *Definitely my type. Definitely cute.*

"Yeah, she is. I'll give you that," Laura said with a nod. "Her name is Jillian. Her team is sponsored by a different bar, which is why she's not here. I don't know her that well, but I'll ask around, see what I can find out."

"Great." Angie didn't expect much, but showing interest in somebody seemed to make Laura happy, and it gave her something to do. Angie wasn't sure how she had ended up as Laura's personal mission, but sometimes she felt like she was disappointing her because she didn't just grab on to a couple of her suggestions and go crazy on them. Or let them go crazy on her. It just wasn't her way. It wasn't how she wanted to do things. Maybe she was old-fashioned, but she hated the idea of having sex with somebody she wasn't in love with.

What she hadn't told Laura was that she hadn't yet actually gone all the way with a girl. Not yet. It was a little odd and a lot embarrassing. She certainly wasn't a virgin. She was twenty-four, for god's sake, and she'd been with a couple different guys. She'd had a boyfriend in high school. She'd had another at the beginning of college. They were nice guys. She'd liked them both a lot. Sex with each of them was . . . well, it was there. At the time, she'd thought she was in love with each of them. Now she knew that she had just been doing what she thought she was supposed to do after being with a guy for a while. And though it was terribly clichéd to say it, it had been true: there was just something missing for Angie. She didn't think much about it at the time, had no idea exactly what it was until an unfortunate (or rather, fortunate, she thought now) game of spin the bottle at a frat party.

Jennifer Barclay, a breathtaking brunette with creamy pale skin and the most stunning green eyes Angie had ever seen—that was her name, and much to the intoxicated joy of their respective boyfriends, Angie's spin landed squarely on Jennifer.

Angie would never forget it. Jennifer's lips were soft, her mouth was warm and wet—and did she know how to kiss! Her hand slid up the base of Angie's neck and under her hair to hold Angie's face to hers. Angie cupped Jennifer's cheek, and it took every ounce of strength she had not to whimper when Jennifer slipped her tongue in and touched Angie's. Somewhere in the back of Angie's mind, she was sure the guys were going nuts, but to her, it was as if the world had gone silent. There was nothing but Jennifer's mouth and endless time.

To this day, Angie had no idea how long they had actually kissed. She would always believe there was no way Jennifer could have kissed her that way unless (a) she was harboring the same secret Angie was, and maybe didn't know it yet; or (b) she was already gay but was using the boyfriend as cover.

Regardless, Angie would be forever grateful to Jennifer Barclay. She had showed her, finally, exactly, what it was that Angie was missing with her boyfriends.

A girl.

Two

"Something smells good in here," Angie said as she entered her parents' house for Sunday dinner. Immediately enveloped in the scents of garlic and tomatoes, she closed her eyes and inhaled deeply. "Hiya, Pop." She kissed her father's cheek and watched him stir the sauce in the stockpot on the stove. Despite his lack of height, Joseph Righetti cut an imposing figure. Built like a bulldog, he was compact and muscular, and with his craggy complexion and buzz cut he radiated authority, even as he stood at the stove in a frilly apron, a dishrag over his shoulder. At his job as head of maintenance at the local high school, few employees disrespected him. But they didn't know his secret. They had no idea that deep down, Joe Righetti was nothing more than a big teddy bear, especially when it came to his daughters.

"Hey there, my girl," he responded, scooping up some sauce and holding it out for Angie to sample. He cupped his free hand below the wooden spoon and asked, "Enough salt?"

Angie smothered a smile as she blew on the sauce, then carefully tasted. He was always asking her if there was enough salt. Or pepper. Or oregano. Or garlic. And it was always just right. It was like a little dance they did each Sunday and Angie loved it. She let the sauce settle on her tongue, reveled in the perfect blend of seasonings, then gave one firm nod. "It's perfect, Pop. As usual. Mama?" As she turned to leave the kitchen in search of her mother, she snagged a meatball off the plate that was piled high with them.

Joe took a swipe at her with his dishrag. "Get!" he scolded as Angie laughed and rushed to escape.

"Mama! Pop's trying to kill me with the *mopine*!"

"Then stop stealing the meatballs," came her mother's matter-of-fact voice from the living room.

"I wouldn't steal them if they weren't so irresistible," Angie replied as she approached the couch and gave her mother a kiss, then bit into the ball of beef. "What are we watching?" She knew already it was likely a classic film; her mother loved the oldies.

"*Rear Window,*" she replied, her eyes not leaving the TV screen.

"Ooo, Hitchcock." Angie sat down next to her mother and munched down the rest of the meatball. She had seen the film more than once and knew it was almost over, so she sat quietly and marveled at the stunning beauty of Grace Kelly.

Across the hall in the den, Angie could see her brother, Dominick, watching the Giants game on a much smaller television, knowing better than to expect his mother to change the channel in the middle of her movie. "Hey, Dom," she called to him.

"Hey, Andi," he called back, raising his arm in the air as a hello but not turning around. He was barely three years older than she, and when the Righettis had brought baby Angie home, the closest he could come to saying her name was "Andi." It had stuck.

As "The End" came up on screen and her mother, Alice, blew out a breath, Angie asked, "What are you doing Tuesday night? Want to go see *Big*? I keep waiting for you, you know."

"That might work." Alice tapped her forefinger against her lips in thought. "Call me tomorrow, and I'll let you know." She stood. "Help me set the table."

"You hear that, Dom?" Angie called to her big brother. "Our mother is such a social butterfly, she isn't sure if she can go to the movies with me two days from now. I have to call her tomorrow. After she checks her schedule."

Alice pushed playfully at her daughter. "Stop that." As dark and Italian as Joe Righetti was, his wife was light and English. They were almost exactly the same height, though if pressed, Joe would swear he had an inch on her. Alice's hair was a light chestnut brown shot through with subtle gold highlights, and most of the time, she wore it in a simple ponytail. Her skin was pale as milk and dotted with faded brown freckles, and her light green eyes didn't miss a trick. Alice and Joe had divvied up their physical attributes pretty evenly among their four children. Dominick and Maria—oldest and youngest, respectively—favored their mother in coloring, though Dom inherited Joe's dark eyes. Tony and Angie—the middle children—looked completely Italian, all olive skin, dark hair, and rich brown eyes. The three oldest liked to tease Alice that she had waited to pass on her beautiful green eyes to the last child, and Maria never hesitated to rub it in.

Sunday dinner at the Righettis' house was a family ritual nobody missed without a damn good excuse. Tony arrived a few minutes later and was promptly handed a stack of plates. Joe may have been an Italian man who loved tradition, but he'd married a modern woman. Alice's sons were raised to do dishes, help with dinner, and clean bathrooms, just like their sisters. No gender gap between chores existed in her house.

"Maria coming?" Angie asked as she laid out flatware.

"She's working today." The pride in Joe's voice was evident as he brought in a giant bowl of linguini. Maria had been Joe's cooking partner in crime since she was old enough to operate the stove on her own. Now halfway through her senior year at culinary school, she was interning at a swanky restaurant downtown, learning the inner workings of a successful kitchen. Job offers were already pouring in. Angie was both proud and jealous of her little sister, but tried her best to focus on the former.

"Speaking of work," Alice said as she walked toward the phone in the kitchen. She tore a piece of paper off the pad and handed it to Angie.

The name *Vince Guelli* was scribbled on it in her mother's handwriting, along with a phone number.

Angie furrowed her brow. "Why do I need Mr. Guelli's number?" He was an old friend of the family, his face familiar to Angie since she'd been a toddler. Though they'd never had a deep conversation, she knew him. He was like family, in a distant uncle kind of way.

"He started up a new business last year, and he's looking for a secretary." With a shrug, Alice continued. "I know you don't love waitressing, and I know this doesn't really have to do with your communications degree, but you'd be off your feet. I'm sure he'd pay you fairly, and I believe there are benefits involved. It's up to you, of course."

Joe set the enormous plate of meatballs on the table next to the bowl of sauce and ordered the family to sit down. As they passed dishes around, they talked about what each of them had been up to, as well as the upcoming election.

"Jeez, Pop, could you have more Dukakis signs in your front yard?" Angie teased.

"I like the guy. What can I say?" Joe shrugged.

All the while, Angie was aware of the phone number in her pocket like it was scorching her pants. Vince Guelli had known her since she was born. If she asked him for a job, he'd probably give it to her, and the idea of getting away from the grind of food service was infinitely appealing. She already knew she would call him tomorrow.

ॐ ॐ ॐ

"Okay, let's get ourselves cleaned up," Jillian called out in the classroom.

Teaching art to six-year-olds wasn't so much "teaching" as it was "letting them make a mess." Though she found it slightly more rewarding to teach the third and fourth graders than the younger ones, Jillian's dream had been to teach older kids—high school and college—show them Rembrandt and Picasso and Pollack. She wanted to awe them the way she'd been awed the first time she went to a museum. But she'd seen the writing on the wall; her friends who were education majors were having trouble finding employment, and she knew she needed to grab on to whatever job she could. Art teacher at an elementary school. It was a paycheck, and right now, beggars could not be choosers. She took it, knowing she didn't plan on staying at the elementary level forever.

For the moment, this would have to do.

"*Now*, Stevie." The pungent smell of finger paint permeated the air as she took the blue away from a redheaded little boy, who made a groaning sound of annoyance. "I know. But you can finish it next week." A good teacher trick she'd learned from her fellow elementary educators: Rather than completely cutting them off, promise the next hour, day, week. By the time it arrived, chances were it had been forgotten by the child, who had a million other things occupying his mind.

It was the end of the day. The kids would be out of her hair in ten minutes, she could clean up her room—a task that always took ages— and then meet her friend Shay for a drink. She needed one. This job was harder, and more tedious than she'd expected it would be.

"Thank god it's Friday," she muttered as the kids' teacher came to collect them from the art room to take them back to their main classroom.

"Amen to that," Marina Bell agreed. "Let's go, kids. Line up." Unlike Jillian, Marina *loved* teaching the little ones; it was exactly what she wanted to do. But it didn't mean she wasn't utterly exhausted by the end of the week, as proven by the way she slumped against the doorjamb. "We still on for tomorrow night?" she asked.

As the only two right-out-of-college teachers in their small school that year, Jillian and Marina had instantly bonded. Despite leading very different lives, they had begun a fun, energizing friendship.

"You bet. I'll meet you there at seven?"

"Perfect. Looking forward to it. Okay, kids, let's go." As the little ones began a slow shambling out the door, Marina dropped her voice to a whisper. "Remind me that I have dirt to share."

"Tease," Jillian hissed at her as Marina winked and led her kids down the hall, single file. Jillian watched them go. Or rather, watched Marina go. The gentle sway of her round hips in the flowing skirt was hypnotizing. Her light brown hair was cut in a hip, short style, and Jillian often found herself wanting to touch it, just to see if it was as soft as it looked. She smelled clean, like laundry soap and fabric softener, and she needed very little makeup to accent her enormous brown eyes. *I know she's straight, but does that mean I can't look?* Jillian smiled at her own thoughts, then went back to cleaning up so she could get out of there and meet Shay.

AJ's was not busy. *Is it ever?* thought Jillian as she stopped inside the door and let her eyes adjust to the dim lighting. The stench of cigarette smoke immediately layered itself on her and she shook her head, annoyed that her entire outfit would have to go into the laundry after only a couple hours' wear. Not to mention the shower she'd need before bed if she didn't want the awful smell burrowing into her clean sheets.

The clacking of pool balls emanated from the back of the room. Two more blinks allowed Jillian to see Shay waving to her from the corner of the bar. Small in stature, Shayneese Jackson had a big personality and a quick wit. She'd gotten her hair cut back from the near-afro she had last time Jillian had seen her, to a light yellow accenting just the tips of her short, dark hair. Jillian smiled and went to her, arms open, then gave a hank of hair a gentle tug.

"Nice 'do."

"Thanks, you sexy thing," Shay said to her as they embraced. "Long time, no see."

"Too long." Jillian took the bar stool next to her as Shay motioned for the bartender.

"What'll you have?"

"Just a Mich is fine."

Shay ordered, then turned her full attention to her friend. "How are you? Hanging in there?"

Jillian grimaced. "You obviously heard the news."

"You know the lesbian grapevine. She left you for a guy, huh?"

"Yep. Just before graduation."

"You should have called me, you know." Shay's expression was stern.

"I know. I'm sorry. Honestly, I just didn't want to talk about it. I played a ton of softball all summer to keep my mind off the whole thing."

Shay took a slug of her beer as the bartender set a bottle in front of Jillian. Then she gave one nod. "Well, it sucks."

"Yes, it does."

"You know you're too damn good for her, right?"

"You don't know her."

"I know you." The gentle kindness in Shay's eyes nearly made Jillian's well up.

Jillian swallowed hard and nodded, trying to change the pain into annoyance but failed. "Yeah. Doesn't make it hurt any less, though."

Shay ran a single finger down the side of Jillian's face, softly tweaked her chin. They sipped in silence before Shay slapped the bar with an open hand and said, "Then here's to being single and moving the fuck on." Her dark eyes twinkled as she held up her bottle. Jillian couldn't help but smile at that look, and she clinked her bottle against Shay's.

"I'll drink to that."

"You'll drink to anything."

"True." Jillian could always count on Shay to make her laugh. Shay was five years older than Jillian and they hadn't crossed paths in school, but their houses backed up to one another's and their mothers were good friends, so they saw each other often. Jillian had spent many of her teen years examining what seemed to be some sort of crush she had on Shay. Then, when Shay came out to her family (and so, via her mother, to Jillian's), things only solidified for Jillian. It was essentially because of Shay that Jillian came to terms with her own sexuality.

"What about you? How are things going at the clinic, *Dr.* Jackson?"

"Yeah, don't you forget that title! I didn't spend eight years in college so you could call me 'ma'am,' did I?"

"I imagine not," Jillian said with a laugh. "So? Is being a veterinarian all you hoped it would be?"

"I love it. I *love* it. The hours are brutal, but I made it through school, so I think I can handle this."

"And have you used your new title to pick up any hot babes yet?" Jillian teased. Shay hesitated a split second too long, and Jillian caught it, squinted at her. "Tell me," she ordered.

Shay finished her beer, ordered another for each of them. "I did actually meet somebody."

"Shayneese! That's terrific." Jillian squeezed Shay's forearm. "At work? Is she a coworker? Because that might not be so terrific."

Shay pointed to her own face, the expression mock-serious. "Does this look like the face of a stupid dyke to you?"

Jillian shook her head, mimicking the stern expression. "Absolutely not."

16

"Thank you. She's actually a patient."

"A patient." Jillian waited.

Shay realized her slip and choked on her laughter, beer dribbling down her chin. "No! No, not a patient. A client. A *client*."

"Thank god we got that cleared up," Jillian deadpanned.

"She came in with her mother's cat a couple weeks ago."

"And she just happened to mention that she loved the ladies? Or did she wear a T-shirt that said *Big Ole Dyke*? How did you know she was gay?"

"Some smooth-ass detective work, that's how. She was not wearing a dyke T-shirt, but a volleyball T-shirt from a rec league over on the east side."

"So she might as well have been wearing a dyke T-shirt," Jillian interjected, well aware of the league and its high percentage of lesbian players.

"Do you want to hear the story or not?"

"Yes. Yes, I do. Sorry."

"All right, then." Shay shifted on the stool, making like she was preparing to tell a very important tale. "I pointed to the shirt and asked her if she played volleyball. She said yes, that she'd been playing since she was in high school, and she'd been so happy to find a local rec league. I told her I was looking for a rec league, too, and where was hers?"

"Wait a minute." Jillian held up a stalling hand. "You don't play volleyball. You're too damn short, for starters."

"Hey. Watch yourself, girlfriend." She winked. "A little white lie in the name of investigation."

"Ah. I see. Continue."

"So she told me that she plays at that little school across from the hospital. So I tell her that, now that she mentions it, I *have* heard of that league, and I even know a couple of the women in it. And I start dropping names."

"Names of lesbians."

"Exactly." Shay pointed at her, then took a drink from her bottle. "And?"

"She knew every last one of them."

Jillian shoulder-bumped her, and they laughed. Shay finished up the story, telling how she'd gone to watch the woman play, and they'd had drinks twice already. Jillian studied her friend carefully as she spoke, and a knowing smile spread across her face.

Shay blinked at her. "What?"

"You like this girl."

The flush that hit Shay's cheeks was visible even on her dark skin. Jillian could see the smart-ass retort come and go, and then Shay simply nodded. "Yeah. Yeah, I do. She's funny and smart and adorable. Yeah. I like her."

Jillian wrapped an arm around Shay's shoulder and gave her a squeeze. "That's great, Shay. Really. I'm so happy for you, and I can't wait to meet her."

"I'm glad you feel that way because you won't have to wait long. She's meeting me here in twenty minutes."

Nineteen minutes later, when the door opened, Shay's face lit up.

"She's punctual, I'll give her that," Jillian said teasingly to Shay.

A cute, boyish blonde walked up to them and gave Shay a hug, then a quick, chaste kiss on the lips. "Hi."

"Hey, baby," Shay answered. "This is my good friend, Jillian Clark. Jill, this is Laura Schaeffer."

The two shook hands, both squinting at each other, each trying to place the other as Jillian scooted back to make room for Laura to sit between them.

"Have we met?" Laura asked.

"I think so, but I've been struggling to remember where," Jillian replied.

They laughed and tried hard to figure out their connection, as Shay ordered drinks and watched them quiz each other.

"Wait," Jillian said finally. "Do you play softball?"

"I used to until I blew out my knee," Laura replied. "But I watch a lot. Go to the games. I bet I've seen you play."

They decided that that was as close as they were going to get to a definitive answer and they settled back, still chuckling and now more familiar with one another.

Jillian sipped her beer and enjoyed the show, realizing that she'd never really seen Shay so enamored with anybody. Her hand was constantly touching Laura; whether on her arm, her shoulder, or her thigh, contact was unremitting. When Laura spoke to Jillian, Shay watched her face as if looking at a masterpiece, something awe-inspiring and breathtaking. It would have been ridiculous if it wasn't so damn sweet. Jillian was happy for her dear friend.

Well, mostly happy. There was a tiny part of her that was envious. Jealous, even. Aware that she was seeing something she missed terribly.

Yes, she knew that she was still young, that there was plenty of time to find permanence. But more than anything, she knew what she wanted, what would make her happy—and it didn't matter that she wasn't even twenty-three yet. She wanted somebody to look at her the way Shay was looking at Laura. She knew that. With every fiber of her being, she knew it.

It seemed like a simple enough request.

She'd felt that way about Linda, her college girlfriend; at least she'd thought she had. Totally, completely, utterly in love. She knew that the look on her face when she'd looked at Linda was an exact replica of the look on Shay's face right now. Jillian had had that, and she'd loved it. She'd like to have it again. What she *hadn't* had was reciprocation. Linda looking back at her the same way, the way Laura gazed back at Shay, that same adoration in her eyes, she hadn't had that. But she wanted it. And what was even more, she wanted to be *worthy* of that look.

Jillian sighed, watched her friends as they laughed at some inside joke, and the warmth in her heart grew.

Yup. I want that.

1989

When I See You Smile

Three

"Good afternoon, Logo Promo, this is Angie. May I help you?" Angie listened, then nodded. "Sure. Hang on while I transfer you."

The small office bustled, and Angie loved it. The ringing phone, the conversations coming from various offices, the copier and fax humming. It was like a machine, the smells of new carpet and freshly brewed coffee taking the place of motor oil and gasoline, and Angie was proud to be a part of it, even if she was overqualified to be the receptionist.

When she'd called Mr. Guelli last fall, she didn't have the first clue what an advertising specialties company was. Some kind of advertising had been her one and only (and lame) guess. She was half right. Logo Promo was a new business that did exactly what its name implied: It promoted companies' logos. A business opening a new location might want to give something out with their name on it, a pen or key chain or calendar. If a company had a crew that did business off-site, landscaping or house painting maybe, it might want imprinted shirts, or something that showed passersby exactly who was doing the work. If an office sponsored an event, it was good publicity to advertise by giving away a mug or a water bottle or decorating with imprinted balloons. Logo Promo had connections around the country with suppliers who specialized in making all those items. LP's salespeople acted as middlemen and placed orders with the suppliers for the products that would then ship to their clients. A pretty simple system, but a surprisingly successful one. Angie was astonished by how many companies used advertising specialties—"trinkets and trash" as they called it.

The gentle *ping* of the door alarm sounded, and Angie looked up to see Gary, the mailman.

"Morning, Angie," he said in his always cheerful tone. He placed a rubber-banded stack on her desk.

"Thank you, Gary."

"Beautiful day out there."

"You'd say that if it was a blizzard," Angie chuckled at him.

"You're right. I think being alive is better than the alternative, so I'm going to enjoy every single day, rain or shine." Two knocks on her desk and then a wave. "See you tomorrow." He smiled a greeting to a tiny woman he passed in the doorway, and was gone.

"I think he's a robot," Hope Maynard commented to Angie on her way past the front desk. "Nobody is *that* cheerful *all* the time." Hope was the only woman on the sales staff at Logo Promo. At just over five feet tall, she probably weighed in at a hundred pounds, soaking wet. She worked hard and played harder, and she and Angie had become instant friends.

Forty-five minutes filled with phone calls and copies went by before Angie had a chance to get to the stack of mail. Half of it consisted of supplier catalogs and she separated those out for sorting later. The rest would be invoices and—hopefully—checks. With her letter opener (emblazoned with the blue-and-white Logo Promo logo), she zipped open the mail piece by piece and divided it into piles. The last envelope in the stack was a little bit thicker than the average invoice, and once Angie opened it, her mind began to race. She spread the textured parchment paper out on her desk and read through the cover letter a second, a third time.

It was attached to a resume.

More than that, it was attached to a résumé from a person she knew, Chris Avanti, a boy from her high school, somebody who'd been just a year behind her.

In any normal situation, she'd feel bad for opening mail that wasn't addressed to her. But in cases here at work, unless something was marked *Personal and Confidential*, she opened all of it. That was part of her job; it was *literally* in her job description. This résumé had been addressed to Mr. Guelli, yet here it sat, on her desk, making her rethink her position at the company.

When she'd started at Logo Promo almost six months ago, it was going to be temporary. Of course, she'd never said as much to the person hiring her, but that was her plan. *Take this receptionist post and make a little money. When something better—something more in tune with my degree—comes along, I'll take it.* A genuine interest in the business wasn't something she'd expected. A tiny desire to manage a business began to form, something she'd never entertained before in her life, and *that* had been unexpected.

And now this. This résumé.

She looked at it again. The cover letter mentioned that Chris had heard Mr. Guelli was looking to hire another salesperson, and though he had no sales experience, he thought he could do a good job, that he'd be an asset to the company.

"*I* am an asset to the company," Angie whispered. Before she could stop to think, she was on her feet and walking down the short hallway to Mr. Guelli's office. His door was open, his head bent over the papers on his desk, a small clock radio blaring a baseball game too loudly. He looked up when she knocked on the doorjamb.

Vincent Guelli looked about ten years older than he was, thanks to the salt-and-pepper donut of hair that circled his head and the extra pounds of paunch that stretched his belt. He smiled at her.

"Angelina."

"Can I talk to you?"

He turned the radio down and gestured to the two chairs angled toward each other in front of his desk. "Of course."

Wordlessly, she handed him Chris's résumé and cover letter.

Mr. Guelli donned his half-glasses—another item that did nothing to promote his real age—and read. When he finished, he looked up at her. "Okay. And?"

Angie wet her lips and fleetingly thought, *Here goes nothing.* "If you hire him for the sales position, I'll be really upset."

Mr. Guelli removed his glasses and raised an eyebrow, waiting for her to continue.

"I have the same degree as he does. Communications. And he has no sales experience. Neither do I, but I do have experience *here*. I've learned a lot about this company and this business in the short time I've been here. I think that gives me a legup on him." She cleared her throat, hardly able to believe what she was saying. "Let me give the sales position a shot. Please. I can do a good job. I can make you money."

That was the clincher. She could see it in his eyes, even when he told her to let him think about it, and that he'd get back to her later in the day. When all was said and done, he was in this business for no other reason than to make money. She knew that, and she had used it. She knew the job was hers. Her parents would be proud.

She was finally moving up in the world.

ȣ ȣ ȣ

"'The Dimpled Pickle'? Really?" Hope shook her head as she handed Angie a beer. "What did it used to be?"

"AJ's," Angie replied. "And as far as I'm concerned, that's what I will continue to call it."

"'The Dimpled Pickle'. What the hell were they smoking when they came up with that name?"

"I'm not sure I want to know."

"I'm embarrassed for your people."

Angie laughed. "Me, too."

Hope held up her beer bottle. "Here's to you, babe, and having another chick in the sales department. Thank god! Now I can talk about my period, and I won't be met only by blank stares or un-comfortable squirming."

They clinked glass and drank. It was Friday night. Hope would begin training Angie in sales on Monday. Since Angie had no existing accounts of her own, Mr. Guelli had hired her on at a small salary—very small—and a commission that was a percentage of the sales she brought in. Plus, he'd given her a handful of small leads. She knew her arrangement was different than the other salespeople, who were mostly on straight commission and with a percentage much larger than hers, but she was thankful for the chance. If she worked at it, she should be able to bring herself in some decent cash, enough to tide her over until she figured out what she wanted to do with her life. She was certain selling "trinkets and trash" wasn't it, but it would do for now.

"Does our usual bet stand tonight?" Hope asked, winking. She settled her diminutive form on her barstool with her back against the bar, while Angie sat forward propped on her forearms.

"No," Angie said firmly. "No way. This is my night for celebrating, not watching while my straight friend gets hit on at the lesbian bar a dozen times more often than I do. *Yet again.* My ego is happy tonight. It does not need to be shot down."

"Fair enough," Hope said with a nod. "You do know it's because you intimidate these poor women, right?"

Angie snorted. "Yeah, that's me all right. I'm so intimidating." She punctuated her words with an eye roll.

Hope leaned in closer. "Most beautiful women are."

Angie felt herself flush and took a pull from her beer.

"I, of course, am special and therefore undeterred by your stunning good looks," Hope went on in her best theatrical tone while Angie grinned. "And if you had that one thing I require of my lovers, I would swoop in and ruin you for all other women."

"Hair on my chest?"

"The other thing."

"Oh yeah. That. I could get one, you know."

"I prefer the real thing, my dear."

"Damn my luck."

They sat looking at each other with twin expressions of joy in their friendship, which was still new but definitely a keeper.

"I've got to hit the little girls' room," Hope said. "Order me another?"

Angie ordered another round and spun on her stool so she could look around the bar. It wasn't busy. Honestly, she wasn't sure it looked any busier—or much different—than when the previous owners had managed it. A small group of older women played pool. A young couple stood in front of the jukebox with their hips touching, bouncing to the Paula Abdul song it broadcast. A burst of laughter emanated from the group at the corner table. Angie squinted at them, wondering if she knew any of them. There were five women, and they seemed to be around her age, or not far from it. Two were an obvious couple, hanging all over each other. The brunette looked vaguely familiar, but Angie couldn't place her. The lighter brunette didn't ring a bell at all. The blonde . . .

Angie swallowed her beer wrong, and turned back around on her stool as she coughed. Trying to cough quietly, or not at all, was no easy feat, but she managed to keep it together. Hope returned to her seat, took one look at Angie's red face and watery eyes, said, "What the hell happened to you?" and rubbed a hand over Angie's back.

Several moments later, Angie finally felt like she could speak. "Ugh. Down the wrong pipe."

"I hate when that happens." Hope dipped her head to catch Angie's eye. "You okay?"

"I think so." Angie took a deep breath. "Now I'm just embarrassed. I hope nobody saw me." She hazarded a glance toward the corner table, but nobody seemed to be paying her any attention. Of course. "I need your advice," she said to Hope.

Hope's eyes twinkled. "I am nothing if not helpful."

"Remember I told you about that softball game last summer? The one my friend dragged me to watch?"

"Even though you hate all things sports-related? Vaguely, yeah."

"Hey, keep your voice down! They can take away my lesbian card for that."

Hope chuckled.

"Remember I told you about that cute blonde?"

Hope squinted as she searched her memory banks. "Oh! The one who slid."

"That's the one."

"I remember you talking about her, yes."

"She's sitting at the corner table with her friends."

"She is?" Hope whirled in her seat. "Where?"

Angie ducked her head down like a turtle trying to retreat into its shell, at the same time grabbing at Hope. "Would you stop being so obvious? Jesus."

"You should go talk to her," Hope said, an unspoken "duh" in her tone.

Angie sighed. "I can't. Too forward. What if she's with one of those other women?"

"Hmm. Good point." Hope took a swig from her beer, thinking. "Maybe we go the old-fashioned route."

Angie raised her eyebrows in question.

"Send the girl a drink."

It was the right call, Angie knew. Her stomach flip-flopped anyway as Hope gestured to the bartender and asked what the blonde was drinking. She did all the work and then pointed to Angie. "It's from her." Angie grimaced at the bartender and received a sympathetic smile in return.

"I can't look." Angie kept her back to the table, surreptitiously glancing at Hope every now and then, as her friend had no qualms about sitting once again with her back to the bar and openly watching the corner table. "God, you're so obvious."

"Well, *somebody* has to see the reaction. Okay, she's got the drink. The waitress is pointing. The blonde is looking."

"Oh, god. This was a mistake."

"No, no. It's okay. She's smiling. Now I'm pointing to you. The whole table is looking over here."

"Christ."

"And she's lifting her glass. Mouthing 'thank you.' Nice." Hope turned back around. "I like her. And you're right. She's very cute."

"I can't believe I did that," Angie said, wishing she could crawl into a hole and disappear.

"Did what? You didn't do a thing. I did it." Hope bumped Angie with her shoulder. "It was good," she said, more serious. "Now she knows you're interested. That was the idea, right?"

With a nod, Angie finished her beer, vowing never to turn around again. "One more?" At Hope's agreement, she put in another order. "So, let's get my mind off of all this. Tell me about work. What can I expect on Monday?"

It didn't take long for them to fall into a comfortable conversation about the job, the company, the customers. Hope had been in sales for nearly ten years, though in the ad specialty business for only five. Angie was infinitely grateful that she was the one who would be training her. She knew Hope would be patient and thorough even as she furrowed her brows, lowered her voice an octave, and threatened, "Don't even think about slacking, little missy. I will have none of that from you. You will work hard and do what I tell you, or I will have you fired immediately." The absurdity of little, tiny Hope Maynard, with her funky glasses and mismatched earrings, swigging a beer while trying to sound harsh and intimidating made Angie burst out laughing. Two seconds later, Hope was right there with her.

As they pulled themselves together, wiping tears, still grinning, the bartender approached them. She slipped a folded piece of paper to Angie and said, "From the woman you sent the drink to."

Angie kept her hand on the paper, her heart in her throat, as Hope swiveled to the corner table. "They're gone."

"I can't look."

"Oh, my god, you are utterly ridiculous, you know that? It's a piece of paper. Look at it!"

"What if it tells me to fuck off?"

"Then it does. So what? Stop being such a wimp."

"Okay." Deep breath in, slow breath out, she unfolded the paper:

Jillian Clark
716-555-0217
Call me.

Four

Angie was not naïve; she knew sales was a tough trade. But it took a week and a half before she closed her very first order. It was more difficult than she'd anticipated.

Today, though. Today was a good day. She'd closed a sale. Her very first one. The order wasn't large, but it was hers. She'd cold-called the company, gotten transferred to the right person, given her pitch. Hope kept telling her timing was everything, and such was the case with Jones Tree. She'd spoken to owner Matt Jones himself. Turned out, his company was fairly new in the landscape business, and he needed to outfit his team. He asked her to bring him some samples of T-shirts. She obliged.

One of the things she'd really envied the salespeople when she'd first started working at Logo Promo was their freedom. They came and went as they pleased, visiting clients and suppliers. Nobody punched a clock. For the most part, they were autonomous. On bright and sunny days, the idea of hopping in her car and zipping along to a client meeting seemed appealing.

Today, she got to experience that for herself as she headed out on her very first sales call.

Matt Jones was a terrific first customer, because he was as new to all of it as Angie was. They laughed as they each stumbled over details. He had a bare bones logo design that needed help. She'd forgotten to bring color options for the shirts. In the end, he'd placed an order for fifteen T-shirts for his five-man crew and one full-zip sweatshirt for himself. They shook on it, he gave Angie a deposit, and she headed back to the office to tell Hope the good news, smiling all the way.

Now, in her apartment, she popped open a beer to celebrate while the mouthwatering scent of garlic and basil from the pizza in the oven filled the miniscule galley kitchen. It was silly to be so giddy. She knew that. The order was tiny by most standards. Her commission would total out at *maybe* twenty bucks when all was said and done. She didn't care. It was still a successful day. It was still a step forward. It was still a taste of what was possible for her. What if she sold fifty T-shirts to somebody? A hundred? More? Hope wrote up an order for a thousand pens the other day and netted herself a couple hundred dollars in commission. From one order! That was the beauty of the ad specialties business. The possibilities were endless. The money was there. You just had to work hard to get to it.

Angie was nothing if not a hard worker.

Using an oven mitt, she took the pizza—her father's homemade—out of the oven to see if it was heated through yet. He and her mother had been so proud of her, she felt like a kid again bringing home an "A" on a test. They hugged her and kissed her and told her to keep up the good work. She smiled as she remembered their faces, her mother telling her the sky was the limit for her. As she plopped onto her couch with a plate of pizza and turned on the television, she thought, *Yeah, the sky may be the limit, but I need to get a bit higher—and fast. Twenty-dollar commissions aren't going to pay my rent. Unless I get a few dozen of them a week.*

"Then I'll get a few dozen of them a week," she said aloud, with determination, refusing to let reality creep in on her good mood. Instead, she savored the pizza, tried hard to solve the puzzle on "Wheel of Fortune" (failed), and finished the beer. As she set the empty can on the table next to the couch, her gaze fell on the piece of paper that had been sitting there for several days.

Angie picked it up, caressed the neat handwriting with her thumb, and saw a flash of blonde hair and dimples. In a split second, she decided to take advantage of the wave of self-confidence she was riding before it washed down to nothing and she became her insecure self once again. She picked up the handset and dialed as quickly as she could, not wanting her fear to catch up to what she was doing.

As the ringing began, Angie nibbled on the side of her thumb and prayed for an answering machine to pick up.

"Hello?" A female voice.

Angie tried to speak, but croaked instead. She cleared her throat and tried again. "Hi, is Jillian there?"

"I think so. Hang on." Rustling sounds followed. A thump. A muffled voice called, "Jill! Phone!" A moment or two crept by. Angie's palms began to sweat. Just as she considered hanging up and trying another time, noise that sounded like somebody had dropped the phone clattered in her ear. A muttered curse. Then a voice.

"Okay. I've got it."

"Um, hi. Jillian?"

"Uh-huh." A little bit of an edge to her voice.

You're annoying her. Pull it together, Righetti. "Um, hi. This is Angie. Angie Righetti."

"I'm sorry, who?" Confusion now.

Realizing Jillian would have no idea what her name was, Angie cleared her throat again. "Yeah. I, um, I bought you a drink at AJ's a week or so ago? You gave me your number? Remember?"

"Angie. . . ." She said it like she was thinking, trying to grasp something. Then, "Oh. Oh!" Jillian's voice lost its edge immediately. "Of course, I remember. It took you long enough to call. I was beginning to give up on you. Angie." She was teasing, that much was obvious. Angie felt herself warm from the inside.

"I know. I know, I'm sorry. I'm . . . a little . . . I've never done that before. Bought a drink for somebody I've never met. Took me a while to work up my nerve."

"Well, I've never given my number to a complete stranger before, so I guess we're even."

The way she said it, playfully accusing, like it was Angie's fault Jillian had handed over her phone number, made Angie smile like a schoolgirl. "I guess so."

A few beats went by. Jillian said, "So, Angie."

"So, Jillian."

"Are you going to ask me out or what?"

Somehow, rather than making her even more nervous, the mischievous lilt in Jillian's voice gave Angie strength, made her feel brave. "I was thinking about it."

"Good. I was thinking about saying yes. Where should we go?"

"Well, how about we start with someplace neutral?"

"Ah, I see. That way, if we decide we can't stand each other, we can retreat easily. I like it. It's smart. Safe."

"How about we grab a drink at AJ's—er, The Dimpled Pickle—during Happy Hour on Friday? Then, if we're enjoying ourselves, we'll get some dinner."

"And if we're not, we're free to leave or mingle or whatever."

"Exactly. What do you think?" Angie held her breath.

"I like it. What time?"

Angie shrugged, even though Jillian couldn't see it. "Seven?"

"Works for me. Should we meet there?"

"Good idea. That way, we're each free to go when we want to."

"Perfect. I'll see you Friday at seven."

Jillian's voice softened. "I'm really glad you called."

ﾠ ﾠ ﾠ

The bar was hopping, surprisingly, but Jillian knew it would only get busier; she hoped it wouldn't get much smokier. The older crowd was always in first, the dykes stopping in for a beer after work. As the night progressed, they'd go home and make way for the younger crowd. At almost twenty-four—and gainfully employed—Jillian couldn't imagine doing the old take-a-shower-at-ten thing in order to stay out dancing and drinking until two in the morning. No, these days, by two in the morning, she wanted to be long asleep.

I'm getting old. Already.

The thought made her smile as she took a sip of her beer. She never liked those hours. She was a morning person. She could remember pulling only two all-nighters in college, and those were only because her friends were studying for the same test and they'd promised to stick together. Jillian had been barely able to function, let alone retain the information they were poring over.

She'd arrived at the bar a little early, mostly because she wanted to be able to snag a couple barstools before the crowd took over. Also because she was nervous and ready too early and couldn't stand the thought of wandering around her house, killing time until seven. Plus, she'd had more than enough ribbing from her two roommates, enough to make her wish she'd never mentioned the gorgeous brunette from last summer or that Angie and the gorgeous brunette were one and the same. She would never live that down, especially if things with Angie went anywhere.

Just thinking about that game, that ridiculous slide she never should have attempted, made her grin. She had really wanted to impress that stunning woman. She was sure she'd blown it, and she'd given herself half a dozen bruises in the process. And now, months and months later, that same stunning woman had asked her out. What were the chances? She'd assumed she'd never see Angie again after that fiasco at the softball game, sure that she'd solidified herself as a complete and utter idiot in Angie's mind.

But that smile.

She couldn't get it out of her head.

That sexy, mischievous smile—Jillian had thought she'd never see it again. And then she'd come here last week, received a complimentary drink from "the brunette at the bar"—and there she was. Not smiling, unfortunately. Looking almost ill, in fact, but that didn't matter to Jillian. It was all she could do to keep from running up to her and spilling out how she never thought she'd see her again, asking her out right there on the spot. But she hadn't been alone, and thank god, Jillian had kept her cool, pretending to waver over leaving her number, though it wasn't even an issue. She was leaving it, whether her friends thought she should or not.

No call had come.

Jillian had been ridiculous about the phone for the next three days. Nobody was allowed to stay on it longer than a few minutes at a time, because what if the gorgeous brunette called and she couldn't get through? And then she gave up and didn't try again? What would Jillian do then?

She was lucky her roommates hadn't killed her in her sleep.

A full week passed, and Jillian had just about given up on ever hearing from the brunette. She was depressed and saddened, but trying hard to just suck it up.

Then the call had come.

And now, here she sat, alone, nursing a beer, hoping she didn't look too pathetic. She gave monosyllabic answers to the butch who approached her to strike up a conversation until the poor woman received the "Not Interested" message loud and clear and wandered back down the bar to lick her wounds. Jillian slid her empty bottle across the bar and raised her hand to the bartender when a voice spoke up behind her.

"I'll have a white wine, please."

Jillian turned, her gaze meeting soft brown eyes.

"Hi," Angie said, taking in the empty bottle. "Am I late?"

Jillian shook her head. "I'm early. Hi." She put her order in with the bartender, then turned to give Angie a quick once-over, wanting to look at her without seeming like she was leering. Angie wore black jeans that hugged her full figure like a lover, a plain gray T-shirt, and a black leather jacket, an outfit that was simple but effectively fashionable. Her dark hair was loose and full, skimming her shoulders in a cascade of brunette that Jillian wanted to bury her face in. Her makeup was subtle, but there, accentuating those beautiful eyes and the full lips Jillian hadn't had the time to take in during the softball game. And she smelled delicious, woodsy without being flowery, a little musk, subtle but sexy. "Wow," Jillian said before she could help herself. "You look amazing."

A gentle pink flushed Angie's cheeks, and she blinked down at her boots. "Thanks," she said quietly. "So do you."

Jillian gestured to the barstool next to her. "Sit. Please." Angie settled herself on the stool as their drinks came. Jillian slid the wine glass to her, then held up her beer. "Here's to finally getting to meet you in person."

"I'll drink to that."

They clinked and sipped and eyed one another as they did so.

"So, Angie."

"So, Jillian."

"Tell me about yourself. What do you do?"

36

"I'm in sales for an ad specialties company." At Jillian's furrowed brow, she explained. "We sell anything to companies that they might want to put their logo on." She looked around the room, then settled on the wine glass in her hand, emblazoned with the Dimpled Pickle logo. "Like these. We could sell these." She made a face. "Actually, I *should* sell these. I wonder if they're buying from a gay salesperson. Hmm . . ."

Jillian chuckled at Angie's sudden distraction. "I know the owner. I can give you her name."

"Really? That'd be awesome. What about you?"

"I'm an art teacher."

Angie cocked her head with a grin. "Not at all what I would have guessed. You don't look like a teacher. Not any teacher I ever had, anyway." She winked.

It was Jillian's turn to blush.

"What grade do you teach?"

"Right now, I'm teaching little kids, elementary. Kindergarten through fifth grade. I really want to teach high schoolers, though. Or even college. I'd love to teach art history or art theory. I just have to wait until the time is right. And the little kids are fun. They're so . . . *open*, you know? Like, the world hasn't jaded them yet, so they're not worried about who's going to think what about their art. They just *create*. It's kind of awesome to see." Angie was watching her with a rapt expression on her face. "What?"

Angie shook her head and drank some wine. "Nothing. I just . . . I like the way you talk about your work. You've got passion around it. I don't think that's common, you know? You're lucky."

Jillian smiled.

"Tell me about your family," Angie said.

They talked for nearly three hours without a break, learning about one another, sharing themselves. As the bar got busier and louder, their proximity got closer until they ended up facing each other, Angie's knee between Jillian's thighs, Jillian's knee between Angie's. Jillian couldn't remember the last time she'd felt so comfortable with somebody, not even Linda. She thought Angie felt almost as comfortable with her, judging by the way she touched Jillian as she spoke, laying a hand on her arm, her knee. At one point when Angie was talking about her sister, Jillian reached out and sifted some of that dark hair through her fingers. Angie stopped mid-sentence and swallowed.

"Sorry," Jillian said, still holding the silky hair. "I've just wanted to see if your hair is as soft as it looks since the first time I laid eyes on you at that softball game."

"Is it?"

"Absolutely."

Angie stifled a chuckle.

"What?" Jillian asked.

"The softball game."

Jillian covered her eyes with her hand. "Oh, god."

"I still can't believe you tried to make it home." Angie was laughing openly now.

"I know. It was so stupid."

"What in the world were you thinking?"

They were both laughing now, and Jillian noticed the way Angie's eyes crinkled in the corners. "I was trying to impress you," she said.

Angie stopped laughing and looked at her. "You were?"

"You don't remember me other than for my stupid slide."

"Oh, I *do* remember you. Other than for your stupid slide. I remembered you for a long time after that game. I didn't think you noticed me at all."

Jillian raised her eyebrows in surprise. "Are you serious? You gave me the sexiest smile on the planet. What do you think made me do something so dumb?"

Angie put her elbow on the bar, propped her chin in her hand, and looked at Jillian. Then she wet her lips with her tongue. Their gazes held. Hot. Intense.

Finally, Jillian spoke, saying quietly in a husky voice, "I want to be alone with you."

"I know. Me too."

"I have roommates."

"I don't."

Another beat passed. Jillian stood quickly, pulled some bills from her pocket, and tossed them on the bar. She held her hand out to Angie, who took it without hesitation. "Let's go."

࿇ ࿇ ࿇

For the first time in her life, Angie silently thanked her mother for being somewhat of a neat freak. Angie hadn't really expected to be bringing somebody home tonight, but her apartment was tidy regardless, because that's the way her mother raised her. All the whining and stomping and complaining she'd done as a kid every time her mom told her to fold something or dust something or clean something fell by the wayside as she praised all the stars in heaven that her home was presentable.

"You've got a nice place," Jillian said, setting her jacket on the arm of the couch and nodding as she looked around.

"Thanks," Angie said. "My uncle owns the house, so he gives me a break on rent. Otherwise, I'd probably have a roommate or two."

"Yeah, I can't afford a place on my own yet, so it was either get a couple roommates or move back in with my parents after college. And *that* was not going to happen."

Angie scoffed. "No way. I love my parents, but I couldn't wait to get out and be on my own." She watched as Jillian's gaze traveled the living room. She ran her hand over the slate blue couch, then gestured to the matching, overstuffed chair and ottoman.

"These are really nice. Soft."

"They're hand-me-downs from my older brother. When he landed a job in a law firm, he celebrated by buying himself leather furniture for his place. So I got these. I don't want to think about what he's probably done on this couch." Angie winced, wanting to take back the words as soon as they left her mouth, but Jillian laughed.

"Oh, my god. You're probably right."

Angie nodded, catching Jillian's smile, nearly swooning over the dimples that marked each cheek. *God, she's sexy.*

Jillian plopped down, spread her arms across the back. "Yeah, he's totally done stuff on this. Comfy." She looked up at Angie with those blue, blue eyes.

39

Angie cleared her throat. "Can I get you something to drink? I think I have a couple beers. And some Coke."

Jillian shook her head and patted the couch next to her. "Come here."

Hoping Jillian couldn't hear her swallow, Angie did as she was told and sat next to Jillian, close enough to fit under the arm draped across the back. With her other hand, Jillian reached toward Angie and played with her hair like she had at the bar. She kept her eyes on her own fingers for long moments, then gave a chuckle.

"You make me nervous," she admitted, surprised by her own shyness.

Angie's eyes widened. "*I* make *you* nervous?"

They laughed together, and Jillian's voice dropped to a near whisper. "You're just so beautiful. You take my breath away." Her cheeks flushed a deep pink, and she looked down to hide her embarrassment. "I know how corny that must sound, but it's true. I feel like I don't breathe right when I'm around you."

Angie had never felt so revered in her life, the feeling rushing through her like a warm wave, and the only thing she wanted at that moment was to erase the discomfort on Jillian's face. Before she could stop herself, she lifted a hand to Jillian's neck, stroked a thumb along her jaw line, and moved in to kiss her.

Never before had Angie Righetti made the first move. Not with the boys she had dated in high school. Not with the young men she tried to date in college. And not with Patti, the first woman she had dated in college . But something about Jillian gave her confidence, and she was smart enough to not stop and analyze it. She kept the kiss gentle at first, tentative, taking the time to feel the softness of Jillian's lips, to taste the hint of beer still clinging to her mouth. Gradually, she deepened things, pushing a bit more firmly, requesting access that Jillian gave immediately, eagerly opening to Angie. When their tongues touched, hot and wet, Angie caught her breath as desire coursed through her like a fire. It caught her by surprise, but she relaxed into it, let it heat her from the inside, and she pushed harder, the kiss becoming demanding, intensifying, both women breathing heavily until Jillian was on her back and Angie was braced over her, their mouths never parting. It was carnal and raw and so incredibly hot, and for the first time since the spin-the-bottle game at the frat party in college all those years ago, Angie followed her instincts.

And her instincts were telling her she wanted this woman.

Badly.

All of her.

It didn't even cross her mind to take the poor girl to the bedroom. Her want was too close, too immediate. She wrenched her mouth from Jillian's and grabbed at her vest and T-shirt, pulling them up, revealing a smooth expanse of belly that she rubbed a palm over. She dipped her head and poked her tongue playfully into the belly button.

"You have an 'inny,'" she lifted laughing eyes to Jillian.

Not to be outdone, Jillian grasped the hem of Angie's T-shirt and pulled the entire garment over her head and off, leaving Angie breathing raggedly in her black bra, her own "inny" exposed.

"So do you." Jillian cocked an eyebrow and smiled, and those damn dimples sent Angie's arousal through the roof once again. She peeled off the rest of Jillian's clothes, baring her completely on her living room couch, forcing herself to take a moment and just look. Just stare. Jillian's body was gorgeous. Lean, athletic, but gloriously female with ample breasts and rounded hips. Her nipples were pink and the triangle of hair at the apex of her thighs was light and curly.

"God, you're beautiful," she whispered.

Jillian smiled, then made a gesture with her finger. "And you're overdressed. Off. Now."

Angie stood and stripped off her own clothing in seconds. Before she could resume her position, Jillian held up a hand. "Wait." Angie stopped. "I just want to look." Angie could almost feel Jillian's eyes on her, traveling from her head down her neck, stopping at her heavy breasts. She'd never been a small girl, would never be a small girl, but she was proud of her body. She was round in some places, had curves in others, and had always hoped the person she ended up with would love her for them. Jillian's gaze moved over her as if she was studying a priceless piece of art. Reaching her toes, Jillian finally looked back up into Angie's eyes and said simply, "You are stunning. Come here." And she opened her arms.

Their lovemaking was wonderful and hot and awkward all at once. They started out quickly before stopping to breathe and then resuming at a more reasonable pace, taking the time to explore one another's bodies, to figure out what each of them liked and what didn't work. Jillian came first, gasping for breath in Angie's ear, gripping Angie's shoulders as Angie's fingers moved through her wetness. Angie closed her eyes as it happened, thinking the sound of Jillian having an orgasm was the most beautiful music she'd ever had the privilege of hearing.

She had little time to revel in it, though, because Jillian had barely caught her breath before she slid her own hand down Angie's stomach and into the slickness that waited there. "Don't look too satisfied," she teased in a whisper. "I give as good as I get." Angie wondered if she should tell Jillian that just the sound of her voice—all sexy and bossy like that—was making her think she'd sprung a leak between her legs, but all coherent thought was driven from her mind when Jillian slipped inside her.

"Oh, my god," Angie ground out, her hips moving of their own accord. Patti had never been there—*inside.* She'd never let her get that far. But with Jillian, she not only wanted that, she wanted more.

More.

She wanted to give more. She wanted to take more. She lifted her head and kissed Jillian deeply, pushing her tongue in as far as she could, wanting to devour this woman, heart and soul. Then she pulled back to look her in the eye. Picking up the rhythm, she rocked on Jillian's hand, felt Jillian's thumb pressing against her, and kept their eyes locked together. It was only a matter of a few short moments before Angie tipped over the edge into oblivion, crying out Jillian's name, one corner of the couch's throw pillow crushed in her fist.

They lay for a long while, until their ragged breathing returned to almost normal. Worried about squishing Jillian, Angie lifted herself up enough to roll off the couch onto the floor, taking Jillian and the afghan with her. Jillian tucked her head under Angie's chin as Angie covered them with the blanket.

"Wow," Jillian said.

"I second that."

Angie smiled against her hair, and they lay quietly, the only sound the ticking of the wall clock. Jillian's breath became even; Angie was sure she was asleep. That's when it felt safe to say it.

"I've never done that before," she whispered.

"Done what? Slept with a woman on the first date?"

Angie swallowed, caught. "Or that."

"I'm not following."

"I've never done . . . that. Felt that."

Jillian lifted her head so she could look at Angie. A mischievous gleam appeared in her eye. "Had an orgasm?"

"Well, no. I've had an orgasm before." Angie cleared her throat. "Not from somebody else, though."

Jillian's eyebrows flew up. "Really? Never?"

With a shake of her head, Angie said, "No. I never let Patti get that far."

"Patti?"

"The woman I dated in college. She was nice, and we made out a lot, but I was always just a little bit too scared to go any further than that."

Jillian nodded thoughtfully. "And did you date guys?"

"I did, but you know." She shrugged. "They were guys."

Propping her head in her hand, Jillian asked, "So. I'm the first woman you've been with? Like this?"

"Yes." Angie tried to tamp down the panic that bubbled up. "Is that bad?"

"No, of course it's not bad." Jillian brushed a strand of Angie's hair off her forehead. "In fact, it's really kind of awesome. I've never been somebody's first before. I'm kind of liking that."

Angie chuckled, hoping her relief wasn't too obvious. "I think you're letting this go to your head."

"Oh, I totally am. So have you never *given* a girl an orgasm before? Because you seemed to know exactly what you were doing, let me just say."

"Well, thank you. No, you're my first there too."

Jillian shifted, moving her body atop Angie's, and took one of Angie's nipples into her mouth, nibbling playfully. "If you've never gone all the way with any girl before me," she began, shifting across to the other nipple and sucking hard enough to make Angie catch her breath. "Then oh my"—she rocked her hips a little, forcing Angie to open her legs to accommodate her—"how lucky am I?" With that, Jillian raised herself to her knees, pushed Angie's thighs as far apart as they'd go, and leaned down. At the first touch to her center, Angie sucked in every particle of air her lungs would hold. Her hips lifted as if trying to reach more of Jillian's mouth. The hot wetness and probing tongue set her heart to racing and her fingers to grasping at Jillian's head, fisting handfuls of her blonde hair as a groan ripped up from deep in her throat.

"Holy Mary, Mother of God," Angie whispered. "Oh my god, Jillian. Oh my god." She swore she could feel Jillian smiling against her own wet flesh. It became impossible to tell exactly where Jillian's tongue was touching her, where her lips met Angie's own skin, how much moisture was her and how much was Jillian. Angie knew nothing but sensation. Hot, beautiful, sensual sensation. And just when she thought she might spontaneously combust, when she was sure her arousal couldn't possibly surge any higher, Jillian pushed her fingers inside—deep inside—her tongue playing over the hot, sticky wet, and Angie exploded.

ॐ   ॐ   ॐ

The clock on the nightstand read 3:24 as the two of them lay spent in Angie's bed, having finally abandoned the living-room floor for something more comfortable. The intention had been to get some sleep, but they'd made a mutual decision that one more orgasm was necessary first.

Now they lay entwined with one another and Angie's limbs felt like they were made of pudding. Very heavy pudding. Jillian's blonde head was pillowed on Angie's shoulder, her breathing deep and even. Angie stroked her fingertips absently along the smooth skin of Jillian's shoulder as she lay awake, reliving the night in her mind and trying to analyze the surprising emotion simmering inside her.

Was it possible to fall this quickly? She didn't really know Jillian, and yet she felt like she did. Was that weird? Was it simply because of the sex? The awesome, limb-melting, mind-blowing sex? Was that obscuring the logic with which she should be looking at the situation? Was she being a U-Haul lesbian cliché? Because at that moment, she never wanted to move a muscle again. She would be perfectly content to stay in her bed with Jillian's warm, naked body wrapped around her own forever and a day.

Angie mentally shook herself, told herself to stop being so silly. She was twenty-five years old, not sixteen. Fairy tale romances happened only in trashy novels, and love at first sight didn't exist. She needed to just take a chill pill or she'd send Jillian screaming into the street to get away from a crazy, clingy lesbian.

Jillian shifted slightly in her sleep, and then a tiny grin turned up the corners of her mouth, causing just a teasing peek of her dimples. Angie swallowed hard, and in her mind, threw in the towel. It was over, and she knew it.

She would do anything to see that smile.

Anything.

1991

Love Will Never Do (Without You)

Five

The entire house shook, causing Jillian to fly down the stairs, worry etched on her face. Something had obviously fallen, she just didn't know what. "What was that? What happened?"

Shay and Laura looked like they'd collapsed onto the couch, Shay sprawled like a rag doll, Laura with her legs hanging over the arm.

"Your couch weighs a fucking ton. That's what happened." Laura groaned. "I think I broke my spine."

"Good thing your girlfriend's a doctor, then," Angie commented as she came around the corner from the kitchen to grab another box, looking only slightly frazzled.

"You are due for your rabies shot, aren't you?" Jillian teased.

"Oh, har har," Laura said. "By the way, why don't you guys buy a house and move in the dead of fucking winter? That's a good idea." She rubbed her hands together.

"You know what?" Angie said. "I think we will. And you know what else? We'll ask our closest, dearest friends to help us."

"And they will. Because they're giant suckers." Shay winked at Jillian, then hauled herself off the couch and swatted at Laura. "Come on, baby. Just a little bit more left in the truck."

"I think my ears might have frozen off. Let me know if you see them on the ground outside."

"I told you to wear a hat," Shay scolded her.

"I'll order the pizza in twenty minutes," Angie called to them as they headed out the front door. "Promise."

Jillian noticed the big furniture truck pulling up out front. "Honey," she called into the house. "I think the bed's here."

Angie gave a little girl squeal as she came up next to Jillian.

A big, burly man with shoulders as wide as both girls standing side by side knocked his snowy boots on the front steps, then came up to the door. "Ms. Clark?"

"That's me," Jillian said.

"I've got a queen-size bed and box springs?"

"Yup."

"Can you show me where it's going?" He bent to untie his boots.

"Oh, no," Angie said. "Please. Don't worry about that. We've been tracking in and out all day."

They led him into the house to the stairs. Before he even took a step up, he made a sound in his throat and shook his head.

"What's wrong?" Jillian asked.

He took his tape measure out and measured the stairway, the wall, the ceiling. He continued to shake his head and finally announced, "The box spring won't fit."

"What?" Angie looked crestfallen, though her voice hitched up a notch.

"See this angle here?" He pointed to the space between the ceiling and the half-wall that formed one side of the stairway. "The angle's too extreme. Box springs don't bend like a mattress."

Jillian glanced at Angie, whose eyes were filling with tears. She always cried when she was frustrated or stressed, and moving had proven very stressful. Jillian squeezed her forearm and said to the man, "What are our options?"

"Well, I'd suggest you order a split foundation. That's a box spring, just in two pieces instead of one."

"Can we do that with you?"

"Sure. Could take up to four or five days to get it."

Angie made a sound in her throat. Jillian squeezed her arm harder. "But you can bring the mattress in right now, yes?"

"Sure can."

"Perfect. Let's do that."

He gave one curt nod and went outside to get the mattress.

Taking Angie's chin in her hand, Jillian looked her in the eyes.

"Baby, it's fine. No worries. We can sleep on the mattress until the box springs get here. Okay?"

Angie cleared her throat and nodded. "Okay. Sorry. I'm freaking a bit."

"I know." Crisis averted, Jillian kissed her quickly on the lips and went to see if Shay and Laura needed more help. Another car was pulling up out front. "Looks like your parents are here, sweetie."

Angie went through the kitchen to open the side door for her mother and father, Jillian right behind her. "Hey, you guys."

"Angelina," Angie's father said in his signature, singsong way. Nobody said Angie's name quite like her dad. "We come bearing gifts."

"Oh, my god, Pop," Angie said over her mother's shoulder as she hugged her and sniffed the air. "Is that your pizza?"

"You know your father," Alice said. "He was afraid you'd order from those Parelli brothers around the corner. You know how he feels about them." She turned, and held her arms open to Jillian.

"They wouldn't know how to make a good pizza sauce if my own grandmother taught them," Joe muttered, his disdain for the local pizza chain always clear.

"Your timing couldn't be better," Jillian commented, her voice muffled by Alice's shoulder. "Our box springs won't fit up the stairs, and our movers are starving. Food will definitely help everybody calm down a little bit. Just"—she slid boxes and papers and garbage around on the counter to make room—"here. Put it here."

Alice came up behind the two of them and held out a bottle of champagne. "This is for you to celebrate. It's not for everybody. Just the two of you. Later."

Jillian's heart warmed, and Angie kissed her mother on the cheek. "Thanks, Mama."

"I'll put it in the fridge."

"Doctor Jackson," Joe called as he headed into the living room. "I thought you were above all of this. How did they rope you in?"

Jillian smiled, watching as Angie's mother dodged the bed guys and joined her husband in the living room, to talk to the women bringing in the final boxes from the truck. A surge of pride and thanks washed through her. The house was small but adorable, and just right for her and Angie. Their furniture was mismatched, their dishes were all hand-me-downs from family members, and their hodgepodge of blue and yellow towels didn't come close to matching the green and beige bathroom. But the house was theirs. They were moving into their own place. Together. They'd been squished into Angie's tiny one-bedroom for nearly a year, and there just hadn't been enough room. Angie wanted a bigger kitchen. Jillian needed a place for her art supplies.

"I can't believe how fast this has all happened," Angie's mother was saying as Jillian tuned back into the conversation. "It seems like you just decided to move yesterday."

"Two months," Angie clarified. "Started looking, found this house, put in an offer, closed. All in the space of two months. I can't believe my head hasn't exploded clean off my body by now."

"Neither can I," Jillian agreed with a wink.

"It was utter insanity."

"But it's the perfect house for us and worth all the stress. Admit it."

"I admit it," Angie said with feigned reluctance, her arm around Jillian's shoulders.

The house was more than they had hoped for. Small, only two bedrooms, but gorgeous hardwood floors, gumwood trim, an enclosed front porch, and a master bedroom with a vaulted ceiling and skylights. With Jillian's regular teacher income and Angie's commission (getting better and better the more sales she made), things might be a little tight to start, but the two of them would be okay.

Forty-five minutes later, delivery guys gone and a lone mattress on the floor upstairs, the six of them sat in the living room, paper plates of Joe's homemade pizza in their hands, bottles of Bud Light all around.

"Thank you all so much for your help," Jillian said, holding up her beer. "We so appreciate it, and we couldn't have done it without you. We owe you."

They all held up their bottles.

"And we will collect," Laura said. As the crew chuckled, she added, "And Mr. R.? This pizza? To die for."

"You remember that the next time you want to order from Parelli's," Joe told her.

Angie shook her head with a grin, watching her parents, while Jillian watched her, searching for words but unable to describe the love and thanks in her heart at that moment. Emotion clogged her throat, and she swallowed it down.

"Jillian," Alice asked, breaking the spell. "Have your parents seen the house yet?"

Jillian shook her head. "No. Not yet. Maybe next week." Alice nodded, but made no comment.

They finished up their meal, the time peppered with much laughter. Afterwards, Joe offered to take the moving truck back so Angie and Jillian could rest and Shay and Laura could be on their way.

"You're the best, Pop," Angie said, hugging her father. "Thank you."

"I can't believe my little Angelina owns her own home now," he said, and the seriousness in his voice was a testament to the emotion he was feeling. "You kids are all growing up so fast." He reached out and pulled Jillian into the hug. "My girls."

"Don't go getting all sappy on them, Joe," Alice said, grabbing his shoulder. "Leave the poor girls alone. They're tired." Over his shoulder, she winked at them. "I'll be over tomorrow to help you with the kitchen."

Angie nodded. "Thanks, Mama."

"Thanks, Mama," Jillian echoed. Alice's grin widened, and she patted Jillian's cheek.

Jillian and Angie stood on the porch and waved as everybody pulled away. Then Jillian closed the front door and turned to Angie.

"So. Here we are," she said. "*Alone.*"

"Finally," Angie said, opening her arms, then wrapping them around Jillian. "In *our* house."

Jillian smiled, placed a kiss on the side of Angie's neck. "Doesn't it feel weird?"

"It kind of does. I mean, I feel like a grown-up now."

"That's exactly it," Jillian said. "I feel like this is the final step from old teenager to real adult." They stood quietly in each other's arms. "We own a house."

"We do. Together."

Jillian pulled her head back to look at Angie. "I think it's time to pop that champagne."

They grabbed the bottle, two plastic cups, and headed up to the bedroom. In the doorway, they stood looking down at the mattress. When their gazes met, they each burst into laughter.

"Just our luck, huh?" Jillian said, shaking her head.

"I'm getting some sheets." They quickly threw some bedding on and pulled their down comforter out of the garbage bag it was packed in.

Looking down at the bed, Jillian said, "Well, it's bigger than that double we had at your apartment."

Angie flopped down on it. "And more comfortable."

"That's because it's not fifty years old like the other one." Jillian sat next to her and opened the champagne.

"Don't throw that cork away," Angie said, taking it from her.

"What are you going to do with it?" Jillian poured two cups.

"You'll see."

Jillian held up her cup. "To us and our new home."

Angie looked into her eyes and said softly, "I love you." They kissed sweetly, then sipped.

Jillian lay back on the mattress, letting her eyes wander across the vaulted ceiling and enjoy all the knotty pine, and big wood beams. Skylights let in a soft moonlight, and Jillian breathed a contented sigh, knowing this beautifully crafted house belonged to her now. "When we first looked at this house, and we came up here, do you know what my first thought was?"

Angie stretched out next to her. "What?"

"That I wanted nothing more than to make love to you under these skylights."

"And now?"

"I want to make love to you under these skylights."

Angie cuddled close and pulled the comforter over them.

They fell asleep.

Six

"It just makes me crazy. I've been waiting for more than two years."
Jillian set her glass down on her mother's kitchen table with a thud.

"At least you were able to get a teaching job right out of school,"
her mother, Liz, said, sipping from her china coffee cup. "A lot of
people are out of work."

Jillian sighed. "I know, Mom. That's not my point."

"I know what your point is. I'm just saying, you shouldn't look a
gift horse in the mouth."

"I'm not." Jillian stopped herself, feeling her frustration build and
her voice rise. She mentally counted to five. "I'm just saying they
promised me first shot at a high school opening, and then they hired
somebody else. From outside."

"What does that mean, anyway?" Ted Clark stood at the butcher-
block kitchen counter and refilled his own cup with the remainder of
the coffee from the pot. "What the hell is a gift horse exactly? Have
you ever seen one? I haven't."

Jillian smiled. It was just like her father to try to allay any tension
that cropped up between her and her mother. A full-time job for him,
she was sure.

He kissed the top of Jillian's blonde head as he sat down at the
head of the table. "Don't you like teaching the little ones?" he asked.

"Actually I do. Sometimes, it's fun. I just wanted something else,
you know? I thought I'd be doing that by now."

"Well, if you get fed up, I can always teach you the ins and outs
of real estate." Her father ran his own real estate company and had
done quite well for himself. So when her brother, Brian, was laid off

from his job at a local advertising firm, he had joined the company and gotten his real estate license.

"I know, Dad. Thanks, but I think one Clark kid is more than enough for you to handle. Two of us in your office would drive you over the edge."

"Your brother has been doing very well there. Hasn't he, Ted?"

"I'm sure he has," Jillian said before her father was dragged in. "I was just kidding."

"How's the house coming along?" Ted asked.

Jillian appreciated his attempt to change the subject, though his choice of topics didn't help with the tension. She dove in anyway. "It's great. We've done a lot in the past month. Painting and unpacking and arranging furniture. Then rearranging the furniture." With a chuckle, she turned to her mother. "Just like you used to do when we were little. Remember how often you rearranged the living room?"

Liz nodded, tight-lipped, and sipped from her cup.

"I'd love for you guys to come and see it." Unable to stand the fact that her mother wouldn't look her in the eye, Jillian turned to her father. "Maybe you could take a look at the furnace, Dad? It makes a weird sound, and we'd love to save the money a service call will cost if we can."

"Sure, sweetheart. I'll give you a call this weekend."

An uncomfortable silence hung around them, but Jillian was determined not to let it pull her down. Part of her wanted to ask her mother, point blank, when she was coming over. She wanted to tell her that Angie's mother had been to the house every weekend since they'd moved in to help unpack things, arrange cupboards, hang curtains. She wanted to yell, to cry, to show her mother that she was hurt by the obvious lack of interest.

Instead, she stood and took her glass into the kitchen. "Okay. Time for me to head out."

"You don't want to stay for dinner?" Liz's expression said she'd simply expected Jillian would.

"Oh, I'd love to, Mom, but Angie's making her famous lasagna. It's to die for. I wouldn't miss it for the world." She'd meant it to sting, and she could tell by her mother's face that it had. So why did she feel no satisfaction?

She gave each parent a kiss on the cheek and left. Once outside—and not for the first time—she was amazed at how much easier it was to breathe.

ॐ ॐ ॐ

Later that evening, Jillian and Angie sat at their breakfast bar counter and ate lasagna.

"I don't know why you let them get to you like that," Angie said.

"I don't let *them* get to me. I let *her* get to me. I always have." Jillian put a forkful from her second helping into her mouth and chewed. "I don't know why. She has this . . . this . . . power. I don't know what it is, but she can make me feel like I'm eight years old again just like that." She snapped her fingers to punctuate the statement.

"You just want her approval," Angie said. "We all want our mothers' approval. It's a basic need."

"I guess." Jillian continued as Angie headed to the refrigerator. "She's always been tough on me, but when I came out? God, I thought she'd disown me right there."

"But she didn't."

"Not officially. She thought I was simply copying Shay. Can you believe that? I really think she thought it would pass. We just never talked about it again. That's my family's M.O. We never talk about anything that involves feelings or emotions."

"God, my family can't talk about anything *without* feelings or emotions."

Jillian laughed. "We couldn't really have come from two more opposite ends of the spectrum, could we?"

"I don't think so. And now, to change the subject." Angie pulled a bottle out of the fridge. "Ta da!"

"Champagne?"

"Well, not exactly champagne. Sparkling wine. Not as fancy, but still something with celebratory bubbles."

"And what's that for? Why do we need celebratory bubbles?"

57

"Think about it," Angie hinted, making a rolling gesture with her hand.

Jillian scrunched up her face, wracking her brains before gasping. "Did you get the Solomon program?"

"I did."

Jillian squealed and jumped off her stool, running over to hug Angie, who joined in the squealing, and together they hopped in a squealing circle. "Baby, that's great! I am so proud of you. How many quotes did you end up sending all together?"

"Six, for god's sake." Solomon was a huge payroll company and Angie had met with the head of marketing four separate times before they chose her. "You know how exhausting all the meetings and paperwork were. But today? Totally worth it."

Jillian opened the wine and poured, then held up her glass. "To my girl, the most awesome," she lowered her voice conspiratorially, "not to mention the sexiest, saleswoman around. Way to go, baby doll."

They touched their glasses together and sipped. Angie took the cork, grabbed a Sharpie from the drawer, and wrote the date and the occasion for the celebration on it. Then she dropped it into a big glass jar on the windowsill, where the cork dated with their move-in date already sat.

"You know," she said. "A program like this means pretty steady orders. I hope. And you know what steady orders mean?"

"Steady commission," they said in unison.

Angie went on. "It'll make a nice supplement to my measly paycheck. And if I can work hard and grow this program, we only go up from here."

∂∘   ∂∘   ∂∘

Angie rolled over in bed. The clock read 1:17, and she sighed heavily. She couldn't seem to shut off her mind. The Solomon logo, in all its reflex blue glory, popped brightly into her head. Again. With a sigh of frustration, she quietly got out of bed, donned sweatpants and a baggy sweatshirt, and padded downstairs in her bare feet. She would never get to sleep if she didn't dump some of this detail out of her head. Pad of paper and pen in hand, she curled up on the couch under the afghan her grandmother crocheted and began to list the things she needed to do.

A long while later, Angie exhaled slowly, set her pen down, and read the list. There. A bit better. There was so much to do; this was an enormous undertaking and creating the list had already alleviated much of the panic that had set in. This was the biggest account she'd ever had, and though she felt like she had a good handle on the business, it still made her jittery and nervous. Hope was confident in her. And proud of her; she'd told her so. Jillian's pride was obvious. Mr. Guelli? Angie had expected he'd be happier. After all, the Solomon account meant a nice profit for Logo Promo. Oh, he'd congratulated her with his signature pat on the behind, but still she didn't feel like he considered her an equal to some of the salesmen, as she'd been hoping. Stupidly, she was beginning to understand.

I'll just have to show him, she thought. *I'll make him a ton of money, and then he'll have no choice but to see that I'm good at this.*

Even in her head she sounded like a petulant child, but she didn't care. This account was a big deal, and she was proud of landing it. And Jillian was proud of her for landing it. That's all that really mattered in the grand scheme of life. She laid her head back against the arm of the couch and closed her tired and scratchy eyes.

"Honey. Come on. Angie."

Angie inhaled deeply and opened her eyes. Jillian's blue eyes looked down at her with concern, hair disheveled, clad in white boxers with light blue pinstripes and a blue tank top. She looked delicious. "Hi," Angie croaked.

"What are you doing down here?" Jillian asked, a flash of hurt zipping across her face.

Angie sat up, stretched. "I couldn't sleep and didn't want to wake you up with all my tossing and turning and sighing." She handed Jillian the list, explaining what had prompted her to make it. "I'm sorry, baby. For what it's worth, I would have much rather been in bed with you."

Jillian kissed her quickly on the lips. "Well, it's after six. You wanted to get in early today, right?"

Angie's eyes widened. "Yes. Crap." She kicked off the afghan and beelined for the stairs.

"I'll bring up your coffee," Jillian called after her.

Seven

The second bedroom was perfect for Jillian's studio. She stood in the middle of the square room, a fingertip between her teeth, and studied each of the walls. She'd painted them a creamy Navajo white, nice and neutral and calming. Deciding on the wall to the left, she used a small level to help hang one of her own paintings, a small abstract in hues of blue and green that had been an experiment at first, but ended up being a piece she was rather proud of. She marked a spot for the nails, tapped two of them in with a hammer, and hung the large canvas.

"Perfect," she said softly to nobody.

The late October sky was growing dark beyond the two windows that during the day let in copious amounts of natural light. Jillian frowned at the twilight, already missing the long days of summer. Winter would be here in no time.

With a sigh, she checked to see if anything else needed adjustment. "What else could I possibly want to do with my Friday night than arrange things?" she asked the empty room. She'd unpacked every-thing over the past few days and the room felt good to her, inviting. She could be creative here. Canvasses, paints, charcoal, paper, easel, desk, everything had fit. It was a bit crowded, but it felt warm and cozy, which was what she'd hoped for. She didn't have a lot, just the basics, because she didn't consider herself an artist—more an aficionado who liked to dabble. She would never sell her work because, honestly, she wasn't all that good; she simply enjoyed creating it.

Jillian didn't love spending this much time alone, but Angie was doing well with the Solomon account, and word of mouth from the Solomon higher-ups was bringing her new clients. That was the beauty of the kind of sales job she had; if she pleased a client, they told their friends. More clients meant more business meant more money. It also meant more schmoozing. She often took clients to lunch, dinner, drinks, insisting that this was all about image. A successful, friendly, generous image. She came home exhausted, but happy.

There were days, though, when Jillian didn't want to forgive the late nights. Yes, Angie was working her butt off. Yes, Jillian was proud of her, but sometimes all she wanted was Angie home, sitting across the dinner table from her, the two of them talking about their day. That was the partnership she wanted. That's what she'd signed up for.

She hadn't embarked upon this relationship so she could spend this much time by herself while her girlfriend wined and dined people she hardly knew.

She tried not to feel like this.

Mostly, she managed.

It was nearing 7:30. Dinner had been a tuna sandwich, since Angie had told her that morning she'd be running late tonight. At the sound of the door downstairs, Jillian peeked out the window and saw Angie's car. A wave of relief washed through her, warm and comforting, as it always did when Angie came home.

"Where's my woman?" Angie's voice boomed up the stairs, low and comical, bringing a grin to Jillian's face.

"Up here, babe."

Following her footsteps up the hardwood stairs, Angie appeared in the doorway. Her black suit still looked fresh—or at least fresher than it should have after a twelve-hour workday—but Angie looked decidedly tired. A faded darkness underscored each eye, and she didn't lean on the doorjamb so much as fall against it. But her dark eyes sparkled, and her smile was genuine. "How's my girl?"

Jillian set down her tools and walked the handful of steps into Angie's waiting arms. "Better now." She snuggled in, burying her face in Angie's neck. "How was your day?"

Angie squeezed her tightly. "Brutal. Guelli was on the warpath. God, he's getting cranky in his old age. My jacket order for Matt Jones is *still* not done. I asked Ivan to show me some art three days ago, and he has yet to get to it. I'm sorry, but after three months, you're not the new graphic artist any more. He has not impressed me. He's disorganized, arrogant, and slow." She shook her head, annoyed. "I'm beat," she said and blew out a breath. "However…" A mischievous grin appeared. "I have something for you."

"For me?"

"Is anybody else in this house having a birthday this week?"

"Hmm." Jillian scrunched up her face, a show of thought. "No, I can't think of anybody."

"Well, then, I guess the little surprise I have is for you. Come with me." Angie led her by the hand down the stairs into the living room and stopped. "Okay. Stay here. Close your eyes."

Jillian did as she was told.

"No peeking." Angie waved her hand in front of Jillian's face.

"I'm not." Jillian listened as Angie moved away from her into the kitchen. There was some rustling of some sort, then what she was sure was a whimper. She furrowed her brow, trying to figure out from the sound what her girlfriend was up to. Finally, she heard Angie come back and stop in front of her.

"Okay. Open." Angie stood with a small, white puppy cradled in her arms. "Happy birthday, baby." The dog turned its head toward Jillian, its eyes a clear hazel color.

"Oh, my god," Jillian said quietly. "You are *beautiful*." She let the puppy smell her hand, get used to her scent, then leaned her face in. "Hi there, sweetheart." Glancing up at Angie, she said, "You're sure?"

"I just wanted it to be the right time," Angie told her. "Here. She's all yours." She handed the puppy over to Jillian, who immediately cuddled her. "She's a pit bull-terrier mix, so she won't get very big. I was going to get you something purebred, but I went to the Humane Society and saw this one and her siblings, and I just couldn't walk away."

It was just what Jillian would have done herself—adopt instead of buying—and she loved Angie even more for it. She held the warm body close. The puppy's fur was almost nonexistent, but what was there was white, thinly layered over soft, pink skin. Her feet and her head were too big for her little body, all out of proportion, which made Jillian smile as she brought a paw to her lips and kissed it. The puppy watched with big, clear eyes. "You look like a little ghost, you know that?" she said to her. "I think your name should be Boo. What do you think? Hmm?" When she looked up, Angie was watching with a big grin.

"I knew she was the one for you."

"I can't believe you did this," Jillian said, and was surprised when her eyes welled up. "Thank you. I love you so much."

Angie gathered the two of them in her arms. "I wanted to do something special for you. You've been so great about work, but I hate that you're here alone. Now you won't be." She touched her lips to Jillian's. As she did so, Boo stuck her nose in, as though wanting to be a part of the kiss. Both women broke away laughing. "I got everything we need, I think," Angie said, and led Jillian to the kitchen. On the floor sat dishes, a bag of dog food, a crate, and a plastic grocery bag filled with toys. "We can get more stuff, but this should tide her over for a bit."

"Tomorrow we can take a ride to the pet store." Jillian shook her head, still a little bit in awe. "You're amazing, Angie. Really." She looked into Angie's eyes. "Thank you."

They spent the rest of their evening letting Boo wander the house and the fenced-in backyard. Angie put the crate together, and they set it at the far end of their bedroom, filled with soft blankets, towels, and a couple dog toys. By the time the clock read 11:00, they were all exhausted. Once their nightly routines were finished, Angie fell into bed.

"Okay, sweetie pie of mine," Jillian cooed to Boo as she put her in her crate and shut the door. "You get some sleep."

Boo whined her disapproval, but Jillian stayed resolute and crawled into bed next to Angie. They cuddled up and turned off the lights.

Boo continued to whine.

"It's okay," Angie whispered as she felt Jillian stiffen. "She's just missing her litter. She'll be all right; she just needs some time."

The whining went on.

At 11:27, Jillian clamped a pillow over her head.

At 11:43, Angie did the same thing.

At 12:19, the whining became a loud scraping/scratching/rattling sound that made Jillian sit straight up in bed.

"What the hell?" She clicked on the light on her nightstand. "Oh, my god."

Angie blinked in the light, squinted. "What?"

Jillian pressed her lips together, not sure if she felt like laughing or crying, and pointed.

Boo had messed in her crate. Not only that, but she'd then acted like she was digging with her front paws and there was dog poop everywhere. On the walls, all over the towels and blankets, and all over Boo. She sat still, looking to her new owners like a white dog with brown spots.

"Boo! What did you do?" Jillian stood before the crate in her boxers and a tank top, hands jammed against her hips, head shaking slowly back and forth. The dog blinked at her, all innocence.

Angie came up next to her. "She obviously thinks this is going to get her a spot in our bed."

Jillian sighed. "Do you want laundry duty or dog washing duty?"

"Duty or doody?"

Jillian laughed. "Either. Both."

"You bond with your puppy in the tub. I'll wash this stuff up."

Jillian reached in and carefully wrapped the dog in one of the least spoiled towels. "You are a piece of work, Miss Boo. Come here." She held the puppy at arm's length and strode to the bathroom. "God, you stink."

By 1:15 a.m., the pup had been taken outside for a pee and Boo was clean (and not all that happy about it), the walls were clean, the crate was clean; there were new towels and blankets lining it, and air freshener had been sprayed liberally.

"Okay," said Jillian, aching for bed. "Let's try this one more time." She put Boo back into the crate. "This time, go to sleep, little one." She kissed the soft head and shut the door, then fell into bed next to Angie, who was sprawled on her stomach.

"Thank god it's the weekend," Angie mumbled, her face half in the pillow.

"You got that right." Jillian clicked off the light and settled in next to Angie, exhaling in relief.

The whining began almost instantly.

"You've got to be fucking kidding me," Jillian said.

Angie pulled the pillow over her head and screamed into it.

The whining continued.

"I can't take it," Jillian said, sitting up.

"What are you doing?"

"I can't take it." Jillian padded across the room, opened the crate, and pulled Boo out and into her arms. "Come on, you little baby. Mama needs her rest." She brought Boo to the bed, ignoring the stink-eye aimed at her from Angie.

"She shouldn't be in the bed with us," Angie stated, so tired her lips barely moved when she spoke. "It's a bad habit. I'm telling you."

"Yeah?" Jillian asked. "Do you want to be right or do you want to sleep?"

Angie looked at her for a beat. "Sleep."

"I thought so. Me too." Scooting down under the covers, Jillian turned on her side and pulled Boo close against her belly so they were spooning. She tucked her hand up along Boo's warm stomach and kissed the top of her head. "Now go to sleep, you bad girl."

Boo was asleep and snoring loudly by 1:23 a.m.

1994

The Power of Love

Eight

"Isn't it cool?" Angie grinned as she held the new black device up for inspection, tilting it this way and that, letting the light from the dining room glint off the buttons. It was smaller than a brick, and not nearly as thick or heavy, but it was solid and almost sleek. "Now you can get ahold of me any time you want, Mama."

"Oh, thank goodness," Alice said with a half-grin, and Angie either missed or ignored the touch of sarcasm in her tone, Jillian wasn't sure which.

Jillian laughed as she lifted a forkful of pasta to her lips. "Please. I've had to hear all about this cellular phone since yesterday. Nonstop. It's only fair that you share in my torture."

"I've had my cell for a year," Dominick piped in as he refilled Angie's wine glass, then his own.

"Yeah, well, we're not all fancy-schmancy lawyers, are we? Besides, you're older than me," Angie stated, and Jillian could almost visualize the two of them as kids, battling over some toy. "I got mine younger than you."

"Why do you need one of those things?" Joe asked.

"Because I'm important, Pop." Angie winked at him. "So my customers can reach me. I'm out of the office a lot."

"Isn't that what voicemail is for?"

"That's what I said," Jillian agreed, pointing at Joe with her fork. "Now she can never get away from those customers."

"I have hours," Angie told them, obviously defending her new gadget. "It's not like they'll be calling me at night or on weekends."

Jillian raised an eyebrow at that, but said nothing. Angie was doing

69

really well at work, and the truth was, the cell phone did make sense. Now if she was held up someplace or caught in traffic, she could reach Jillian and tell her. And the look on her face when she brought it home—she was like a child with a new bike. No way did Jillian want to extinguish that light. Angie was proud of herself, deservedly so, and Jillian was proud of her, too.

Jillian loved Sunday dinners with Angie's family. They were so warm, open-armed, and open-hearted, utterly different than dinners with her own parents. At her mother's house, she was tense, always on guard, careful not only of what she said, but of the subjects on which she spoke, avoiding such hot-button issues as politics and religion. Here, she felt welcome. More than welcome, part of the family. Alice Righetti always greeted her with a heartfelt hug and a kiss on the cheek. Joe Righetti teased her just as mercilessly as he did his own kids. She felt a tenderness and a comfort with the Righettis that she'd never felt in her own house. Her mother had never made her feel safe enough to fully be herself, but with the Righettis, she never felt the need to hide anything, to fake anything. With the Righettis, she was who she was, and that was good enough for them.

Jillian watched the family now as if removed, as if she wasn't in the room. Angie brushed a hank of dark hair out of her eyes and leaned toward her brother Tony, pointing out different features of her new phone. Tony was the wild card of the bunch with his questionable friends, vague employment, and history of drug use—Jillian was reasonably sure he was high now, judging by the redness of his eyes—but today was a good day, and there was no tension between him and Joe, as there was on bad days. Instead, Joe tipped his head nearer to Angie's younger sister, Maria, as they debated the best method of mixing the ingredients for meatballs—wooden spoon or bare hands. Maria looked nothing like Angie, nothing like Joe. Instead, she was the spitting image of her mother, all light brown hair, green eyes, and pale skin. Jillian flashed to her own brother's face, so very much like hers, people thought they were twins. Dominick sat at the opposite end of the table from his father and chewed thoughtfully, watching his family. He caught Jillian's eye and shot her a wink. As he did, his cell phone rang on his hip. Without looking at the screen, he answered it, then rolled his eyes as his sister dissolved into giggles, her phone pressed to her ear.

"You're ridiculous, Andi," he said, but he chuckled anyway.

This is my family.

The thought hit Jillian's mind loud and clear, and it warmed her from her heart out. She laid a hand on Angie's thigh and squeezed. Angie was still laughing and joking with her brothers, but put her hand on top of Jillian's and squeezed back. Across the table, Alice met Jillian's gaze and smiled. Jillian scooped more pasta into her mouth, and felt completely, utterly content.

This is my family.

Nine

If Boo could have disappeared into the floor tiles of the waiting room, she would have. The Chihuahua sitting in the next spot over barked— or more accurately, yipped—incessantly as Boo tried her hardest to become invisible, burrowing behind Jillian's legs and under the bench on which she sat, avoiding any and all eye contact with the tiny dog.

"You are such a baby," Jillian muttered, unable to hide a grin at the contradiction that was Boo: a dog barrel-chested, strong, and solid, with an intimidating pit bull head, who cowered at small dogs, garbage trucks, and the vacuum cleaner.

Jillian adored her.

A door opened to the left of the front desk, and a young vet tech stepped out. "Boo?"

"That's us, sweetie," Jillian said to her dog, then tugged gently at her leash.

Inside the room, Boo was a model patient, which also made Jillian smile. That contradiction again. Whimpering and scared in the waiting room, brave and confident for the vet tech, who poked and prodded and examined, then told them Dr. Jackson would be right with them, and gave Boo a treat.

She was still munching happily when Shay came in and immediately gave Jillian a hug.

"Hey there, good lookin'. Why aren't you at work?"

"Midwinter break. I'm off all week. It's good to see you, Shay," Jillian told her as she looked her friend over and grinned. "I still can't get over how impressive it is when you walk in here in your lab coat, all doctor-like." She could still picture high-school age Shay, her unruly hair having gone from afro to cornrows, athletic and always sure of herself. Now she kept her hair short, still colored it a bit so it was light, almost blonde at the tips, and that confidence always radiated from her, drew people to her. Shay was one of those people who always made you feel comfortable, no matter what.

"You look so good," Shay said, talking to Boo. "You're such a pretty girl. Let me see those teeth. Ooo, look at those babies, all pearly white. Mommy's been brushing them, hasn't she?"

Boo let Shay lift her lips to check her teeth, look into her eyes and ears, play with her feet, even held still for her puppy shots. As she worked, Shay directed her questions to Jillian. "So how's life? Work okay?"

"It is," Jillian said, and meant it. "I'm actually liking working with the little ones."

"Yeah?" Shay stopped what she was doing to look at her friend. "That's great. I know you were getting antsy there for a while."

"I was." Jillian blew out a breath. "And I don't like the politics. I didn't expect there to be so much in education. They don't prepare you for that in college."

"Newsflash, honey: there's politics in every business. Every business."

"I suppose. But I work with some really great people, and the kids are fun. I'm kind of enjoying myself."

"You know, Laura and I were just talking about you last night, about your whole job situation, and she had a terrific idea. I bet you could volunteer at the art museum. I imagine they'd love to have somebody educated to help out."

Jillian blinked at her, then slowly nodded. "I never thought of that. How did I never think of that? That's a fantastic idea."

"My girl's pretty creative."

Jillian bumped her friend with a shoulder. "So? Sounds like things are good."

Shay stopped what she was doing, took a big breath, and let it out loudly. "Things are amazing. Really. She's smart and funny and sexy. I never thought I could be so happy."

"We did good, didn't we?"

"We sure did. How's your girl? Doing pretty well at work, I hear."

73

Shay tugged at her lab coat, which was embroidered with her name and the animal hospital's logo. "She did these for us."

"I remember her telling me she'd done a job for you. Thanks for getting her the meeting."

"I was happy to."

"I think she's much better at this job than she expected to be. She's developed quite a sizable clientele, and I think her boss has been pleasantly surprised."

Shay cocked her head to the side slightly and studied her friend. "What's that look?"

"What look?"

An arched brow. "Don't mess with me. I've known you since you were a kid. What's wrong?"

Jillian sighed. "Nothing's wrong. I just don't get to see her as much as I'd like, that's all. She works a lot."

"Honey, I know what that's like," Shay said with a snort. "She's doing well, right?"

"Yes."

"And you're proud of her?"

"Very."

"And when she comes home, is she happy to be there?"

"Absolutely."

"Then relax. It won't be like this forever. She's still making her way."

Jillian grinned at her old friend. "Sounds like you're speaking from experience."

"I went through a billion years of school, remember? I know what it's like to try to juggle a career and a relationship. I think she's doing okay."

Somehow, just hearing Shay's positive tone made Jillian feel better—this was the first time Jillian had given voice to her concerns. "You're right. She is. We are."

"Good. Now take this gorgeous mutt home, and when you get a minute, call my girlfriend and set up a dinner date for the four of us." Shay kissed Boo on her white head and gave her another treat from the jar on the counter. A parting hug for Jillian, and Dr. Jackson was on to her next patient.

"Come on, Boo. Let's go home."

споль

ぞ   ぞ   ぞ

"I just want to thank you, Matt." Angie lifted her wine glass.

"Is that why we're drinking at lunch?" Matt Jones asked her with a grin. "So you can thank me?"

"Exactly." She clinked her glass against his beer bottle. In the three years since Angie began her sales career, Matt had remained a loyal customer. As his business grew, so did hers. Jones Tree had gone from a small handful of employees to nearly thirty. Matt and Angie had become surprisingly good friends along the way and they tried to meet for lunch or drinks—or both—at least once a month.

"Cool. What are you thanking me for?" Matt's brown hair was neatly combed, and though his regular attire consisted of jeans, a T-shirt, and work boots, he always looked tidy. She liked that about him. Presentation was important to him. Like she was always explaining to Jillian, image mattered.

"For being my first customer and for continuing to be the customer who is the least of a pain in my ass."

Matt laughed, a loud guffaw that surprised Angie even though she'd heard it a hundred times before. "Well, you are very welcome."

"Seriously," Angie said, leaning in over the table they shared. "You are a dream. You're rarely in a rush. You understand that shit happens, and that if something of yours is late, it's not because I'm trying to screw you. You pay your bills on time. And you don't give me an ass ache."

Matt's bushy eyebrows climbed up to his hairline. "Wow. Somebody been giving you a hard time?"

"Understatement." Angie sipped her wine. "You have customers you can't stand?"

"Oh, god, yes. Everybody does. It's part of doing business."

Angie shook her head and watched as people mingled, sifted in and out of the restaurant. "This is not what I went to school for."

"No? Join the club, sweetheart. I have a psychology degree," Matt said.

75

Angie blinked at him. "Really?"

"Scout's honor. I fell into the landscape business, liked it enough, and decided to stay."

"Ever regret your decision?"

Matt heaved a breath, gazed out the window. "Once in a while, maybe. When I have more money due in collections than I do in my checking account. Or when my crew works its ass off on a job only to have the customer say they don't like it or it isn't what they expected. But"—he swigged his beer—"I love the freedom. No time clock. I'm outside much of the time. Makes it almost all worthwhile. I would like to see my wife a little more often."

"Oh, I so understand that. Jillian's been great and super supportive, but I know she gets frustrated with my hours. Did I tell you I had a customer call me last week on my cell at eight o'clock?"

"At night?"

"He was on the west coast, so it was only five for him, but he didn't seem terribly apologetic when I explained to him that I was home with my family. Jillian was not happy about that."

"I know. Beth can be the same way."

"I do love the freedom, though, that's for sure." It was true. As long as Angie was making sales and writing orders, nobody lurked over her shoulder. She could come and go as she pleased, be out of the office all day long, and nobody questioned her. She'd never expected to be so autonomous so early on in her career, but she liked it. "I have a communications degree, but I minored in business."

"Oh, yeah?"

Angie nodded. "I think I could run this company, easy."

Matt's eyes lit up. "That'd be great. Is Guelli looking to sell?"

"Not that I know of," Angie said with a shake of her head. "But he's no spring chicken. He's got to be at least thinking about retiring in the next five or ten years." The idea of actually running Logo Promo had been rolling around in her head for several weeks, but this was the first time she'd spoken aloud about it. To anybody. As the owner of a small business himself, Matt seemed like the perfect sounding board. But even as she spoke to him, she felt guilty for not talking to Jillian first.

"It'd be good to have the company run by somebody younger. Times are changing quickly, and so is business and the way it's done."

"Guelli thinks computers are a fad."

Matt gaped at her. "No."

"Yes. He's an old friend of the family, but the guy's a relic. I start talking about sorting sales records on the computer, and I can see his eyes just glaze right over."

"Maybe you should spend some time working up an automation plan, see what he thinks. It's worth a shot."

Angie nodded. "I'll give it some thought."

Matt glanced at his watch. "Ugh. I've gotta go." He looked around and signaled the waitress.

"No, no. You're the customer. I'm buying." Angie's cell rang at that moment. "Go," she said to Matt, who gave her a quick kiss on the cheek. "Thanks for lunch." And he was off.

"Hi, this is Angie," she said into the phone.

"Angie, this is Margie from Keystone Bank. Those pens we ordered came in, but the phone number is wrong." Margie's tone held a combination of irritation and panic. They had a grand opening scheduled for their newest branch next week, and the pens were one of their giveaways.

Angie closed her eyes and took a deep breath. "Okay. Don't worry. I'm in the neighborhood. I'll be right over and we'll get it fixed. Okay?" She finished the call and wondered where the mistake had happened. Had Ivan screwed up the art and she didn't catch the mistake? Or did the pen supplier drop the ball? The answer would mean the difference between eating the cost of a thousand pens or having the pen company pick them up and take care of things in time for the opening.

She picked up her wine and downed the remaining half a glass in two big gulps.

∾ ∾ ∾

The March night was beautiful, the air still crisp, but with that distinct smell of impending spring, and Jillian cracked one of the bedroom windows open just enough to fill the room with that scent.

"Oh, this is nice," Angie commented as she came through the doorway, shedding her suit as she walked, careful not to spill the remainder of the wine in her glass. Jillian had a few squat candles burning on each nightstand, the covers turned down, the pillows fluffed. Angie looked at her girlfriend and arched a brow in question.

Jillian smiled. "You've been working so hard, I wanted to help you relax. So . . ." She held up a bottle, tipped it back and forth in her hand. "I bought some massage oil."

"Ooo. I like the sound of that."

"Then get undressed and come over here." Jillian injected a sexy undertone into her voice as she pointed to the bed. It was close to eight o'clock, and Angie had been home for only a half hour. Long enough to eat and grab a glass of wine. Jillian had plans for her woman tonight. It had been too long since they'd been together, and she was tired of waiting for Angie to make a move. She pointed to Boo's bed in the corner, and the dog obediently curled up on it.

Angie set her glass down and undressed while Jillian watched. Even after nearly six years together, Jillian was still in awe of her girlfriend's body. Tall, bronzed even in the winter, rounded and curvy in all the right places. Angie hung up her suit and blouse, put her heels in the closet, then turned to stand before Jillian in her bra and underwear.

"Oh, no." Jillian gestured with a finger. "All of it."

Angie grinned then removed the rest of her clothing until she stood completely naked.

"Much better." Jillian stepped close to her, touched a finger to her throat, ran it all the way down the center of her torso to the thatch of dark hair at the apex of her thighs. "You are so beautiful, Angelina," she whispered.

Angie tilted her head down and their mouths met, then their tongues, hot and hungry. Jillian held tightly to Angie's hips, slid her hands up Angie's bare back, dug her fingers into the flesh at Angie's shoulders. God, it felt like it had been so long, and she wanted nothing more than to turn their bodies, push Angie onto her back on the bed, and take what she wanted. She stopped herself, forced herself to slow down, to keep control. This night was supposed to be about Angie, about making *her* feel good, not about Jillian having her way—though she hoped that's the direction things would end up going.

She pulled away from the kiss, and took a step back from Angie. Waving an arm at the bed, she said, "Okay. Lie down on your stomach."

Angie blinked at her for a moment, all swollen lips and ragged breath. Then she smiled and complied, stretching out on the taupe sheets.

Jillian surveyed the sight for a moment, admiring the gentle lines of Angie's calves, her thighs, her rounded ass and hips, and that strong, strong back. There was something about the wide planes of Angie's back and shoulders that turned Jillian on, and she told Angie so as she climbed onto the bed and straddled her, sitting lightly on Angie's behind.

"I've always wondered if I should try lifting weights," Angie said. "Maybe that would develop the muscles more."

"I love them just the way they are," Jillian responded as she poured massage oil into her hands and warmed it by rubbing them together. "They're perfect, and I love them." She punctuated her words by placing both palms in the middle of Angie's back and sliding up, using her own weight as pressure.

The groan that escaped Angie made all the effort Jillian put into the evening worthwhile.

"Fair warning," Jillian said. "I'm sort of winging this massage thing."

"Wing away," Angie muttered, her face half in the pillow. "You're doing just fine." Jillian wrung another groan from her, then focused on Angie's shoulders and arms. She used liberal amounts of the oil and found herself enjoying the process nearly as much as Angie seemed to be. Something about rubbing her oil-slicked hands over Angie's smooth, warm skin was intoxicating, and she kept at it, kneading not only Angie's back and shoulders, but her arms, her hands, her thighs, her calves, and even her feet. By the time she felt her own legs tingling from being crunched beneath her on the bed for too long, she'd had her hands on just about every muscle group in Angie's body and had molded each one into submission. And much to her delight, her own underwear was damp.

Happy about the discovery, she hopped off the bed and quickly divested herself of her clothes, then scooted up next to Angie.

Whose eyes were closed.

Who was breathing deeply, evenly.

Who was sound asleep.

Jillian turned onto her back and blew out a huge breath of defeat, trying to think that she'd done a great job at relaxing her girlfriend, not that her plan had backfired. With a turn of her head, she studied Angie, ran her eyes over her face, the smooth skin, the full, pink lips that were the shape of a perfect bow, the chicken pox scar at her right temple, the small brown mole low on her chin. Using her thumb, Jillian stroked the length of one dark eyebrow once, twice. This was the only time lately that Angie seemed relaxed . . . when she slept. During her waking hours, her face was tenser, her brows a tiny bit furrowed. Not for the first time, Jillian worried that Angie was working too hard.

"I love you," she whispered, and leaned forward to place a feather-light kiss on Angie's nose.

They lay face to face until Jillian followed Angie into slumber.

Ten

When the office-wide intercom clicked on and Guelli's voice filled the room, Angie and Hope were in Hope's office chatting about a couple of Angie's accounts.

"Please, everybody, let's take a moment to congratulate Keith Muldoon for closing a jacket order today with Cavit-McTavish for a hundred thousand dollars. Nice job, Keith."

Angie and Hope blinked at one another for a moment until Hope broke the silence with a fiercely whispered, "What the *fuck?*"

Angie shook her head as muffled applause could be heard throughout the building. "How the hell does he do that? *I* want to close a hundred thousand dollar order."

"I don't even want to think of the commission on that one. I'll want to kill myself."

Even as they spoke, Angie was doing the calculations in her mind. On an order that size, Keith had probably marked it up by twenty-five or even thirty thousand dollars. Angie knew he got a bigger commission percentage than she did. He stood to make somewhere in the neighborhood of fifteen thousand dollars. On one order.

"That prick," Hope muttered. Keith got a larger percentage than she did as well, and judging by her face, she obviously knew it. Hope did just fine with her own sales, but Angie knew that it had to grind on her a little bit. "I'd be happy for him if he wasn't a chauvinistic asshole."

Angie grinned, but nodded her agreement. "I know. I get that if you make more sales, you get a bigger cut. But he's just such a jerk."

There was no love lost between Hope and Keith. Frankly, there was no love lost between Keith and most women. He had the supremely annoying habit of calling them all *sweetheart* or *honey* or *babe*, and often expected them to do such things as bring him a cup of coffee or box up a package for him. On top of that, he didn't see anything wrong with his behavior; he actually thought he was being nice. When anybody called him on it, he'd simply shrug it off. And her previous job as office manager meant that Angie felt obligated to do what Keith asked of her, despite Hope continually reminding her that she was now his peer. She had as hard a time accepting that as Keith did—a fact that annoyed her to no end.

"His advantage is that he knows *everybody*," Angie said. "He's got contacts all over the place, and if there's some place he doesn't have one, one of his contacts will know someone and introduce him." Keith had locked up dozens of companies as customers before many of the other salespeople at Logo Promo even had time to think about trying to get in. His customer list was twice as long as everybody else's, and his salary reflected that. He wore designer suits, drove a Cadillac, and had the biggest, most well-furnished office in the building.

"I'd better get back to my own office and get to work," Angie said as she stood. "I've got issues coming out of my ears."

She'd been in Hope's office looking for guidance on how to keep the stress from making her feel like her head was going to explode. Flopping into her chair, she scoured the list she'd made of problems that needed her attention. She had three embroidery orders that were late. Six customers were waiting on quotes, and in turn, Angie was waiting on six quotes from her own suppliers. Four orders were waiting to be written, two new and two reorders. Ivan owed her art for three separate projects.

When she got this bogged down, she didn't know where to begin, so she didn't begin at all. Instead, she clicked on the small radio on her desk and just sat looking at the things she needed to do. Her head was clogged. Blinking at her list seemed to be all she could do.

Scrubbing her hands over her face helped to wake her up a little. She glanced at the clock and made a sound of surprise. It was after four. How was it possible she'd spent all day in the office and still had this seemingly insurmountable list in front of her? "Because I spent half the day bitching," she muttered to herself. "That's how." Frustration bubbled up, adding to the stress; her stomach was a cauldron and whatever was in it was boiling over. She glanced up through her window onto the hall just as Hope approached. A tap on the door, and then she entered.

"It's after four," Angie said as she reached for the cupboard door above her credenza. Her fingers closed around the bottle of Absolut. "I have a ton of work to do, but I need to relax for five minutes. Join me?"

Hope hesitated.

"Come on, Hopie. My day has sucked balls, and I need to de-stress before I have a heart attack. I don't want to drink alone, but I will."

"Okay. But just one. I've got to get home." She scooted down the hall to the company kitchen and returned with two cans of 7UP and two plastic cups with ice.

Angie poured, and they touched glasses.

"Sixteen thousand, one hundred twenty-seven dollars," Hope stated. "That's what Muldoon is making on that order."

Angie shook her head. "Why can't I find a client as big as Cavit-McTavish? Do you know what I could do with money like that?"

"I've been trying not to think about exactly that since we got the announcement. I could pay off my car. Go on a trip. Put a new roof on my house."

"I would take Jillian away somewhere," Angie said. "I feel like I never see her. I practically live here." As if on cue, her phone rang. She glared at it until it went into voicemail, changing the little 4 on its screen to a 5. "I feel like I can't catch up."

"Yeah, that's one of the things I like least about this job." Hope took a sip from her cup. "There's never any plateauing. In most sales jobs, you spend years building your clientele, but once you have one, you can ease off and relax a bit. Not here."

"'Any customer can desert you at any time. There will always be somebody who can do it cheaper.'" Angie sighed, quoting one of the first rules Hope had told her when they began working together.

"That's why our customer service is so important; it's the only thing that sets us apart from everybody else. And *that's* what you need to keep focusing on." Hope leaned forward, caught Angie's eye, and said, "And that's why you shouldn't let your phone click over to voicemail when you're sitting right here."

Angie grimaced, then nodded.

Hope took another sip of her drink, reached across the desk, and spun Angie's list around so she could read it. "Okay, first things first. What on this list is going to make you money?"

Angie didn't need to look. "The orders and reorders."

"Exactly. Do those first."

Angie nodded.

"Taking care of the late stuff consists of—"

"'—nothing more than quick, angry phone calls.' I know. I know."

"So get the embroidery shop on the phone and rip them a new one. One late order is understandable. Three late orders are unacceptable."

"Okay."

Hope tapped the paper with her forefinger. "Then get these quotes done. Same thing with the suppliers. Get angry. They are holding you up. If they don't get numbers to you, you don't get an order, which means *they* don't get an order, which means *they* don't get any money. Tell them so. And tell them there are a dozen people just like them who supply the same item, and you'll be more than happy to go to them." She glanced once more at the list and rolled her eyes. "And get in Ivan's face. He is slower than molasses in January. My god. It might be time to scream at him."

Angie grinned. "Wow. You're a hard-ass."

"And you're not enough of one." Hope shot her a pointed look.

"I know." Angie blew out a breath.

Hope finished her drink. "If you want to close orders like Keith does, you need some balls the size of his, and you need to get tougher with some of these people. *They* work for *you*." She stood. "There's no reason you and I can't make that kind of money, too. It's all about how much you want it." With a wink, she left.

"Sixteen thousand dollars in commission," Angie whispered. "God, would that be nice!" Gulping down the remainder of her drink, she made herself another, then picked up the phone and left a message on their home answering machine for Jillian. She had a staff meeting after school today and wouldn't be home quite yet. Angie left a message that she'd be working late.

Then she got to work on her list. She could make more money.

She absolutely could. Dominick wasn't the only Righetti who could rake it in. She could. And when she did, when she hit the next big order, she was going to take Jillian on a romantic getaway weekend.

She deserved it for being so patient.

෨   ෨   ෨

"God damn it."

Jillian slapped the delete button on the answering machine after listening to Angie tell her she was going to be late. Again.

"'Don't wait up?' Really?" Boo cocked her head as Jillian spoke. "A girl could start to worry that she was having an affair." She stopped, looked at her dog, blinked several times. "No. She's not. She wouldn't. I know her." Satisfied she'd curtailed that train of thought, she grabbed Boo's leash off its hook and clipped it to her collar.

Jillian hadn't had a dog growing up. Her friends had, and she'd enjoyed them whenever she visited somebody else, but her mother had never wanted one in her house. So Jillian had never understood till now the head-clearing peace of simply walking her dog through the neighborhood in the evening after work. It helped her to decompress from her day, to slow down her racing mind and body, to just take some time to breathe in the fresh air, admire the trees, and smile at passersby and their dogs.

Boo loved everybody and every dog; she always wanted to say hi. There were a few people who would get that look when they saw her, that *Oh, a pit bull I think I'll cross to the other side of the street* look, but many of them recognized Boo and knew she was anything but a threat. Dog owners were funny. They rarely introduced themselves, but they were quick to introduce their dogs. She didn't know the names of any of the people they crossed paths with during their walk, but she recognized the older woman and Gus the pug, the retired couple and Molly the miniature dachshund, and the young jogger and Sofie, her black Lab mix. She was fairly certain she was known as the blonde woman with Boo the pit bull mix.

An hour later, Jillian and Boo returned home. Boo wolfed her dinner as Jillian made herself an omelet and ate it, alone. After dinner, she busied herself with some housework—cleaned the bathroom, mopped the kitchen floor, made a grocery list for her shopping trip the next day. Then she took a glass of white wine up to the bedroom and read, Boo curled up at her feet. The book was engrossing, and she fully intended to wait up for Angie—partly to spite her for that irritating "don't wait up" message, and partly because she missed her terribly and wanted a hug.

She was asleep long before Angie got home.

Eleven

Jillian blew out a breath as she flopped onto the couch, alone there for all of two-and-a-half seconds before Boo joined her, crawling up her body so her front paws lay across Jillian's chest. Jillian couldn't help but laugh.

"You are so not a lap dog, young lady," she said with a grunt. "Didn't they tell Mama you'd stay small? Fifty pounds is not small." She kissed the top of Boo's head as her thoughts swirled around her brain.

By the time Memorial Day weekend rolled around, Jillian was angry, frustrated—and worried. Angie's work hours hadn't eased up. True, they hadn't gotten any worse (as if they could), but she wasn't coming home any earlier. They'd been going around and around about it until Jillian's head spun. She felt like she had a girlfriend half the time. They had dinner together once a week, for sure, and that was at the Righettis. No way would Angie miss Sunday dinner at her parents'—and that was another thing: Angie would blow off dinner with her girlfriend nine times out of ten, but not once did she miss a family dinner.

Jillian lay on the couch stroking her dog. Something else was causing her worry. Angie was drinking a lot more than usual. Her excuse was that she was schmoozing the clients—and if she wasn't drinking, her clients wouldn't be drinking, wouldn't be comfortable enough. And she needed them comfortable. She'd been taking clients to dinner or out for drinks at least a couple times a week now, and even at home she was drinking quite a bit.

"Sweetie, do you really need another glass?" Jillian had asked just two nights ago when Angie had refilled her wine glass for the third time.

Angie shrugged off the question. "It helps me relax. I'm too wound up. I'll never get to sleep if I don't calm down. No big deal."

Jillian wondered now if she should have been less gentle about it, firmer, more obvious that she didn't approve. Or maybe she should have just said, flat out, "I'm worried that you're drinking too much." Why did people always tippy-toe around things that needed to be said? Her mother was like that, never coming right out and saying what she meant. Now Jillian was taking after her.

She hadn't even tried to bring up their sex life. Or lack thereof. The biggest drawback of Angie's long hours was that she was tired. Too tired to make love. It had been weeks. *Weeks.*

As if sensing Jillian's frustration, Boo slipped out her hot pink tongue and coated Jillian's cheek with affection. Jillian wrapped her arms around the solid body that was anything but soft and cuddly and squeezed.

"I love you, too, Boo-Bear."

Their lovefest was interrupted by the sound of the side door. Another grunt was pushed from Jillian's body as Boo bounded off of her to check out the visitor. A glance at the clock told Jillian it was just after six, normally much too early for Angie to be home. But the sound of her voice cooing to Boo brought warmth and a smile as Jillian popped up from the couch and headed for the kitchen.

"Hi," Jillian said, wrapping her arms around Angie's neck. "You're home early."

Angie hugged her tightly. "No, I'm home at a normal time. I'm home early for me."

"That's what I meant."

"Hardy har har." Holding Jillian at arms' length, she said, "What are you doing?"

"Right now? Hugging you. Why?"

"No, I mean are you in the middle of something?"

Jillian made a face. "No."

"Good. Go pack a bag. Three nights' worth."

Jillian blinked at her. "What?"

"I'm taking you away. My sister's coming over to watch Boo."

"Where?"

"It's a surprise."

Jillian backed away, a grin spreading across her face, then raced up the stairs to do as she was told.

෨ ෨ ෨

It was just before eight o'clock when Angie parked the car. Strathmore-on-the-Lake was gorgeous in the dusk: a stone, almost castle-like building tucked away on the shores of a small, secluded lake. Lit sconces at the door, and subtle, ankle-height lights marked the several walking paths that led from the inn to the lake and back. The late-spring breeze carried with it the scents of water, trees, and fading lilacs.

Jillian had drifted off to sleep about a half hour earlier; Angie gently shook her awake. "Babe. We're here."

Jillian inhaled deeply and rolled her head around on her neck, working out the kinks that came from napping in a car. She blinked several times. "Oh, Angie. It's so beautiful." She'd figured out their destination after an hour on the road (there wasn't much else in this direction worth sneaking off to), but she'd only ever seen pictures before. "Oh, my god."

Angie smiled at her. "Ready?"

"Hell, yes."

They grabbed their bags, and headed for the front entrance. Despite the beauty of the outside, the opulence and elegance of the lobby inside surprised Jillian, given that they were in the middle of nowhere in up-state New York. A fountain of marble stood in the center, directly beneath a circular skylight, its water gurgling pleasantly. Angie couldn't wait to see it in the daylight, especially with the sun gleaming through the skylight and reflecting on the water. Hanging plants and potted trees lent an almost tropical feel. Soft music came from an open door to their right, the restaurant and bar, Angie guessed. Their next stop. She approached the front desk and gave a friendly woman their reservation information. They were directed to follow a young, clean-shaven man who led them to their room. Within ten minutes of pulling into the lot, the door clicked shut behind them, and they were alone.

"Oh, my god, Angie." Jillian's voice was quiet, just above a whisper. "I can't believe you did this." She let go of her duffle bag and wandered farther into the room. Her breath caught as she looked in the corner and noticed the Jacuzzi tub. "We are so getting in this," she told Angie.

Angie laughed. "Yes, we are. Want to get something to eat first? I know it's kind of late, but I'm starving."

Jillian stepped to her, wrapped her arms around Angie's neck, and pulled her down for a searing kiss. When they parted, both women were slightly breathless. "I can't believe you did this."

Angie's expression softened. "You deserve it. You've been so patient with my ridiculous hours. I told Hope the next big order that I closed, I was taking you away for a weekend. That happened earlier this month."

Jillian's blue eyes widened. "You've been planning this for nearly a month?"

Angie nodded. "I had some details to take care of—somebody to watch Boo, make sure you didn't have a meeting or something that would keep you late at school tonight, be certain I could actually get us a room. This place is almost always booked on the weekends, especially long ones."

As she shook her head, Jillian's smile was huge, her dimples in plain view, and Angie realized that it had been far too long since she'd seen that big, genuine look of happiness.

"I can't believe you did this," Jillian said a third time and rested her head on Angie's shoulder.

"Well, this won't be the last time, you know. My long hours and schmoozing have really been paying off. I got my biggest commission check yet this month."

Jillian wanted to tell her that the money didn't matter, but Angie was so excited, her face shone with such pride, that Jillian simply smiled and said, "I love you."

"I love you, too."

"I'm still starving."

A laugh bubbled out of Jillian. "Okay. Let's go eat."

☙ ☙ ☙

Throughout their entire meal, Jillian felt like she had the old Angie back. The Angie that wasn't worried about work, the Angie that didn't seem preoccupied and stressed out. She'd even left her cell phone back in the room. Turned off. They ate by candlelight—filet mignon for Angie and broiled scallops for Jillian. They drank a bottle of full-bodied, delicious cabernet, and they talked about everything and nothing. By the time they returned to their room, it was nearly eleven.

"This night has been incredible," Jillian said as they entered their room. She turned and wrapped her arms around Angie. "I've missed it being just the two of us."

"The night's not over." When Jillian looked up, Angie gestured to the Jacuzzi with her chin. "You up for it? Or are you too tired?"

"Too tired to soak in a hot tub? Never."

It didn't take long for them to fill the tub—adding some of the scented bath oil provided by the Inn—and settle down on the seats. They groaned simultaneously as the luxuriously hot water sluiced over their naked skin.

"Oh, my god," Jillian said, her eyes closed, her head back against the pillowed edge of the tub. "I never want to leave this spot."

Angie scooted her body closer so their thighs were touching. "Maybe when we get a bigger house, we can get our own hot tub."

Jillian smiled, but didn't open her eyes. "Maybe." Her tone said she knew Angie was just talking, her ideas were just that: ideas.

"No, I'm serious."

Jillian opened her eyes. "About what?"

"A bigger house."

"We don't need a bigger house, babe."

Angie nodded, settled back so her position mimicked Jillian's. "I know. I'm just thinking out loud. I'm making decent money. I can make more. Dominick moved to something bigger when he started making money. Maybe it's time for us to start thinking about leaving the city and finding a place in the suburbs. Don't you think Boo would like a bigger yard to run around in?"

"Of course she would." Jillian could tell by Angie's reasoning that this was something she'd been thinking about. Resting her head on Angie's shoulder, she voiced her worry. "I don't want you working any harder than you already do. You're doing amazingly well at your job, and I can't tell you how proud I am of you. We're doing just fine financially. And I like our little house."

"Me, too."

"I'd rather have you home at dinnertime than have more money in our bank account and a bigger house for me to wander around in by myself."

Angie sighed, rubbed water over her arms. "I just want to make sure you're happy." The way she said it—a mix of worried lover and small child—made Jillian's heart ache.

"Babe, what's brought this on?"

"I don't know. I just, I see my parents, and my dad works so hard to make sure my mom's happy, and I just want that for us. I don't want you to ever think you're not important."

Jillian cocked her head and smiled widely. "And I see *my* parents and how miserable my mom can be, and I *know* how lucky I am to have you. I wish you wouldn't worry so much. You make me very happy."

"Yeah?" Angie leaned closer.

"Absolutely," Jillian assured her before their lips met.

Despite all the time that had passed since their last bout of love-making, there was no rush. Jillian crawled over Angie, straddled her lap, and let herself become lost in their nakedness. The wet skin, the ragged breaths, the familiarity with one another. Angie wrested the lead from Jillian and flipped their positions, taking over, taking charge, and taking Jillian to heights she hadn't felt in longer than she cared to think about. She came hard, clamping her mouth down on Angie's bare, wet shoulder as she did so.

When they were spent, they dried each other off, gently, lovingly, and cuddled in the enormous bed as if they were one living, breathing being. When Jillian was awakened by a sound outside somewhere at 3 a.m., she turned to kiss Angie, but Angie was awake as well, and took Jillian again with her fingers. And then again with her mouth. By the time they went back to sleep, Jillian couldn't feel her legs. She couldn't remember the last time she'd felt so completely sated. She drifted off with a single thought in her head.

We're back.

Twelve

Jillian hit the snooze button on Tuesday morning with a groan, then snuggled into Angie, drifting in and out of sleep and remembering the fantastic long weekend they'd shared.

Jillian had come embarrassingly close to crying when they'd left the Strathmore early Monday afternoon. They meandered through various tiny country villages, stopped for a delicious, relaxed lunch, hit a few antique shops, and drove on roads with a speed limit no faster than 45mph—but they still had to come back to real life. They held hands on the trip, and Angie said more than once, "I wish we didn't have to go back."

"We need to take a weekend away more often," Jillian suggested, something she'd been thinking about the entire morning. "I feel like we've recharged, you know?"

Angie lifted Jillian's hand to her lips and kissed her knuckles. "I know exactly how you feel."

Despite their less than enthusiastic return home, Boo was ecstatic to see them, running in circles and howling, her nub of a tail going a mile a minute. That made things a little easier to bear. They unpacked, did some laundry, ate a light supper, and once in bed, they made love again. Jillian tried not to cheer with glee, but she couldn't remember the last time they'd been intimate more than two nights in a row—at least not since they were newlyweds. She loved this "new" side of Angie—which was the old side, the Angie she had first loved

Tuesday morning arrived like a hangover. Jillian didn't want to get up, to officially signify the end of the weekend by actually dressing for work. Her head was muzzy, and she was slightly nauseous—

94

though she suspected both symptoms derived from "I Don't Want to Go to Work Syndrome." She hit the snooze one too many times, and both she and Angie ended up running around like crazy people, trying to make up for lost time. On Angie's way out the door, Jillian forced them to stop, face to face, by grabbing Angie's head with both hands.

"I just want you to know that I had an *amazing* weekend," she said softly. "I can't wait to do it again. Thank you so much. I love you." She kissed Angie's lips.

"I love you, too." Angie's smile was radiant. "See you tonight." And she was off.

Jillian was just giving Boo her treats and saying her goodbyes when the phone rang.

"Jill?"

"Brian?" Jillian hadn't spoken to her brother in weeks, and having him call her first thing in the morning was odd. He was more of an evening guy.

"I was hoping I'd catch you." His lack of preamble combined with the slight crack in his voice put her on red alert.

"What's wrong?"

"It's Mom. Dad just called me here at the office. The ambulance is taking her to the hospital."

"What? Why? What happened?"

"I didn't get a lot of detail. She told him she felt light-headed last night. Then this morning, she said her chest felt tight. When she started having trouble breathing, he called the ambulance."

"Oh, my god." Her heart was racing at triple time as she dropped onto a chair.

"I know."

The siblings were silent for several moments. Jillian finally asked, "What if it's serious? What do we do?" As soon as the words left her mouth, she felt like she was ten years old.

She heard Brian exhale. "I don't know. I'm going to head over now."

"Where are they taking her?"

"St. Mary's."

"I'll meet you there."

Angie felt helpless.

She wasn't even thirty yet. It hadn't even crossed her mind that she would lose her parents one day. Okay, yes, she could lose them *any* day, but hell, it just wasn't something she thought about. They were young, barely sixty. This was the 90s. People didn't just drop dead before they were sixty. So why would she even think about such a thing?

But Jillian was only twenty-seven. And her mother, at fifty-six had done just that: dropped dead. Not immediately. Not until she'd reached the hospital. Heart attack at fifty-six.

Sitting in the corner of the couch, her arms wrapped around Jillian, trying her best to keep her warm, keep her safe, keep her from crumbling or hold onto her if she did, she had no idea what she could possibly say or do to make things better. So she sat and she held her girlfriend, and she did her best to pour every ounce of love she had from her heart through her arms and into Jillian, hoping she'd feel it, hoping she'd know.

Jillian kept talking about the same thing. She was not ready for this. She was not prepared. *Who in their twenties thinks about the mortality of their parents?* She'd asked the question over and over, as if somebody would finally materialize and give her the answer she wanted. *Why, nobody, Jillian. You're absolutely right! This has all been a terrible mistake. Here's your mom back.*

The wake had been rough. Endless parades of people hugging Jillian, her brother Brian, their dad, telling them how shocking it all was. As if they didn't know. As if the three of them didn't look like the dictionary definition of the word "shocked." Mr. Clark was slack-jawed, and he looked like he hadn't slept in days as he tried to put up a strong front for his kids. Brian was a taller, handsome version of Jillian, his sandy hair freshly cut, his black suit classic, his lavender and black tie somber. Angie thought it was a blessing that he'd gone into the real estate business with his father because he slipped easily into business-man mode, shaking hands, thanking people for their attendance, keeping himself one step removed from the reality of the pain. Jillian's expression could only be described as bewildered. Like she was a backstage manager who'd just found herself directly in the spotlight, in front of a full audience. Her blue eyes were wide, too wide. Bloodshot and swollen and too wide. Her face was drawn, her skin so pale as to be nearly translucent. She had barely eaten in three days, and it made her dress hang loosely off her body, as if she were a child in her mother's clothes.

Angie had hung back. Mr. Clark and Brian knew who she was to Jillian and were glad she was there for moral support. But most of Mrs. Clark's friends and family—aside from Shay and her parents—either didn't know or didn't approve, and Angie knew it wasn't the time or place to make a stand for gay equality. She stayed close, supplied Jillian with water, tissues, mints, whatever she needed. At one point late in the evening, she approached Jillian to see how she was holding up. Jillian simply grasped her hand and held onto it for the next twenty minutes until the last mourner left the funeral home.

The funeral itself had been a blur. Much quicker than Angie—a Catholic used to long masses and services—had expected. Then she stood by feeling useless while Jillian talked and smiled and greeted people for as long as she could until finally tugging her partner into a corner, she uttered seven words that gave Angie something she could do.

"Get me the hell out of here."

They'd come home, changed into comfies, and cuddled on the couch. They'd been there ever since, just breathing, just being together. Boo paced and circled, sensing Jillian's sadness, wanting to help. She came up on the couch, licked a stray tear off Jillian's cheek, lay down with her head on Jillian's thigh, where she'd remain for a few minutes before pacing some more.

I know just how you feel, sweetie, said Angie to Boo when the dog made eye contact. She tightened her hold on Jillian and spoke aloud. "Honey, you should eat something."

"Not hungry." Jillian's voice was gravelly.

"I know, but I still think you should eat. You've hardly put a thing in your belly in days." When Jillian inhaled, about to protest, Angie interrupted her. "And no, the three spoons of yogurt this morning don't count." Jillian blew out the breath in defeat. "How about some scrambled eggs?"

It wasn't really a question, but Jillian gave a curt nod. "Okay."

"Come and sit while I cook."

In the kitchen, Jillian sat on a stool, propping her elbows on the counter with her chin in her hands.

Angie pulled eggs, tomato, cheese, and spinach from the fridge, determined to get as many vitamins and minerals into the meal as she could. Frying pan on the stove, butter melting in it, she quickly chopped the tomato, then the spinach, surprised when Jillian spoke.

"It's so weird."

What could she say to that? It was *totally* weird. It was *absolutely* weird. She grimaced and nodded.

"My mom's gone."

Angie glanced over her shoulder, expecting another breakdown, but Jillian was the most dry-eyed she'd been all day, picking at a spot on the counter with a thumbnail.

"I mean, we had our issues. It's not like we had this super fantastic relationship…" Jillian began.

It was the most she'd said in two days, so Angie let her talk.

"She could be a total pain in my ass. And she was. Often."

Angie sautéed the tomatoes and spinach in the butter, nodding encouragingly.

"She did *not* handle the gay thing well."

"If you consider ignoring it completely the same as not handling it well, then yes, she did not handle it well."

Jillian barked what almost sounded like a laugh. "Exactly."

Angie cracked the eggs into the pan, stirred them into the veggies.

"I was hoping she'd come around eventually. I was hoping time would help, you know?"

Angie glanced over and this time, Jillian seemed to expect a reply. "I know, babe."

"And now there isn't any. There isn't any more time."

"I know."

"It's not fair."

"No, it's not."

"It fucking sucks."

"Big time." Angie added the cheese, let it melt, then scooped the eggs onto two plates. She fished two forks out of a drawer and set the plates at the breakfast bar, side by side.

"My mom's gone, Angie."

"I know, honey. I'm so sorry."

Jillian exhaled, picked up a fork, and stabbed at her eggs.

1997

Semi-Charmed Life

Thirteen

"Am I going to be the only straight girl there?" Maria gave her sister Angie a look of hesitation as she passed the plate of meatballs to her left. "I don't want to be the only straight girl there."

"I promise I won't let any of my friends hit on you," Angie said, coupling her words with an eye roll and sending the meatballs on to her mother. "I can't make any promises, though, what with you being all irresistible and stuff."

Across the table, Angie's father grinned. Dom barked a laugh.

Maria laughed and swatted Angie with her napkin. "I'm sorry. That was ridiculous. You know how I am around new people. I just get all nervous and jerky."

That was true. For every ounce of gregariousness Angie had, Maria had an equal amount of reserve. In a group of people she knew well, nobody would ever accuse the youngest Righetti of being shy. But surrounded by strangers, she clammed up and needed to be coaxed into conversation. Angie had spent much of their childhood serving as the transition-easer between her little sister and potential new friends.

"You've probably met a lot of them. Tinny from Jillian's softball team, you've met her. She's coming with her girlfriend. You've met Shay and Laura. They're bringing a couple friends with them. Hope from my office will be there."

"I love Hope!"

"Who doesn't? Kevin and Keisha, our new neighbors are coming. And the Kleins from across the street. Brian might come, and Jillian's friend from work. And any of you guys are welcome." She made a circular gesture with her fork to include her parents and big brother.

103

Turning back to Maria, she went on. "It's going to be fun, and I just need you to help me with food. I told Jillian she wouldn't have to worry about feeding the company, she can just relax and enjoy the show, but I can't do it by myself. I'll freak out. I need your help. Please? Pretty please?"

"All right. All right." Maria put her hand up, palm out. "Stop begging. It's beneath you."

Angie threw her arms around her sister. "Thank you."

"I still don't understand why an episode of a sitcom deserves a party."

"Because it's a milestone," Angie's mother said, causing Angie to smile and silently thank the stars above for the amazing family she'd been born into. "Right, Angelina?"

"It's huge," Angie agreed, turning to Maria. "No lead character has ever come out on television before. Ever. There has *never* been a show with a gay or lesbian *lead character*. It's unprecedented. It's a very, *very* big deal." She saw her father nodding as he ate. "Pop, you want to come to our 'Ellen's Coming Out' party?"

He chuckled. "I think your mom and I will watch it here. You kids have fun. And watch your drinking." He added the last line in the same stern voice he had used when Angie was in college, poking his fork at her for emphasis.

"That's why it's at my house. So I don't have to go anywhere." She tapped her temple. "My mama didn't raise no dummies."

"Angelina," Alice said. "How does Jillian like volunteering at the art museum?"

"Loves it," Angie said around a mouthful of bread. "She's helping with tours now, did I tell you?" She grinned, proud of her girl.

"Really?"

"They needed an additional person who knows about art to help with visiting groups. She's having a blast, although she hates missing Sunday dinner."

"Well, we'll make sure to pack up a plate for her when you leave." Alice had been subtle but Angie had noticed the extra attention she'd been giving Jillian since the death of her mother. Had Jillian? Alice turned to her son. "And one for Pam, poor girl."

Dominick's wife of two years was seven months pregnant and relegated to bed rest for the remainder of her pregnancy to avoid further complications. He didn't like to leave her alone, but she insisted he visit with his family on Sundays. Angie watched her brother's brow crease slightly and knew he was trying to hide his worry. Their parents tried not to get overly excited, but sometimes, Angie thought her father's face might explode from trying to tone down his grin. It wasn't just his first grandchild; it was his first grandchild from his eldest son. She was excited too: this would be her very first niece or nephew. She hadn't expected the idea of being an aunt to be so . . . wonderful.

"How's she feeling?" Angie asked Dom.

"She feels okay; she's just bored out of her skull." He shook his head. "We'll both be happy when this is all over."

"Won't be long now," Joe said. "Just think, in twenty-five years, you too can be having a dinner like this every Sunday at your house." He waved his butter knife around the table.

Dominick smiled through his worry. "I should be so lucky, Pop."

"You let me know if she needs anything," Alice ordered him. "I can come right over."

"I know, Mama. I told her. Thanks."

Nobody asked after Tony, though it crossed Angie's mind. Her brother was in one of his phases again, the kind where he'd submerge himself too deeply in whatever he was into at the time: alcohol, coke, weed. He'd show up again eventually. They were having a pleasant enough dinner; she didn't want to ruin it by poking at her parents' open wounds.

Angie had a moment as they cleaned up where she felt almost removed as she observed her family, like she wasn't there and was watching from afar. She watched her big brother flick soapy water at their little sister, who giggled and tried to snap him with a dish rag. Alice popped the lids closed on Tupperware containers so she could feed her missing children as Joe put a hand on her shoulder and kissed her cheek.

Do you have any idea how lucky you are?

She could still hear Jillian's voice from the first time she'd taken her home with her to Sunday dinner, amazed, almost bewildered as she stressed to Angie that most normal people would kill to have the family Angie did, quirks and all.

She knew how right Jillian was.

It wasn't perfect. Of course it wasn't. How could it be? Nothing was. Joe had a short temper and a long memory and could hold a grudge better than his great-grandmother (and that was saying *a lot*). Alice didn't always know when to leave well enough alone. Dominick was bossy and could come off like a know-it-all, and before Pam, he'd gone through women like toilet tissue. Maria was far too comfortable in her parents' home, so much so that Angie sometimes wondered if she'd ever move into her own place. And Tony . . . yeah. There was Tony.

So, no. They weren't perfect. They were absolutely *im*perfect. But they loved each other unconditionally, and it wasn't until Jillian had pointed it out to her, until Angie had recognized the blatant indifference or frequent hostility of Jillian's family—her mother in particular—that she'd really begun to grasp just what a gift she'd been given.

"Here, sweetie." She was yanked out of her reverie by her mother handing her a Tupperware dish. "You give Jillian a hug for me."

"I will, Mama. Thanks."

Thanks? It could never be enough.

Fourteen

"You guys have about twenty minutes before the show starts," Jillian said to Angie as she hugged her from behind, her arms tight around Angie's middle.

"No problem," Maria told her, pulling a tray of stuffed mushroom caps from the oven. "I've got one more sheet to deal with, and we'll be all set."

"Man, you don't mess around, Maria. When we said hors d'oeuvres, I was thinking cheese and crackers and some chips. Our guests are very impressed. The bacon-wrapped chicken bites were a huge hit."

"And that's why I asked for her help." Angie kissed Jillian quickly on the lips. "How's it going in there? Everybody having fun?"

Jillian nodded. "It's great. I can't believe it's really happening."

The news coverage had been nonstop, and Jillian had been following it for weeks. Magazine covers, talk shows, news reports. While it was fairly common knowledge that Ellen DeGeneres was a lesbian, she had never openly, publicly announced any such thing. Eventually, and apparently tired of being grist for the rumor mill, she decided to put the entire subject to rest once and for all. In just over fifteen minutes, the lead character she portrayed in her sitcom, *Ellen*, was going to come out. On national television. For the first time ever. *Ever.*

Jillian stood on the threshold between the kitchen and living room. Perched on an arm of the couch was Kevin Webster and his wife, Keisha, leaning against him. They were a young newlywed couple who'd moved into the house next door just three months ago. They were friendly, fun, and open, coming over for dinner, the fact that they'd moved in next to a lesbian couple not fazing them at all. Tinny, from softball, sat in the corner of the couch, sipping a Labatt's Blue Light. Her current girlfriend—they changed on a frequent and regular basis—sat in her lap. Deb was a tiny little thing with a nose ring and a buzz cut. The rest of the couch was occupied by Mike Klein and his wife, Gina. They lived across the street and had been the first people to welcome Jillian and Angie to the neighborhood by bringing them an apple pie hot out of the oven. On the floor near Gina's feet, leaning her back against the couch, sat Marina, and Jillian thought she looked less like an elementary school teacher and more like an old friend. Their initial bond from that first year of teaching had only solidified, and Marina had told Jillian in no uncertain terms that she wanted to be with her for the "big reveal," as she called it. Boo was stretched out next to her, her head on Marina's thigh, totally in love judging from the look in her brown eyes. Next to Marina sat Hope, the two of them with their heads bent close, lost in conversation. In the overstuffed chair in the corner, Shay sat comfortably with a glass of white wine while Laura perched on the arm of it, beer in one hand, her arm around Shay's shoulders. Jillian's brother Brian stood at the end of the couch, quietly taking it all in, but smiling just the same.

Jillian's heart warmed as she moved her gaze from one person to the next, marveling that there were more straight than gay people in the room. But that was typical, wasn't it? There were many more straight people in the world, so it made sense. The important point was that these people loved her. They loved Angie. And they loved the two of them as a couple. That was the most important factor. She and Angie had managed to surround themselves with people who loved them *together.*

Her eyes misted.

"Hot stuff coming through!" Maria bumped Jillian out of the way with a hip so she could set a plate of goodies on the coffee table.

"Yeah, but what about the food?" Jillian asked with a wink.

"More food?" Kevin said, happily bewildered. "I might just move in." He grabbed a mushroom cap and popped it into his mouth.

"Wouldn't be long before you weighed three hundred pounds," Keisha teased him.

"Only if Maria moved in, too," Angie joked, coming up behind

Jillian and wrapping her in an embrace. In her ear she whispered, "You okay, babe?"

Jillian cleared her throat and nodded. "I'm great."

"Here." Angie held a glass of wine in front of her.

"Is it weird that I'm nervous?"

"Not at all. I am too."

As if overhearing them, Laura looked over at them and said, "I've got butterflies."

"So do I," Marina chimed in. "And I'm not even gay."

"Same here," Hope said with an infectious grin. "It's so exciting!"

Deb stood up. "Before we get caught up, I'd like to propose a toast." She held up her beer; the rest of the room followed suit. "To Jillian and Angie, for opening their home to us, to all of you who are here to celebrate with us, and to Ellen DeGeneres for making history."

"Cheers!"

Moments later, the show began.

It moved along at seemingly breakneck speed, despite Jillian willing it to slow down so she could savor. The writing was tight and snappy. She laughed out loud on several occasions, along with everyone else. Laura Dern playing Susan, an out lesbian, made the fictional Ellen Morgan question her own sexuality. Jillian watched Ellen be told by Susan that she gave off a "gay vibe," then try to reject that ridiculous notion by throwing herself at a man, before finally talking with her therapist about her confusion—and she wondered how many lesbians watching right that moment had gone through exactly the same thing. She was lucky that she'd understood and accepted her own sexuality at a fairly young age. But she knew many lesbians who hadn't come out until their thirties, forties, or even later. Here was their story, playing out on national television for the first time. It was liberating, stunning.

At one point, Tinny commented, "I've always liked Laura Dern. Is it wrong that I'm now completely in love with her?" earning her a playful slap from Deb.

And when Ellen leaned too close to the airport microphone and said out loud to Susan, "I'm gay," tears filled Jillian's eyes and then streamed down her cheeks. She felt Angie's grip on her tighten, and when she turned to look at her face, her eyes were full, too. Shay and Laura were locked in an embrace, and both their faces were etched with emotion. The next second, just as it happened on the show, the entire room burst into applause. As the show broke for commercials, everyone stood and hugged each other, kissed cheeks and lips, slapped backs.

When the buzz died down, and the credits rolled, Jillian spoke to her friends.

"I don't know how to thank you all for being here, for supporting us, for being our friends. We just witnessed history. It sounds a little corny, but it's true. Not only that, but I can honestly say that I can't ever remember feeling quite as proud of who I am than I do right this second." She sniffled. "And now I will stop talking before I start sobbing."

Later that night, as Jillian stood at the bathroom sink brushing her teeth, she tried to analyze the unfamiliar emotions that hit during the show. The part about being proud? It was absolutely true. She'd always thought she was comfortable in her own skin, but now she knew that wasn't quite honest, that there'd always been a small sliver of her being that was hidden, just in case. As she rinsed her mouth and glanced up into the bathroom mirror, she caught a quick flash of her mother's eyes in her own reflection. Not for the first time, she debated over whether she wished her mother had been there to see the *Ellen* episode or if it was better that she hadn't. She could almost hear how the conversation would have gone.

"Mom, we're having a party to watch Ellen's coming out. You should come over."

"I will never understand the need to announce such a thing." Jillian could see her face, how she'd purse her lips in disapproval, arch one eyebrow as she spoke.

"It's historical, Mom. It's visibility for the LGBT community."

"You know, this is why you people have such trouble. Because you need to talk about it incessantly. It's private. Private things should stay that way. What you people do in your bedroom is your own business, but I don't need to hear about it."

It would have been awful.

But still, having her here and irritated would be better than not having her here at all. Wouldn't it?

She still couldn't decide.

"Honey." Angie's voice pulled her from her musings. "I'm cold. Come to bed and warm me up."

Jillian finished up and crawled into bed, snuggling in close to Angie even as her thoughts whirled. "I kind of wish my mom had been here."

"Really?" Angie didn't disguise her surprise, which made Jillian chuckle.

"Yeah, I know. She would've hated it. Honestly, she wouldn't have come. I don't know what I'm thinking."

Angie squeezed her tight, placed a kiss on her forehead. "Sweetie, it's okay to miss her, to want her here."

"But it's ridiculous, isn't it? I wish she'd been present at an event she would have despised. Vocally."

"It's not ridiculous."

After a pause, Jillian propped her head on her hand, looked down at Angie, and said quietly and with no small amount of wonder, "I feel proud tonight. Of being gay. I'm *proud* of who I am. I've never really felt that."

Angie nodded. "That's why you wish your mom had been here."

Jillian dropped back down to Angie's shoulder and blew out a breath. "Yeah, but she would've hated it."

Her thoughts continued to swirl long after Angie had fallen asleep.

అ అ అ

In the weeks that followed, the shift that Jillian had felt stayed with her, and it was on her mind often. She remembered reading somewhere that your thirties are the "age of enlightenment," and she wondered now if maybe that was true. Somehow, she felt newly invested in her life, as if she'd suddenly started paying more attention. There was no way to explain it, though she tried on more than one occasion. Instead, she sat with it, embraced it, and then ran with it, feeling free and solid.

Unfortunately, the same feelings didn't seem to be affecting Angie, who was a million miles away during dinner on a night in early June.

"You should have seen Bradley today," Jillian said, referring to one of her shyer students. "He had a color mix going, and I swear his paper looked like a Jackson Pollock painting. I'm not sure what got into him, but he found a combination he liked, and he just went with it." She scooped a forkful of potato into her mouth and watched Angie push her food around her plate. After a moment of silence, she went on. "And then a mob of angry leprechauns broke into my classroom and demanded all the green paint."

Angie gave a faint nod and took a slug from her wine glass.

Jillian blew out a breath. "What is wrong with you?"

Angie blinked at her. "What?"

"You haven't heard a word I've said. What's going on?"

With a grimace, Angie shook her head. "I think I'm on the verge of losing Davis Direct."

"Seriously?" It was one of Angie's larger catalog companies. Jillian knew she'd worked hard to get it, that it contributed a nice percentage to her commission—and that the Davis head of marketing, Jim Carmen, was notoriously fickle. Angie had told her all of this when she'd landed the account over a year ago. "What happened?"

Angie's expression was grim. "Freaking Carmen. He's such a jerk. He's making me bid now. I set the whole program up for him, get everything stocked and printed and logo'd, present him with *very* fair pricing—honestly, I should be marking his stuff up a lot more than I am—and what does he do? He starts collecting quotes. So he gets a lower price, then shows it to me like I'm ripping him off." She grabbed the wine bottle and topped off her glass. "How many times have I taken him out to dinner? *Nice* dinner. Or drinks? He's never paid for a thing. I take care of him. And this is the thanks I get? Asshole."

It had been a while since Jillian had seen Angie quite this angry, and she winced as some of the red wine sloshed onto the table. "Babe. Calm down. It's okay."

Angie shot her a look, and Jillian pressed her lips together. Obviously, Angie was in no mood to be talked down. *Maybe it's better to just let her vent,* she decided and kept quiet.

"Do these people think I'm not supposed to make any money? That I'm working for free?" She downed a third of her glass in one gulp. "Do you know what the worst part is?" Without waiting for Jillian to answer, she went on. "It's that the next guy who does the Davis Direct catalog will have it so easy because *I've already done all the work.* I found the products, I priced them out, I estimated shipping costs. All Carmen has to do is pass my catalog on to the new guy and tell him to come in just a little lower. It's so unfair."

"I know, babe. What about Mr. Guelli? Can he help? Talk to Carmen maybe?"

Angie barked a sarcastic laugh and drained her glass. "If there's one thing I've come to realize, it's that Guelli is a guy who owns a sales company but has no idea how to sell a thing. He's a freaking dinosaur. Honestly, I'd rather keep him away from my clients than have him meet any of them. He's embarrassing. I hate this business."

"I'm so sorry, honey. What can I do to help?"

Angie's scoff made Jillian flinch almost as much as Angie's next words. "No offense, Jill, but you work with six-year-olds all day. This is way beyond you."

Jillian poked at her cheek with her tongue, nodded slowly, and stood from the table. "Okay. Got it." She whistled for Boo, grabbed her leash, and was on her way out the side door when she heard Angie finally speak up.

"Jillian. Wait."

She kept going.

Fifteen

The merlot in her system made it impossible for Angie to remain awake until Jillian and Boo finally returned home. She must have passed out on the couch because the next thing she knew, it was after seven in the morning according to the cable box clock, and the sun was spearing her eyelids like tiny ice picks. There was barely time to register the clicking of Boo's nails as she scrambled down the hardwood stairs before her body landed like a boulder on top of Angie's chest, forcing all of the air and a loud "oof" from her lungs.

Jillian followed a moment later and didn't glance at Angie as she walked past and into the kitchen to let Boo out back.

"Hey," Angie said, her voice a mere croak.

Jillian quickly tossed some leftover salad into a bowl for lunch. She didn't turn around as she moved to the back door and let Boo out.

"Jillian. Honey. I'm really sorry." When Jillian continued to stare out the sliding glass door, Angie tried again. "I mean it. I'm sorry. I was a jerk last night."

Jillian spun around, her blue eyes hot with anger, and it was only in that moment that Angie realized she'd really crossed a line. "No, Angie, you were not a jerk. You were an *asshole*. I'm really sorry that you had a shitty day. I have them, too, even though my job is apparently a piece of cake and not nearly as complex and as important as yours."

Angie swallowed. "Yeah, that was out of line."

"You think?"

"I'm sorry, Jill."

"You should be." She turned back to the door and let Boo in. On her way through the kitchen, she stopped, rinsed Angie's late-night

114

dishes, and put them in the dishwasher. "Was that so hard?" she said out loud, and Angie knew it was a direct shot at her. Then Jillian picked up the empty wine bottle, held it for Angie to see. "And this? Not helping." She slammed it back to the counter with a thud and grabbed her keys off the rack. "I'm going to work. When I come back, I'll be going to see my father. And I'll be taking Boo with me. I don't know what time I'll be home."

And she was gone.

Angie flopped back onto the couch with a groan. Boo sat on the floor so her face was inches from Angie's and cocked her head at the sound. "Oh, Boo. Mommy fucked up. Big time." Boo blinked. No kisses, no nudges to play. It was as if the dog knew. Angie looked into the light brown eyes and felt judged. "I know. Big time," Angie said again.

She knew she should get up, get moving, but the impending stress of the day kept her pressed into the couch. She didn't want to get up because her head was pounding, as if a little man with a sledgehammer were wandering around inside her skull just banging on random things. The idea of dealing with Jim Carmen made her want to retch. She hadn't yet told Mr. Guelli about the likely loss of business. He'd pretend he understood what happened, though he wouldn't have a clue, so he'd blame her. Subtly and indirectly, but blame her he would. And on top of all of that, she really, really needed to suck up to her girlfriend. What had she been thinking, saying something like that last night? What was wrong with her? She'd been so edgy, so furious over the situation, it was like a fog had invaded her brain, obscuring everything but her anger. She knew how hard it was to teach small children; she *knew* she could never do what Jillian did, and she had said as much, more than once. On any other day, she'd tell any person who would listen what an amazing and talented teacher Jillian was. What the hell had happened yesterday to turn her into a complete shit?

"Ugh." She sat up slowly, then gradually stood. Shuffling like an eighty-year-old, she made her way into the kitchen for a glass of water, hoping it would help her headache. Had something died in her mouth? She needed to get rid of that taste, too, before she threw up all over the counter. Boo sat watching.

115

Angie stared at the empty wine bottle and then flashed on Jillian's glass of water with last night's dinner. Jillian hadn't had any wine at all.

"Christ," she muttered. Popping a slice of bread into the toaster, Angie gazed out the kitchen window. The early June sun shone brightly on the patio set in the back yard, and she wished she could just go sit there, relax and breathe, and think of nothing for a few hours. She loved June in upstate New York. Not too hot, not too cold. Flowers in bloom. No bugs yet.

In a few short weeks, her girlfriend would be done with school, and then she'd get to spend her days outside, working on the flowers and the garden, determined to harvest bushels of tomatoes this year. That had been her goal every year they'd lived in the house . . . except she seemed to have a green thumb with everything except tomatoes. She'd never ended up with more than six; it had become a running joke.

"I'm growing tomatoes this year," Jillian would say. "I mean it."

"Again?" would be Angie's reply, and she'd wink at her girlfriend.

Angie could see them sitting out there at dusk, the portable black metal fire pit they bought last year filled with branches, Jillian arranging the wood to make her fire just so, Angie smacking at her own arms, legs, shooting a look of sheer frustration at Jillian, who was always left untouched by the bugs.

"Why don't the mosquitoes ever bite you?" she'd ask, just as she had a hundred times over their years together. "Why do they only feast on me?"

Jillian would chuckle, give the same answer she always did. "If you had the choice, which would you rather suck on? Olive oil or white bread?"

Looking out the window now, Angie smiled.

Summer was coming. There were so many good times ahead.

She blew out a huge breath.

"Shit."

෬   ෬   ෬

The day didn't get any better, and not for the first time, Angie wondered why she hadn't just stayed in bed.

"Oh, yeah. That's right. Because I was on the couch," she muttered aloud as she waited on hold for a supplier to come back on the line with pricing.

Hope popped her head in through Angie's office doorway and tipped her hand to her lips, miming the universal sign for "Want to get a drink?" Today's mismatched earrings were a dangling teal cupcake and a red maple leaf.

"Oh, god, yes," she hissed in response, just as a voice came on the line and began rattling off numbers that Angie jotted down.

"I'll buzz you," Hope stage whispered, then scurried on down the hall.

Angie didn't love the pricing she'd been given, but it was the only supplier who had stock on that particular pen, and Angie's customer had a firm in-hand date. They had no choice. She added in any incidentals, marked it up to cover her own costs, typed up the quote, and hit Print. She walked to the printer, which sat behind Rosie at the reception desk, and grabbed the quote. Then she signed it, and dialed the fax number of her client just as the front door buzzer went off to signal a visitor.

"There she is," Matt Jones said with a grin. "Just the woman I was looking for."

"A customer who doesn't hate me," Angie said. "Boy, are you a sight for sore eyes." Turning to Rosie, she said, "Can you drop that fax in my office once it goes through?"

"Of course."

To Matt, she waved a come-this-way gesture. "Follow me, young man."

Once settled in her office, Matt said, "I need some tank tops. Do you have something that won't make my guys look like a bunch of losers in wife beaters?"

Angie laughed. "I know exactly what you mean, and I think I've got a solution. One of my clothing suppliers was here last week and showed samples of sleeveless T-shirts. They're a bit neater than a tank, but still let your guys stay a little cooler." Rifling through a file cabinet, she found the catalog she was looking for, thumbed to the page, and handed it to Matt. "Here."

"Oh, perfect. Those'll work."

Rosie peeked in as Matt was perusing. "Here's the fax you sent; it went through. And this one came for you." Angie took the papers from her with a nod of thanks.

The fax was from Jim Carmen, telling her he had enjoyed working with her, but they'd decided to go with another company to handle their catalog program from here on out. He'd send further instructions about where to ship the remaining stock she had on her premises.

Knowing it was coming and actually reading the words turned out to be two different things. Angie closed her eyes, inhaled slowly, exhaled even more slowly, swallowed hard, willed the lump in her throat to leave, hoped she wouldn't cry.

The sound of pages turning had stopped, and when she opened her eyes, Matt was gazing at her with concern.

"Are you okay? What's wrong?"

Slowly, she shook her head back and forth. "I just lost a really big account. I guess it was easier to tell me in a fax than actually call me on the phone and talk to me about it like an adult."

"Aw, that stinks. I'm sorry."

Her attempt to shrug it off was lame. "I knew it was coming."

"Doesn't make it easier," Matt said, his expression one of sympathy and understanding. "Happens to me all the time."

"Really?"

"In a tree and landscaping business? Absolutely. You think there aren't a hundred other guys out there just like me?"

"I guess I didn't really think about it," Angie said honestly.

"Oh, I know who my loyal customers are. Then there are the fly-by-night ones. Those are the people who will drop me like a hot potato if they get a bid that comes in five dollars cheaper than mine. Those sting. I try not to let them because I know there's nothing I could have done any different to have kept them, but they still sting."

"That's exactly it. I did a good job for this guy. My prices were fair. My products were of good quality. I'm sure some schmuck working out of his basement came in with a cheaper price and Jim's eyes lit up."

"You've been doing this for a long time now," Matt said, his voice gentle. "Aren't you used to guys like that?"

Angie thought about that. Matt was right. She should be used to this kind of thing. It came with the territory. "Yeah, this one's bothering me. I don't know why. I can't stand the guy anyway."

"Well, he'll be sorry when Basement Guy can't keep up, won't he?" Matt winked.

"This is why I keep you around, Matty. You cheer me up."

"Wait, you mean it's not my good looks?"

       ॐ   ॐ   ॐ

By the time four-thirty rolled around, Angie'd had enough. Remembering Jillian's plans to grab Boo and go to her father's, she hit her intercom button and buzzed Hope.

"Hey, sexy," she said into the speaker.

"Is it wine o'clock?" Hope asked.

"It is."

"I'll be right there. Five minutes."

They decided to keep it simple by sticking with the little bistro just down the block from the Logo Promo office. It was a place they visited often, and Mindy, the bartender, knew them well.

"What can I get for you ladies today?" Mindy couldn't have been older than twenty-five. Her straight, dark hair hung halfway down her back, and her large brown eyes were made up with subtle color. An easy smile made her approachable, and probably earned her some good tips. That, the ass-hugging jeans, and the unbuttoned blouse.

"Martini," Hope said without a second thought.

Angie blinked at her. "Wow. You're not messing around."

"No, I am not. I had one of those days."

After ordering a vodka tonic, Angie said, "Yeah, when you asked me before lunch if I wanted to drink, I figured something must be up."

Mindy delivered their drinks, and they clinked their glasses together.

"Why do we stay in this job?" Hope asked suddenly. "This business? Why do we stay?"

"Oh, that's easy," Angie replied. "I've thought about this long and hard. It's like golf. I hear you can suck at it for seventeen holes, but that one beautiful drive on the eighteenth keeps you coming back for more, because all you want is to hit another one. And you're willing to wade through seventeen more sucky holes if you can get it."

Hope nodded, sipped, nodded some more. "That is the *perfect* analogy, Angie. I spend my days dealing with assholes and writing orders that will net me a hundred bucks here and eighty bucks there because I know that if I just hang in there long enough, that big order will come in, the one that pays me a few thousand in commission."

"And then you can breathe."

"And then I can breathe."

"But only for a little while, because then it starts up all over again."

"Ugh."

"I know."

They were quiet for a moment.

"Then," Angie said, "there's the added joy of having a lucrative program, but worrying all the time that you might lose it."

"Along with the steady income you've gotten used to."

"Exactly." The slug of vodka was too big and burned Angie's throat as it went down. "I lost Davis Direct today."

Hope set down her glass and stared at Angie. "Shit. Really? I'm so sorry."

Again, as she'd done with Matt, she tried to wave it off. "I saw it coming. Though dumping me by fax was a nice touch."

"That guy is such a prick," Hope said.

"I haven't told Guelli yet."

"Speaking of pricks." Hope sipped.

"He's going to think it was me. It wasn't, but he's going to give me that look, like I'm just a *girl*, and if he'd set up Jim Carmen with a male salesperson, this wouldn't have happened."

"Tell me again why we stay." Hope winked, and Angie snorted a laugh.

"Fuck him," Angie said. "Forget it. I don't want to give him another ounce of energy. Tell me about your day. Why were you ready to drink at ten o'clock this morning?"

They commiserated for the next hour as the crowd around them thickened and the volume of the music increased. This time with Hope was vital to Angie, vital to her sanity. Somebody who didn't work in the ad specialties business had a hard time understanding the stress, the hoops that needed to be jumped through, the bubble gum and string and paper clips it sometimes took to close an order. Not to mention the fancy footwork that was often the only way to hold on to a good customer. Talking with Hope, complaining, bitching, and supporting each other, was often what helped Angie stay sane in a business that could seem utterly cracked.

As Mindy hit them with thirds, Angie asked suddenly, "Do you think we drink too much?"

"Yes," Hope answered immediately.

"No, no, take your time. You don't have to answer right away."

Hope laughed, but at Angie's suddenly serious expression, she asked, "Why?"

With a resigned sigh, Angie told her about the previous night. All of it, even the horrible thing she'd said to Jillian.

"Ouch."

"I know. The look on her face . . ." Angie shook her head, not wanting to relive it. "I'm a complete fuckwad."

"I hope the sucking up has already begun," Hope said, arching one eyebrow.

"I sent flowers to her work."

"That's a good first step. Why are you out with me and not home making it up to her?"

"She's at her dad's."

"Until when?"

"No idea."

"Okay, come here." Hope ducked her head down low, as if she had a secret plan to share. In a way, she did. "Here's what you're going to do . . ."

Sixteen

Hyacinths had the most amazing smell of any flower Jillian knew; it was one of the few things she and her mother had agreed on. The purple, pink, and white plants lined the side of the house as well as the garage, and she could still picture her mother from years ago, on hands and knees, painstakingly burying each bulb in her family's backyard. Surprisingly, some of them were still in bloom. As far as Jillian was concerned, their only drawback was that they didn't last long enough.

Boo came bounding through the yard toward her and dropped a tennis ball at her feet. She dutifully threw it.

This was Jillian's favorite time of year. The evenings began to stretch, the sun staying up a little longer each day. Warm air was pushed around by a gentle breeze. The smell of freshly cut grass was one of the biggest, most prominent markers of the season. In the distance, she could hear the buzz of a lawn mower, probably Mr. Jacobs a couple of houses down. He was a freak about his lawn.

Her dad handed her a glass filled with ice cubes and Sprite. "Here you go, sweetheart." It was the only soda he kept in the house, but she didn't mind. Folding himself into the patio chair next to her, he groaned.

"You okay?" she asked.

"Just old," was his usual reply. Then he patted her knee and gave his other usual reply. "Don't worry about me."

Since her mother's death, Jillian *did* worry about him. She supposed that was natural. It made sense that losing one parent would cause a child to become overly concerned about the other. He seemed to have handled his wife's death as well as could be expected. He'd dropped weight in the first six or eight months, but then seemed to turn a corner. Jillian had dinner with him once or twice a week, to keep tabs on his eating habits, among other things. She tried hard not to be ridiculous about showing up unannounced, and she knew that her brother was doing the same thing. They visited often, popped in unexpectedly with some lame excuse—he wondered if he could borrow a tool, or she needed to get something she thought was packed in the attic. To his credit, it was pretty obvious that Ted knew exactly what his children were up to. Also to his credit, he didn't tease or mock them about it. Jillian thought he probably understood, and she was grateful that he let them do what they felt was necessary to check up on him.

He sipped his Sprite. "So what's new with my girl?"

Boo's ball was getting slobbery. Jillian picked it up and tossed it with her thumb and finger, grimacing as she did. After a moment of gathering her thoughts, she asked, "Did you ever wish you did something different? For a living, I mean."

"Do I wish I didn't run my own business? Or do I wish I'd done something other than real estate?"

Jillian smiled, thinking how much she loved her dad. He didn't ask her why she'd posed such a question. He didn't try to analyze. Instead, he simply clarified it. "Do you ever wish you had a career other than real estate?"

"Hmm. That's a good question." He scratched his head. "I'm sure I've had times where I wondered if I should've done something different. Instances when deals fell through or clients jerked me around a few too many times or the market was in the crapper. I think mostly, though, I've enjoyed it. I'm good at it, and I've made an okay living. I've been lucky." He gave her a shrug. "Do you wish you did something other than teach?" he asked. Boo had shifted her attention to her grandpa, so he picked up the soggy ball and threw it.

"That's just it," Jillian replied. "I don't. I love my job. And I'm even finding that I like teaching the little ones. I don't care if I move up to the high school any more."

Ted studied her. "That's good, to be happy where you are. Isn't it?"

"It is." The rest of it was harder to put into words. Angie's comment had rolled around in her head all day. Had she settled? She was only thirty and was completely content in her career. She'd wanted to teach art. She was teaching art. And she was happy doing so. Was it supposed to happen so easily? When she looked at Angie, guilt flooded her. Angie was not using her degree. When asked what she did for a living, Jillian knew she did not want to answer, "Oh, I sell T-shirts and pens and other useless crap to people who don't really need it." But that wasn't Jillian's issue. It wasn't her concern. Angie's unhappiness with her job didn't mean Jillian should have to rethink her own happiness. Did it?

"You sure?" Ted was studying her face now, trying to read her thoughts.

"It is," Jillian said again, this time adding some firmness. "I'm good."

"Good."

Boo dropped her tennis ball to the patio, the sound like a wet sponge falling to the ground, and loped over to the bowl Ted left out for her. The sound of her slopping up water made both father and daughter chuckle.

"She's so dainty, isn't she?" Jillian asked as she watched water pool around the bowl. "Thanks for helping me poop her out. She'll sleep good tonight."

"I'm always happy to play ball with my grand-doggie." Boo came to him and he grabbed her big, square head with both hands, ruffling her ears even as she dripped a combination of water and drool on his pants. "Where's Angie tonight?"

So many things had shifted in the three years since her mother's passing, and this was one of them. Jillian wasn't sure if her dad was trying to make up for the past, if he'd had a change of heart, or if he just finally felt that he could express his own opinion because he no longer had a wife he worried about pissing off. Whatever the case, he was much more receptive to Angie, and to Angie and Jillian as a couple. Even now, it caught Jillian off guard, made her take a moment before answering.

"She had to work late." It wasn't a lie. It was more like an educated guess. The chances that Angie was working late were pretty high, so Jillian was most likely not lying. Plus, she didn't really want to get into the details of the previous night with her father. He didn't need to know that stuff. He'd worry. Then she surprised herself by blurting, "She sent me flowers today."

"Really?" Ted smiled. "That's a nice thing to do. Every woman should get flowers once in a while. I sent them to your mother all the time."

Jillian looked at him. "You did?"

"Yep. Probably once every month or two."

"Why?"

He looked at her like she'd asked something silly. "Because it's romantic, Jilly. Why do you think?" He gave her cheek a gentle pinch, something he had done often when she was a kid.

"It is romantic."

"She loved getting them. No matter how mad she was at me, what stupid thing I'd done or said, the flowers were always the first step in my apology." He gave her a wink. "And they always worked. What did she send?"

"Roses. A dozen."

"Oh, nice. She must have really ticked you off."

Jillian found herself chuckling, despite the unfamiliarity of *almost* talking about her love life with her dad. "She did."

"She's obviously trying to fix it." He asked no details, his gaze on the bird feeder, straight ahead from where they sat.

"I think so." Jillian, too, kept her eyes forward.

"You going to let her?"

"I probably should."

"You love her?"

"Big time."

"Then you probably should."

They became quiet, but the smile stayed on Jillian's face as she and her dad avoided eye contact and sipped their Sprites and lounged in the evening air. Boo snuffled in her sleep, crashed out between their two chairs. Jillian inhaled the floral scent that would always remind her of her mother. And for a short moment, she wished not only that her mother was sitting there with them, but that she'd heard their conversation, that she'd participated and was of the same opinion as her father. If only . . .

125

"Thanks, Dad."

"Any time, sugar."

❧   ❧   ❧

Jillian smiled as she glanced in the rearview mirror. Boo was barely conscious in the back seat of the car on the ride home. She loved visiting Grandpa. His yard was much bigger than theirs, so she ran her furry little butt off chasing the ball. Not to mention all the new, fun things there were to sniff and pee on.

Jillian's father was a good man. She had always thought so. Despite that, they'd never been close, although if she were to be honest, that probably had as much to do with her trying to keep her private life away from her parents' scrutiny or criticism. In her family, if you didn't talk about it, it didn't exist. Simple.

But things had definitely shifted. The idea that it had taken the death of her mother to bring her closer to her father was heart-wrenching, but true. And the ironic thing was, now that she felt she was developing a real relationship with her dad, the person she wanted to tell most was her mother.

Life could be so cruelly unfair.

Pulling into the driveway, she was surprised to see Angie's car. It was almost eight o'clock, and after this morning, Jillian expected it would be a late night of work for her. She grabbed her bag, let Boo out of the back seat, and headed in.

The lemony smell was the first thing she noticed.

Boo scrambled past her, galloping into the house to find her other mommy. Jillian walked in slowly, following her nose into an astonishingly clean and sparkling kitchen. The counters, the sink, even the floor glimmered with the shine of a good, thorough cleaning. A vase of fresh daisies in pink and white were centered on the breakfast bar. Another vase, this one bearing four enormous sunflowers, sat on the coffee table.

"Angie?" Jillian called, hanging her bag from the coat tree in the corner.

"Up here, babe."

The stairs were totally dust-free, as was the landing windowsill. Jillian kept going, found Angie in the bedroom making the bed with what smelled like freshly laundered sheets.

Angie stood up straight, gave what Jillian thought was meant to be a smile, but looked more like a grimace of uncertainty. "Hi."

"Hi. What's going on?"

"What do you mean?"

Jillian's eyebrows shot up. "What do I mean? It looks like the Merry Maids spent a week in here, that's what I mean."

"Oh, that." Angie smoothed the duvet cover, then sat at the foot of the bed. Boo jumped up to sniff her face, and Angie petted her absently. "I'm sorry. I'm so, so sorry."

Jillian stepped into the room and noticed a third vase of fresh flowers, this time pink roses, sitting on the dresser. "You've been busy," she said. "The house looks great."

"I wanted to make it up to you. For last night. For being such a jer—asshole, I mean. I wanted to do something nice, something you'd appreciate. And since I'm always working, and you're always stuck doing the cleaning, I decided to do it. I scrubbed everything I could find. I think I took the top layer of skin off my hands." A nervous chuckle escaped her lips. "I just . . . I thought maybe if I could clean for a change, so you didn't have to, if I could do it for you, it would . . . make you happy." She fizzled out at the end, as if deciding halfway through that everything she was saying was stupid, and her gaze dropped down to her lap. "I'm sorry, Jillian," she said, her voice barely above a whisper. "I should never have said what I did. It was hurtful and mean and I'm so sorry. I love you."

Jillian waited a beat on purpose, letting Angie suffer one more moment of misery before letting her off the hook. Three steps got her across the room and to the bed, where she sat. Taking Angie's face in her hands, she lifted it, made Angie meet her eyes. "I love you, too." She kissed Angie's lips lightly. "You're forgiven."

Angie blew out an enormous breath. "Oh, thank god," she said, wrapping Jillian in her arms. "Thank you, baby. Thank you."

Jillian pulled back so she could look Angie in the face, but kept their bodies close. "But," she said. Angie's face fell, and Jillian shook her head. "No, it's okay. I still forgive you. I love you. We're good. And the house looks amazing. But." She held up a finger. "You need to do something about work. If you hate it, you need to make some changes. I am not going to feel guilty about liking my job because you hate yours. It's not fair."

Angie nodded. "You're right."

"Figure it out." Jillian looked at her seriously. "I mean it, Angie. Figure it out. Take a different path at Logo Promo. Or make a change and leave. Go back to school. Whatever. I don't care; I just want you to be happy. But figure it out."

"I will."

"And you have to cut back on the drinking."

Lips pressed together, Angie nodded again. "I know."

Jillian held Angie's gaze for another moment before releasing her breath and leaning her head against Angie's shoulder. "Okay."

"I love you," Angie murmured into Jillian's hair.

"I love you, too." They sat like that for a long while, Boo spread out on the bed behind them, snoring softly. Eventually, Jillian stood and moved to the doorway. Angie looked at her, a question in her eyes. "What? Who knows when my house will be this clean again? I want to wander some more. Sue me."

1999

Kiss Me

Seventeen

"I have to say," Shay pointed out as she sipped a beer and watched a burly young man walk past her carrying Angie's coffee table. "This sure beats the last time you moved."

"We're in our thirties now," Angie said with a grin. "In our thirties, we hire movers."

"Amen to that. I'm too damned old to be hauling your shit around."

"So am I." Angie perched on the edge of a chair and watched as Jillian directed the movers, pointing this way and that, giving instructions as to where each box, piece of furniture, or other item should go. "I will never not hire movers again."

"We're never moving again," Jillian snapped as she disappeared into the kitchen.

"She seems a little edgy," Shay whispered.

Angie grimaced. "She's probably tired." She didn't add that Jillian had done the majority of the packing, given Angie's hours, and was none too happy about it. Her brain tossed her a quick flashback of last night's conversation.

"You're the one who wanted this move," Jillian said as she made lists and packed up the last couple of boxes. "The least you could do is be here to help."

"I know. I'm sorry." Angie meant it, but it didn't seem to make Jillian feel any better. She reached for a box, not really knowing what to do with it, feeling—and, she was certain, looking—useless.

Jillian's sigh was filled with annoyance. "Just leave it. I've got it."

Angie tried to shake the memory away. "I hate it when she's mad at me."

131

"I get that," Shay said with a nod.

"It just seems like lately, she's always mad. You know? She's got a really short temper and I feel like I've got to tiptoe around her sometimes, but I have no idea why."

"Have you asked her?"

Angie almost laughed at the ridiculousness of that suggestion. First of all, Jillian was just like her mother—though she'd never admit it. She held things in. Bottled them up. She let Angie try to figure out what was wrong. "If I ask her, she'll just say it's nothing."

"Typical woman," Shay said, reaching across to playfully push at Angie's shoulder.

"Right?" Angie grinned, but it didn't reach her eyes. Angie wasn't sure what was going on, if Jillian was still annoyed about her hours. Boy, had that become an old argument. And yes, Angie was still working hard, still working long hours, but she was making really good money. They were able to afford nice things, including this house.

Angie had been looking at houses on a whim. Over the past few months, she'd noticed herself paying close attention to "For Sale" signs whenever she was out on a call. There were neighborhoods she really liked, houses less cramped, streets with more privacy, properties that had less of a city and more of a suburban feel. She began to think maybe it was time for them to make that move—to the suburbs. Bigger, better. She didn't go intentionally looking. She just started to observe.

This wasn't the first house that caught her eye. It was more like the fourth or fifth. But it was definitely the best. In the suburbs, on almost two acres, far enough from the city to see the stars. There were four bedrooms, enough for a guest room and a studio for Jillian. A finished basement, a formal dining room, a brand new kitchen, a big yard for Boo. She'd called Jillian's brother Brian, and he got her an appointment. It was perfect. She felt it, and she wanted Jillian to feel it too.

Convincing her wasn't easy.

"Why do we need to move?" she'd asked.

"We don't need to. But don't you think it's time?"

"What does that mean? 'It's time.' I don't understand. Is this because Dom and Pam have a new house?"

"No. Of course not." Angie bristled at the comparison. "I just thought maybe a change would be good." Angie searched for the right words. "This is what couples do when they grow up, you know?" Her laugh came unbidden at the reference to their age. "They move to bigger houses. They move out of the city, away from the hustle and bustle to someplace nicer, more peaceful."

"It just seems kind of, I don't know, unnecessary," Jillian shrugged, but Angie could tell she was at least entertaining the idea.

"Just take a look with me." Angie grabbed her hands. "Come on, baby. We can afford to have a bigger place. Why shouldn't we?"

"All right," Jillian allowed as her smile broke through. "But only to look."

That was all Angie had needed: Jillian making a visit.

The rest was history.

Their new house was at the end of a cul-de-sac in a nice, quiet neighborhood that straddled the line between suburbs and country. Angie loved that. She loved the idea of driving home from work and watching the office buildings and stores become parks and farms and fields. Unlike their house in the city, the neighbors here were a good distance away. They wouldn't be looking out their bathroom window and into the window of a bedroom next door. They had space now. Privacy. Peace and quiet.

"I'm going to have a chat with her," Shay said, yanking Angie back to the present. She shot a wink over her shoulder and followed Jillian's path up the stairs.

Angie inhaled deeply, blew out her breath slowly. Yes, the house was perfect. Now if she could only find a way to make it so with everything else.

જ   જ   જ

"Hey." Shay found Jillian in a bedroom tapping a finger against her lips, scrutinizing a wall.

Jillian blinked several times as if coming out of a trance. "Oh, hey, you." She stepped towards the doorway and wrapped her arms around her much shorter friend. "I'm ignoring you. I'm sorry. Arranging the furniture on the fly is harder than I thought it would be."

"You don't have to get it all right today, you know."

"I know. I just like things to be somewhat in order."

Shay nodded, then pointed to different parts of the room. "I think the dresser there, I like where the bed is, nightstands, and maybe the other dresser . . . here?"

Jillian considered the suggestion. "You might be right." As two movers came in carrying a large dresser, she pointed them in the direction Shay had chosen, then gave one nod of affirmation. "Perfect." Turning back to her friend, she asked, "Where's Laura?"

Shay's dark eyes slid away from hers. "Oh, she had some stuff to take care of."

Jillian studied her face and softened her entire stance when she caught the look of uncertainty zip across. "Hey." Shay's arm was strong under her fingers. "Are you all right?"

Shay met her gaze, raw confusion in her expression. "I don't know. I just don't know."

"Come here." Jillian took Shay's hand and led her to the foot of the bed where they sat on the bare mattress. "Talk to me. What's going on?"

"I don't know," Shay said again, then blew out a breath of frustration. "Laura's been kind of weird lately. She's quiet, a little distant. We're not talking like we used to. Something's not right."

"Have you asked her about it?"

Shay scoffed. "I've touched on it, but she brushes me off." Her eyes filled with tears. "Honestly, Jill, I don't think I want to know."

Seeing her old friend so emotional worried Jillian, it was so uncommon. Shay was stoic, tough, no-nonsense. Jillian wanted to skirt the issue but she asked anyway, "Do you think she's having an affair?"

A half-sob escaped Shay's throat. "I don't know what else it could be."

"Oh, sweetie." Jillian pulled Shay close, hugged her tightly as quiet tears flowed. They stayed like that for several long minutes, Jillian silently pointing to direct the occasional mover who appeared with a box.

Finally, Shay sat up, wiped her wet, blotchy face, and gave a self-deprecating chuckle. "God, I hate this. I feel like a twelve-year-old."

"Sweetie, you're hurting. That's nothing to be ashamed of."

A breath in, a breath out. Shay looked in Jillian's eyes. "What do I do?"

"You need to talk to her."

"Ugh."

"I know. It won't be easy. But you need to know what's going on and what you're up against. Right?"

"Probably."

"Shay." Jillian took her hands. "If you do nothing, nothing will change," and she thought bitterly over how little improvement had taken place in her own relationship.

"You're right." A bitter laugh. "I know you're right. But . . . what if she is having an affair?"

"Well, that'll suck." Their gazes held until they both laughed. "But you'll know, and you'll be able to decide what you want to do." Her shrug said, *What other option is there?*

ॐ   ॐ   ॐ

It was nearly nine o'clock before Jillian and Angie were alone in their new house. Physical exhaustion rivaled emotional as they took paper plates of pizza, cans of beer, and Boo up to their new master bedroom. They collapsed on the still unmade bed, leaning their backs against the wall.

"Oh, my god, I don't think I've ever been this tired. I don't know if even I have the energy to chew this pizza."

Jillian laughed. "I'm too hungry not to, but there will be no strength left to make the bed. Hope you don't mind sleeping on a bare mattress under a comforter."

"I could sleep on the basement floor right about now."

Even Boo seemed too tired to show any interest in their food. She turned in a circle twice at the foot of the bed and settled down to sleep.

They ate in silence. Jillian looked around the room as she chewed, finally pronouncing, "I like this room."

With a nod, Angie agreed. "Me, too. It's got a good feel, doesn't it?"

"It's the windows. All the light. And I like this tan on the walls. I know I talked about painting it, but I think I'd like to keep it. It looks like melted chocolate ice cream."

"It does." They ate some more, then Angie said, "I think this house was meant for us."

"Yeah? How come?"

"I'm not sure." Squinching her eyes up in thought didn't help Angie find the right words. "It's just a feeling. I had it as soon as we walked in the first time."

"I like that." Jillian grinned. "All I can say is, I'm so glad we didn't move in the dead of winter this time."

"Who says we don't learn from our mistakes?" Angie laughed, and they tapped their beer cans together in solidarity.

They ate their pizza in companionable silence for several long moments before one of them spoke again

"Shay thinks Laura's cheating on her." Jillian wasn't even aware she'd been thinking about it until the words blurted out of her mouth.

Angie's head snapped around. "What?"

Jillian nodded. "She's worried."

"Oh, man. That's rough. Do you think she is?"

"You know her better than I do."

"I know, but we've kind of drifted." Angie shrugged.

"Well, I do know Shay. She's not the kind of person to worry needlessly. Of course, I've never seen her so head over heels for somebody the way she is for Laura, so maybe she's overreacting." She sighed. "I don't know."

"Well, all we can do is be there for them. Her. Them." Angie grimaced. "I hope it's a big misunderstanding. I don't want to have to pick sides."

"We wouldn't," Jillian said, then looked at Angie. "Would we?"

Angie lifted one shoulder. "Wouldn't we?"

"I have no idea. I say we cross that bridge when we come to it. If we come to it."

"Deal. Let's talk about our new house some more instead."

Jillian was surprised that despite their exhaustion, Angie unpacked a couple small boxes as they talked, setting the marketing and business books she'd recently purchased on her nightstand. She'd been reading a lot of that type of thing lately, Jillian had noticed, and she regarded them warily.

When Angie settled back down, they spent a while longer talking about each individual room, paint colors, furniture arrangement, future remodeling projects, and other changes they hoped to make. The ideas would have energized Jillian if she hadn't been so bone tired already. Her summer break had just started, though, and she had two long months with nothing to do but work on her new house. And maybe her art.

"First thing tomorrow, I'm going to head over to Home Depot and grab a ton of paint swatches. Are you sure you need to go in to work? We could look at colors." Jillian poked out her bottom lip, earning the intended playful reprimand from Angie.

"Hey, don't use the boo-boo face on me. I only have to go in for a couple hours. If I get a few things off my plate, Monday will be that much easier for me, and we can look at colors then. Okay?"

"Fine." Jillian continued to work the pout until Angie laughed. Plates aside and beer cans drained, they sat in silence, Boo's soft snuffling the only sound in the room. Jillian leaned her head on Angie's shoulder and said quietly, "I wish my mom was here. She'd really like this place."

Angie wrapped an arm around her. "You think so?"

With a nod, Jillian said, "She always liked this neighborhood, and she'd love the layout of the house. She was great with interior design. I wish she could've helped. Don't you?"

"Of course. Especially since she never came to our last house."

Jillian sighed. "I know. Who knows if she would've even come here? Still. I wish she could."

Angie pressed a kiss to the top of her head. "She's with you, honey. Don't get me wrong, she hates that you live here with me, but she knows it's a great house."

Jillian laughed, which—she knew—was Angie's intention.

"It was really cool of your dad and brother to stop by. I think your dad liked the place."

That remark kept the smile on Jillian's face. "I think he did, too. And I think Brian was really glad you called him."

"So was I."

Jillian snuggled down into the comforter. "Time for sleep. Tomorrow is all about color."

Eighteen

Blue was not Jillian's favorite color, but there'd been something about the serene, almost slate-like shade she had ended up choosing for her studio. Now, as she sat at her desk facing the window, looking out at the lush green of the trees in the backyard and surrounded by the peaceful blue, she felt weirdly artistic. Full of creativity. She'd woken up that morning with the burning desire to sketch with charcoal.

She didn't try to analyze it when the creative bug hit. That lesson was learned a long time ago. Don't question it, just go. Just do.

Sarah McLachlan crooned softly from the stereo in the corner. Boo was curled up on her fluffy dog bed, her big paws with the white nails cradling her chin. Jillian spun in her chair, sketchbook on her knee, and went to work, because really, there was no better subject than her beloved pup. She smiled as she worked, changing charcoal thickness, smudging with her fingertip to shade where necessary. Boo's flanks were hard to get just right. Her nose was easy. Her paws were tough, her ears a bit simpler.

It was early August and hot. Not a fan of air conditioning and how it dried her sinuses, Jillian found herself thankful this house had it. She never cranked it, and she couldn't understand people who did. Angie told her that Keith at work was always turning the a/c down to 65 degrees. *That's not even warm enough in the winter,* Angie would say. *Why is that acceptable in the summer? The office is freezing!* Jillian agreed and set the house a/c at a comfortable 75.

Boo shifted in her sleep before Jillian was completely done with the picture, but it was okay. She could wing it the rest of the way. She didn't want to stop. Something about the sound, the smell, the feel of charcoal

139

against the paper, the blackening of her fingertips, made Jillian feel more relaxed than anything else. It didn't matter to her that she wasn't a terrific artist. She was okay, and that was good enough. She felt at peace when she was drawing or painting. That was all that mattered.

When the ringtone on her new cell phone sounded, it took Jillian a moment to realize what is was, then where it was. Angie had just purchased it for her, telling her it was a really good thing to have in an emergency, but Jillian still wasn't used to it. She never remembered to carry it with her, causing Angie to point out more than once that having it with her was sort of key to having it help during an emergency. Jillian was working on it.

Following the electronic-sounding ringtone brought her to her dresser in the bedroom, and she picked up just in time to keep the call from going into her voicemail—which was a good thing because she had no idea how to retrieve her messages.

"Hello?"

"Misplace your cell again?" Shay's voice was tight, but held the hint of a smile.

"I don't know why she thinks I have to have one of these. I don't travel for work. I don't go very many places without her. If I'm not at the school, I'm here. Why didn't you just call the house?"

"I was testing you. You barely passed."

Jillian snorted.

"Mark my words, everybody's going to have one of these things."

"I know. I'm a relic." Jillian chuckled. "How are you?" She glanced at the clock, saw that it was still before noon, an unusual time for Shay to be calling. "You have today off?"

The clearing of her throat told Jillian something was off with her friend. "No, I'm at work. I just needed to hear a friendly voice."

"What's the matter?"

This time, it sounded like Shay sniffled before she cleared her throat again. Jillian recognized it as an attempt to keep emotion at bay. "I was right about Laura," Shay said softly.

"Oh, Shay. Oh, no."

"Yeah. She's been seeing somebody else. She wants out." Shay sniffed.

"Oh, honey. I'm so sorry."

"Can you meet me for lunch?"

"Of course. Tell me when and where."

            ৡ   ৡ   ৡ

That night at dinner, Angie kept shaking her head and muttering, "I don't believe it." She sipped her wine, took a bite of her chicken, shook her head. "I don't believe it."

"I know," Jillian said with a nod.

"Did she give any reason?"

Jillian spooned some potatoes onto her plate and blew out a loud breath. "Just that Shay works too much, they've drifted apart, that she's felt that way for a long time."

"Well, Jesus Christ, how 'bout you talk about it instead of fucking somebody else?"

"Pretty sure that's how Shay feels too."

"I don't believe it."

Jillian chewed for a moment, then said, "Laura never called you about it? Never said anything?"

"Not a thing. Frankly, I'm a little miffed about that, too. I mean, I know I said we've drifted some, but we're still friends, for Christ's sake. Maybe I could have helped set her straight before she did something stupid." She was quiet for a beat, then added, "She's seemed distant lately. I did notice that, but really didn't think anything of it. Now I wish I'd called her on it."

"I don't know that it would have made any difference. Shay said she's totally made up her mind. Doesn't want to talk about it. Doesn't want to see a counselor. Nothing. She wants out so she can be with this other person."

"And do we know this other person?"

Jillian shrugged. "I have no idea. Somebody from her office building, I think."

"God, poor Shay."

"I told her she was welcome to stay here if she needed to, at least until Laura gets her stuff out of the house. That's okay, right?"

"Absolutely." Angie pushed her plate away. "I can't eat any more. I feel sick about this."

That was something about Angie that Jillian loved: her ability to empathize. Coming off like a stoic businesswoman was a lot of work for her because that wasn't really who she was. Jillian blamed Joe's Italian genes for Angie's emotion, and Alice's English genes for Angie's attempts to conceal that emotion. It was quite the battle that went on inside her girlfriend, but at times like this, when the emotion was clear-cut and palpable, Jillian felt like she was really seeing Angie's heart.

"I want to call Laura, but I don't," Angie said. "I want to ask her what the hell is going on, but I'm afraid I wouldn't be nice about it."

"She may end up calling you, you know."

"Yeah." She was quiet for a moment. "Not sure what I'd say."

Jillian stood and started clearing the table. Angie joined her. As they were putting the last of the dishes into the dishwasher, Angie said, "We're there, in that spot where we'll have to choose sides between our friends."

Jillian furrowed her brow. "Why do we have to choose sides? I mean, I don't like what Laura did, but does that mean we can't be friends anymore?"

"It's what happens, babe. You've seen it. What about when we have a party or go out with a group? We can't invite both of them."

"Why not?"

Angie stopped what she was doing and looked at Jillian. "Honey. Shay has been your friend since you were a kid. Would you really want to put her in the position of having to be in the same room with the ex that broke her heart?"

"But Laura is your friend. Don't you feel the same way?"

"I haven't known her as long as you've known Shay. And . . ." Her voice drifted off, and she simply shook her head.

"You don't like the way she handled things."

Angie looked at her, her eyes flashing. "I hate the way she handled things."

Jillian inclined her head. "Me too."

Nineteen

The New Year's Eve party at Tinny's was in full swing, and at full volume. The stereo was blasting—appropriately—Prince's *1999*. There were plenty of guests talking, laughing, and in varying states of intoxication, some having been there for much of the day. A trio of women sat at the dining room table, talking over a bottle of merlot while two women Jillian recognized from her early softball days were competing to see which of them could stand on her head longer while holding a beer, as half a dozen others watched and cheered them on.

On the television, a muted Dick Clark was pointing out the ridiculous number of people in Times Square waiting for the ball to drop at midnight. Jillian shook her head in awe as she watched. *You couldn't pay me enough to be there,* she thought, watching the throngs of people packed up against one another like so many thousands of sardines. Just the thought of being *that* close to *that* many strangers made her want to wriggle out of her skin.

"What happens if you have to pee?" Angie's voice was soft as she wrapped her arms around Jillian from behind, kissed her temple.

"I was just wondering that same thing," Jillian said with a laugh. "I think you either hold it or you wear a diaper."

"I'd love to be there for New Year's Eve." Angie reached around and pointed to a window on the TV screen, high above the crowd. "But only if I'm in one of these apartments. Warm, dry and near a toilet."

"Amen to that."

They were interrupted by the ringtone of the office. Jillian rolled her eyes and stepped out of Angie's arms.

"Seriously, Angie? It's New Year's Eve."

143

With a grimace, Angie fumbled in her pocket for her cell phone. "I know. It's got to be an overseas supplier. I'm sorry. I'll get rid of them." She handed her empty cup to Jillian, moved to a corner and plugged one ear with a finger as she pressed the phone to the other.

Tinny staggered across the room to Jillian. "Hey!" Tinny's voice was booming, not surprising since she'd been drinking since early afternoon. "I'm so glad you guys are here." She leaned heavily against Jillian, and Jillian laughed even as she worked to help her keep her balance. "Jill. We need you this year. Come back to the team."

This was not the time to get into it—Jillian was pretty sure Tinny wouldn't remember this conversation tomorrow, let alone at the beginning of softball season in the spring—but it was something Jillian had been thinking about. With a glance at Angie, still on the phone, she said to Tinny, "I may take you up on that. You never know."

"Really?"

Jillian nodded. "I miss it. And I've got the time." She purposely did *not* look at Angie as she said that.

"Excellent. Wait. Why are your cups empty?" Tinny's stood up straight. "Gimme those." She snatched the two plastic cups out of Jillian's hands and disappeared with them, leaving Jillian grinning and shaking her head.

"What are the chances we get refills before Tinny gets distracted by a conversation and forgets us altogether?" Angie asked as she reappeared by Jillian's side, the phone tucked away once more.

"Slim to none," Jillian answered with a laugh.

"I'm on it." Angie followed Tinny into the kitchen where the keg was.

Across the room, Jillian saw Shay in conversation with a cute redhead, and she studied them. It had taken a ton of convincing to get her to come along to the party with them, but Angie had been very persuasive. Plus, Jillian suspected that seeing nobody socially except herself and Angie was starting to bore poor Shay to tears. The redhead was taller—though that didn't take much when compared with Shay—and seemed to be absorbed in what Shay was saying, her eye contact remaining steady. Shay looked better than she had over the past few weeks. She was still too thin—Jillian had done her best to invite her to dinner often in an attempt to put back on the twenty or so pounds she'd dropped since the breakup—but her face didn't look quite so gaunt any more, and she was actually grinning at the redhead. Only in that second did Jillian realize how much she'd missed that smile. As if feeling Jillian's eyes, Shay turned and caught her gaze, then excused herself and headed in Jillian's direction.

"God, I'm so glad the holidays are almost over," Shay told her.

"I bet." She gestured with her eyes toward the redhead. "She's cute. She doesn't look familiar."

"She's new in town. Just started working in Tinny's building a couple months ago. Got roped into coming to this party, but she only knows, like, four people." Shay sipped her Coke.

Before they could continue, Tinny's latest squeeze stopped by with a tray of small, plastic shot glasses, her voice about a hundred decibels louder than necessary. "End of the world Jell-O shots! Have one!"

Shay declined, but Jillian grabbed a green one. Using her tongue deftly and making Shay laugh in the process, she sucked down the shot just as Angie returned with two cups.

"Hey! You're only supposed to do that when I'm here to watch," she whined. Noticing Shay, she asked, "Do you need a drink?"

"Nah. It's better for me to avoid that stuff tonight. Besides, somebody's got to drive your two drunk asses home."

"I am not drunk," Jillian said. "Quite yet."

Cheers rang out from across the room as one of the head-standers fell to the floor, along with her beer.

"Ah, to be in our twenties again," Angie said, feigning wistfulness.

"I don't miss that," Jillian replied. "I do miss softball, though."

"Tinny hit you up?" Shay asked. "She said she was going to."

"Yup, but I've been thinking about it anyway. I got away from it once I got a job and a house and a life, and I just never went back. I worry that I'm too old to play now, that I'll break a hip, but I miss it."

"I've got some friends starting up a golf league. You should join us." Jillian glanced at Angie. "I have no idea how to golf," Angie said.

"My dad golfs," Jillian reminded her. "I bet we could get the basics from him."

"Think about it," Shay told her.

Guests had been coming and going steadily since Angie, Jillian, and Shay arrived around eight. At 11:30, the doorbell rang and the front door opened. Jillian knew who it was before she looked, simply by the way Shay's face fell and she muttered, "Fuck."

Laura looked good. Better than Jillian wished she did. Her eyes were sparkling, her skin aglow. She looked happy. She was hand in hand with a tall blonde with stunningly blue eyes and a pretty face. Jillian could feel Shay stiffen before she excused herself and left the room. Laura watched her go, even as she greeted Tinny and Margo, smiling and handing over her coat.

"Should I go get Shay?" Angie asked Jillian in a whisper.

"Let her be for a minute." Jillian took a swallow from her cup and almost choked on it as she saw Laura look their way, then head towards them.

"Shit," Angie muttered.

"Just be nice," Jillian warned. "Don't make a scene."

"Hey, you guys," Laura said, her grin just a little bit too big and a little bit too forced. "How are you?"

"Good. We're good," Jillian said. "And you?"

Laura nodded. "I'm good, too." Turning to the woman whose hand she still held, she said, "This is my girlfriend, Kerry. Kerry, this is Jillian and Angie."

Kerry gave a genuine smile and reached out a hand. "I've heard so much about you two. It's nice to finally have faces to go with the names."

They all shook hands politely, but the conversation faltered. Laura shifted from one foot to the other, obviously uncertain how to navigate around the elephant in the room. Angie never looked her in the eye, not once. Jillian was at a loss. They all stood there in uncomfortable silence. Finally, Kerry provided the necessary out when she waved to somebody across the room and tugged Laura away with a, "Nice to meet you both" tossed over her shoulder.

"Okay, that could not have been more awkward," Angie said, relief obvious in her tone.

"Oh, my god, I was afraid we'd all just stand there looking at each other forever."

Before they could continue, Shay returned. "You guys, I've got to get out of here. I'm so sorry, but I can't do it. I can't stay here with them being all lovey-dovey. I can't take it."

Jillian and Angie exchanged a glance, then set their drinks down.

"But, it's almost midnight," Tinny whined, loudly, when they told her they had to head out.

"I know," Angie soothed. "But Jillian's got a stomach thing going on, and the last thing she wants to do is puke in your newly remodeled bathroom."

On cue, Jillian burped and covered her mouth with her fingers.

Tinny grimaced. "Oh, all right. But feel better." She hugged all three of them, the smothering, too-tight bear hug of a large woman who's had way too much alcohol. "I love you guys."

Once tucked into the car, Shay spoke from behind the wheel. "I'm so sorry. I didn't mean to ruin your New Year's Eve."

Angie was in the passenger's seat, Jillian in the back, but they held hands over the seat. "You didn't ruin anything," she said.

"I just—I couldn't do it. Just when I think I'm okay, I get knocked back down a few pegs again." Shay blew out a frustrated breath.

"Screw her," Angie said. "You stay with us tonight."

"Oh, no," Shay protested. "I couldn't. I've already encroached on you two enough for one night."

"Well, you are staying with us tonight." Jillian was surprised when she heard herself. She'd hoped to have a quiet, romantic evening with Angie to ring in the New Year, maybe even an orgasm or two. But her friend needed them, and it's not like it would be the first time Jillian had hoped to make love with Angie and ended up disappointed. "We've got some champagne. The guest bed has fresh sheets on it. Angie's cooking a fabulous breakfast in the morning. Right, honey?"

"Absolutely," Angie said. "Besides, we might need help if all the electronics go kaplooey and the world ends."

That was all the convincing Shay needed.

2001

Hanging by a Moment

Twenty

Angie was cursing at her calculator, unable to figure out how she'd screwed her markup so badly, when the frantic intercom call from Hope yanked her attention away.

"Angie. Get in here. Keith's office. Hurry up!"

Two questions hit her brain as she stood. One: Why did Hope sound so freaked? And two: What the hell was she doing in Keith's office? She hated him. Angie hurried down the hall, noticing several others heading in the same direction. When she got to Keith's office, four of them were already standing in the middle of it, eyes glued to the small television he had set up on top of his armoire. Keith was one of those people who needed constant noise—television, radio, whatever—to help him work.

The television was tuned in to what the bottom of the screen said was breaking news.

"What's going on?" she asked, her question echoed by the three others who'd followed her in. Even Mr. Guelli was standing in the group.

"A plane flew into the World Trade Center," Keith told her, his eyes never leaving the screen.

"What?" Angie was incredulous. "How the hell does that happen?"

"Half hour ago. They're trying to figure out if it was an accident or a terrorist," Guelli said.

Before any more could be said, the TV reporter's voice raised in pitch, and he became more animated.

"Oh, my god," Hope said. "There's another one!"

The group watched in horror as a second plane crashed straight into the building, an explosion of flames shooting out into the New York City sky.

"Holy shit," Angie said, as her colleagues shrieked. . They watched the news for long moments, everybody trying to absorb the fact that this had definitely been an attack on the United States. Then the unthinkable happened.

The South Tower began to collapse, each floor caving in on the one below it. Angie covered her mouth with her hands. People around her gasped and cried out.

"Oh, my god," she whispered. "All those people. *All those people.*"

Nothing could be done. Nobody could do anything but watch, horrified, as the World Trade Center collapsed on itself, taking the lives of thousands in a matter of minutes.

The group, watched, paralyzed. Finally, Ivan, the graphic artist, spoke up.

"My college roommate lives in Manhattan. I need to make sure he's okay." He left the room without a backward glance, and his words spurred on the rest of them to head for a phone or a computer to check on their loved ones.

Somebody had attacked the United States.

It was almost unfathomable. Back in her office, Angie scoured the Internet and gobbled up any reports she could find. Her mother called her cell phone.

"Ma. You okay?"

"Oh, Angelina," her mother said, distraught. Angie could hear the tears in her voice. "How could anybody do something so awful?"

"I don't know, Ma. I don't know."

Several more calls came in a similar fashion. Maria. Matt. She tried Jillian's cell several times, but with no answer. She wondered if she'd even heard, or if she was closed up in her classroom with finger-painting six-year-olds. She left messages.

Focusing on work was next to impossible. Her intercom crackled with Guelli's voice.

"Everybody. Go home. Nobody can concentrate. We shouldn't bother. Go home. Be with your families. We're closing early."

Angie blinked at her phone. Closing early? That never happened.

But this day . . . there was something that linked them all. Angie'd never considered herself any more or less patriotic than the next girl, but this day—they were all Americans and they all needed to stick together.

She was packing up her briefcase when her cell rang again.

"Angie Righetti."

"Angie? Did you hear?" It was Jillian, her voice cracking.

"I did. Baby, are you okay?"

"We're sending the kids home early. Everybody's leaving. It's so awful."

"I'm on my way home, too. I'll meet you there. Be careful driving. A lot of people are closing early, so traffic will be heavy. Take your time."

It was nearly another ninety minutes before they stood in the kitchen, their arms wrapped around one another. Jillian cried in Angie's arms, then chastised herself for doing so.

"I don't know why I'm crying. I don't know anybody in Manhattan. I didn't lose anybody." She swiped at her tears.

"Oh, honey, we all did. We've all lost somebody. We've lost some of our peace, our sense of security. We should all be crying."

They spent the remainder of that day and well into the evening in front of the television. They held hands, their petty squabbles forgotten and even their difficult issues set aside for the time being. News reports were plentiful. Film of the planes was abundant, and it was played over and over and over again.

"I don't want to see it anymore," Jillian whispered, her head on Angie's shoulder. "But I feel like I have to. For the sake of everybody who died, I feel like it's my duty to sit here and watch it happen as many times as they show it to me."

Angie wrapped her arms around Jillian and held her tightly.

"I don't think the country will ever be the same again," Jillian said.

"I know, baby. I know."

They sat.

They watched.

They ached.

Angie dialed Jillian's cell with the phone on speaker. She answered on the second ring.

"Hi, babe."

"Hey," Angie said. "Are you home?"

"Where else would I be at dinnertime?"

Angie tried to ignore what she felt was an implied "the time of day when you're never here," and stuffed extra cheerfulness into her voice. "Good. Stay put. I'm almost there."

"Already?" Jillian's disbelief was evident.

"Go outside. I have a surprise for you."

Ten minutes later, she coasted into the driveway, put the car in park and hopped out. She gestured to the Lexus, with a grand flourish worthy of Vanna White. "What do you think?"

Jillian's eyebrows raised into her hairline. "It's beautiful. Whose is it?"

Angie dropped her arms in a move that said, *Duh!* "Mine, silly. Ours. I just bought it."

"You did? When?" Jillian's tone fell somewhere between happily startled awe and irritation. Angie tried hard to keep it squarely in the former.

"Yesterday. I went over on my lunch hour. The dealer is a client of mine, so I knew he'd steer me in the right direction."

Jillian walked slowly around the sedan, running her fingertips along the sleek, midnight blue exterior, her eyes taking it all in. "But do we need a Lexus? It's not exactly an affordable brand, Ang."

Angie nodded. She had prepared for this. "I know. I know. But I was going for image."

Jillian's barely suppressed her eye roll. "Image again? Angie."

"Seriously. I read a couple articles in the sales magazines that Keith gets. They talked about how important image is for somebody in sales. It's like I keep telling you. You need to look successful. Look the part. You need the right clothes, the right shoes, the right car to give the impression of success to your customers. You know? Nobody wants to buy stuff from somebody in an off-the-rack suit who drives a beater."

Jillian came around the front of the car, having circled it once. "You didn't think it was something we could have maybe discussed together?"

Angie nodded her agreement. "I know. I should have mentioned it. But it all happened so fast. It just felt right. Remember when Dom joined his firm? He got really nice furniture for his office and traded in his Toyota for a BMW for the same reason. Image." She watched Jillian's face, and could see that she wasn't happy about the purchase and was fighting to keep from lashing out, chewing instead on the inside of her cheek—until suddenly, instead, she accepted it.

"Well?" she said, arms thrown out to the sides. "Are you just going to stand there or are you going to take me for a ride in your new luxury automobile?"

Angie jumped into motion and opened the passenger door for her partner. "Wait until you see the interior. It's going to blow your mind."

～ ～ ～

Angie watched from the copier as Vincent Guelli led the strange man around the office. The guy was young—maybe midtwenties—and Angie was pretty sure she'd seen him before, though she couldn't place him. *Must be a new sales guy,* she thought, slightly irritated because she knew she'd probably be tapped to train him. She had enough on her plate with her own clients, but she'd been trying to do anything and everything Guelli asked of her in order to help her work up her nerve. A sit-down with him was her goal. A closed meeting, just Guelli and Angie, talking frankly. He wasn't getting any younger. His health wasn't great. He was looking more seriously at retirement; she could feel it. She could see it in the way he'd been spending less and less time in the office, delegating more tasks to others. Guelli was contemplating an exit, and Angie wanted to be there to help him make that transition.

She was more than ready to run the company. She knew it. He had to know it. She'd been there for over a decade and had more than proven herself. She knew sales, and more importantly, she knew the ad specialties business. It had been quite a while now that she'd been studying marketing projections and reading business books. She'd joined a couple of small business organizations so she could network. She knew that changing with the times was paramount, and that Guelli didn't have a clue. Logo Promo needed a leader to help it slide seamlessly into the new century, to help it use the Internet rather than fight against it. Angie spent countless hours of her free time doing research on how to implement the World Wide Web as part of a growing, timely business, and she had tons of ideas. Logo Promo was solid. She wanted to keep it that way.

Guelli and the young man were headed her way. Angie finished her copies and looked up as they approached her, pasting on a smile and thinking maybe now was the time to set up that meeting. Why wait?

"And this is Angie Righetti," Guelli said to the young man as they stopped in front of her. "One of our best salespeople. Angie, this is my nephew, Jeremy Guelli."

Jeremy was nice-looking and clean-cut. With broad shoulders and an athletic build, he stood a few inches taller than Angie, and his handshake was firm. His khakis and polo shirt were neat, his leather shoes shiny, his hair combed. He looked every bit the young urban professional. "I've heard a lot about you," he said, flashing a perfect, white and very expensive smile. "Uncle Vince has nothing but good things to say about you."

"What a relief," Angie said with a grin. "Are you coming on board?"

Jeremy nodded and Guelli said, "I was hoping you could give him a crash course in the ad specialties business, Angie. Jeremy's got a business degree, but is unfamiliar with how our particular industry works. I told him you could show him the ropes."

"Of course," Angie said, suddenly uneasy. Smiling extra broadly, she said to Guelli, "On another topic, do you have some time for me this afternoon?"

Guelli nodded. "Sure. I've got to be out of here by five, though, so come see me before that." Gesturing to his nephew, he said, "I'll show him around the rest of the office, then send him to you when we're finished."

"Sounds good."

"Nice to meet you, Angie," Jeremy said as they continued on their way.

Around noon, Guelli buzzed Angie on the intercom and told her she wouldn't need to spend time with Jeremy until the next day. They'd gotten waylaid. Angie didn't ask for clarification. Instead, she took the time to get her ideas and information all organized for her meeting with Guelli later.

She'd printed out several articles about using the Internet to help grow a small business. She'd contacted several local chapters of different networking organizations and had compiled information on all of them, along with notations of how joining a few of them could benefit Logo Promo by helping them reach new customers. She'd researched sales managing and how to set up realistic quotas for salespeople, as well as information about sales meetings and how to pump up your sales team. Sales was a very difficult job, and incentives and positive reinforcement were key to keeping your sales force from slipping into frustration. Guelli thought sales meetings were a waste of time, so this one would be a delicate point to make, but Angie was determined. Optimism flooded her. This was it. This was what she'd been waiting for. She knew this company inside and out, and despite the difficulties she occasionally faced, knew she could run it and run it well.

Time to prove it.

At 4:30 on the dot, she rapped on Guelli's office door, and at his gruff "Come!" she entered. He was in the middle of figuring commissions for one of his salespeople. Angie could tell by the handmade chart on the desk in front of him and the adding machine at his right elbow. Guelli was intimidated by computers, and he hand-calculated and wrote out all the commission sheets for the sales staff. Time and time again, Angie told him a computer program would be faster and more accurate—he'd made dozens of numerical mistakes over the years—but he remained undeterred.

And stupid, in Angie's opinion.

She sat quietly, if not quite patiently, as Guelli finished up what he was doing, then set it all aside. Folding his hands neatly in front of him, he gave her his attention.

"Okay, sweetheart. What can I do for you?"

Angie bristled at the pet name. He talked to all his female employees that way. Angie knew he shouldn't, that she should ask him not to, but he was an old, old friend of her parents', and respect and manners always won out. She could almost hear her father's voice. *He doesn't mean anything by it. He's just old school.*

Uncertain just where to begin, Angie folded her hands as well and asked, "How's the golf game?"

That brought a big smile to his face. Though he didn't appear to have an athletic bone in his body—short with a roundness that was rapidly approaching obesity, thick glasses, and a donut of salt-and-pepper hair—Vincent Guelli was an avid golfer. And quite a good one. Angie was reasonably sure that when the weather was nice, and he wasn't in the office, he was at his golf club.

"It's not bad. Had a really good round yesterday."

"The weather has certainly been cooperating."

"It has. Much nicer than playing in the wet. I'll be bummed when it gets too cold. Winter always feels so much longer than summer."

Time to zero in, she thought. "Seems like you've played a lot more this year. Haven't you? I don't remember you ever playing this late into the fall."

If she hadn't been expecting his eyes to narrow slightly in suspicion, she would have missed it. "I play when I can," he said.

"With all due respect, you've got to be thinking that retirement is just over the horizon, yes?" There really wasn't a delicate way to say anything resembling, *You're no spring chicken . . . don't you want to retire soon?* But she tried her best, making sure to pair her words with a gentle smile. Part of her plan was to appeal to their family connection, so she went on. "As you know, my dad retired last year. He says it's the best thing he's ever done. Never been happier." Wait a beat. "Not sure my mom agrees."

Guelli laughed, which was her intention, and he visibly relaxed. "Funny you should mention it. I *have* been entertaining the idea of retirement lately. A lot."

Bingo.

Without waiting for an invitation, she handed over one piece of research at a time, explaining each one and how it could pertain to

Logo Promo. To his credit, Guelli actually seemed to be listening to her ideas, rather than tolerating them, which was what she usually felt like he did. A nod here, a curious hum there. She had him; she could feel it. He was interested. He liked her suggestions.

A glance at the clock told her she was just about out of time. "I know you have to be out of here in a minute, so we can go over more of this tomorrow if you want."

He finished looking at the paper in his hand, then gathered them all up and tapped them into a neat pile. "I do have to run." He stood up, grabbed a jacket off the hook on the back of the office door. Angie stood as well. "This is really impressive, Angie. Really." Her grin widened. Guelli picked up the whole pile she'd given him and slipped it into his briefcase. "I'm meeting with Jeremy tonight, and I'm going to show it all to him. Then you two can go over the details tomorrow."

Angie's eyebrows furrowed as she stood. "Jeremy?" she said, confused.

"My nephew? You met him this morning."

"Yeah," Angie blinked several times. "Yeah, I know who he is. Why are you going to show him my ideas?"

"For when I retire, silly," Guelli said, rather slowly, as if he was talking to a child. "Jeremy's going to take over the business. Didn't I tell you that this morning when I introduced you?"

Angie felt like she might throw up. "No," she said, barely above a whisper. "No, you didn't mention that."

"Bah." Guelli waved a dismissive hand, one that said *no big deal.* "I introduced him to a dozen people in about ten minutes. I must've forgot. Yeah, Jeremy's my brother's kid, just out of college with a business degree, really bright kid." He went on as he gathered up his things and turned off the lights. "We've been talking about it for months, him and I. Younger blood will do this company good. He's got some great ideas, but—" he held up his briefcase containing all the information Angie had so painstakingly collected and winked "—nothing like this. This is great stuff. Thanks, babe." He leaned over and kissed her on the cheek. "See you tomorrow."

He left Angie standing there, in his office, in the dark. She felt as though she'd been ambushed. How had she not seen this coming? She liked to think of herself as a pretty attentive person, as somebody who was well aware of the world around her. How had she missed a family member taking over the running of the company? And why on earth had she ever thought an Italian, old-fashioned male chauvinist like Vincent Guelli would even entertain the idea of leaving his beloved company in the hands of a female? What a stupid thing to hang her hat on. Moronic. Naïve.

Her knees buckled, dropping her back down into her chair. The office was dark. The building was quiet and Angie had the sudden, discomfiting feeling of being utterly alone.

The only sound was the ticking of the second hand on the wall clock.

Angie's voice was little more than breath. "Fuck."

The clock ticked on.

Twenty-One

Jillian walked into Starbucks and inhaled the warm, comforting aroma of freshly brewed coffee. She was almost always there before Shay, and today was no exception. They'd set up a standing twice-weekly coffee date: Wednesday afternoons and Saturday mornings. It had started during Shay's breakup with Laura, something to help keep her sane and focused, and it had continued on even after Shay had recovered and begun dating again. It was good for both of them to have a touchstone of sorts.

The same barista, Jen, was there every time. She was cute in a pixie-like way, but with a very subtle edge demonstrated by the silver hoop at the end of her eyebrow and the teasing glimpse of a tattoo at the base of her neck, sometimes covered by her dark hair and sometimes not. Her sexual preference was no mystery at all, since she flirted mercilessly with Jillian every time she came in, today being no exception.

"Grande nonfat Chai latte," she'd announced before Jillian had even opened her mouth. With a grin, Jillian nodded, holding eye contact. "Coming right up. Love that jacket, by the way." With a wink, Jen was off to make the order.

There was something pleasing—and flattering—to be so recognized by an attractive woman. Jillian didn't try to deny that. Why should she? What was wrong with liking attention? She certainly wasn't getting much at home.

The guilt immediately oozed in, as it always did. Jillian knew Angie was exhausted. She worked too much. She tried too hard to keep up with the standards that Dominick set—though he had no idea at all that there was a competition. She'd been cramming her brain full of research and ideas, and though Jillian admired this hard work, she didn't understand it. She had insisted to Angie over and over that it wasn't worth it, that Guelli obviously had no idea what an asset she was to his company, and that she should concentrate her efforts elsewhere, take all that research and excitement and find someplace where it would be appreciated. It wasn't like Angie loved the place, either.

Sometimes Jillian thought she might be getting through. Other times, it was like she was talking to a shoe, that's how much response she got. And all the while, Jillian felt herself slipping down Angie's priority list. Work came first. Work, clients, and money. Clients called at all hours; that damn cell phone was rarely out of her sight and she never turned it off. Jillian entertained fantasies of smashing it to bits with a hammer, baking it to ash in the oven, burying it in the backyard under mounds of dirt and grass.

"Here you go, beautiful," Jen said, handing over Jillian's drink and effectively pulling her out of her own head.

"Thanks," Jillian said, flashing a grateful smile. As their fingers grazed, Jen gave her a sexy little wink.

Jillian's smile widened as the feeling of flattery washed over her. She found a table in a faraway corner near a window.

She didn't have to wait long for Shay.

"Hey, sweetie," she said as she hugged Jillian and plopped her bag on the table. Fishing out her wallet, she went to order her coffee, and was back in a few minutes. "So. What's new? And why are you blushing like a schoolgirl?"

A shake of her head, a dismissive wave of her hand, and a comment about it being warm in the shop convinced Shay that she was fine and let her get back on track, away from contradictory thoughts about Angie and the barista that were cluttering her mind.

"How's Angie?" Shay asked as she sat. "Still working like a dog?"

Jillian made an exasperated face. "Always. I can't seem to get her to understand that she should be happy in her job. Her boss is turning over the reins to his nephew before long and Angie is beside herself. She wanted to manage the business, and now that's not going to happen, and she's so disappointed. Tell me, Shay, what's wrong with actually liking your job? I'm not sure she sees that as possible. It's like she thinks if she just hangs in there, it'll magically get better."

"Have you suggested she look for something else?" Shay started to sip her coffee, then thought better of it and blew on it instead. "There have to be more companies like hers."

"There are. Quite a few. But she's stubborn, and she hates change. Look at her parents. They've had the same jobs forever. I think her dad worked at the same place for forty years or something ridiculous like that before he retired."

"She's a hardhead, that's for sure."

"The most frustrating thing is that she's all over the place. One minute, she's become a freak about money. It's so weird. She acts like we don't have any—we're fine—and that she's the only one bringing it home—she's not, obviously. No, I don't make as much as she does, but I do just fine, thank you, and I take care of our health insurance. The next minute she'll do something that's the complete opposite of what somebody worried about money would do. She actually bought a Lexus a few weeks ago. A freaking Lexus! She thinks it will help her project a more successful image to her clients." She shook her head. "I don't know what's going on with her."

Shay took a deep breath. "How's the drinking?"

Jillian shrugged. "It's not worse, but it's not really better. She's so stressed lately. And angry. That's new. She seems angry. Sometimes a drink calms her down. Sometimes it revs her up. I don't know."

They sipped their coffees in silence. Seemingly out of suggestions, Shay changed the subject. "And how's my baby Boo?"

At the mention of her beloved pooch, Jillian's eyes lit up. "She's adorable, as always. A little stiff in the mornings, I think."

"She's getting up there," Shay said. "Those old bones and muscles aren't as limber as they used to be. What is she now, eleven?"

Jillian agreed. "Yeah. I hate to think about it. Why can't our dogs live as long as we do?"

"Not a day goes by for me that I don't have a client ask me that very question." Shay gazed out the window, her voice growing almost wistful. "I think dogs are much too valuable to stay in this world for very long. It must be exhausting, constantly handing out all that love and devotion and loyalty. I think they move on to the next place so they can recharge."

Her eyes glassy, Jillian agreed. "That's beautiful. I like it."

"It's the only explanation I've got," Shay said, shaking herself with a chuckle.

With a glance at her watch, Shay mentioned she needed to stop by the office.

"What?" Jillian scoffed. "It's your day off. You're supposed to avoid that place like the plague on your day off."

"I know, but Melissa had a couple things I promised I'd help her with." Shay looked everywhere but at Jillian, which made her friend laugh loudly.

"Oh, Melissa needs help with a 'couple things' does she?" Jillian made air quotes with her fingers, her tone gently teasing.

Shay shook her head, unable to hide a shy grin. "Come on! She's new. She isn't sure how it all works at the clinic, so I told her I'd go over some things with her."

"And does going over things with this new vet include doing so over a meal?"

Shay cleared her throat. "It may."

"I knew it!" Jillian pointed an accusing finger at Shay, her delight palpable. "You're dating her, aren't you?"

Playful defeat colored Shay's face. "Maybe a little."

"This is good news," Jillian pronounced, meaning it. Shay'd had a terrible time recovering from the loss and betrayal of Laura. It had been over a year before she'd even considered going on a date, and when she did, she'd told Jillian she was uncomfortable and self-conscious the whole time. She stopped about three months ago, telling Jillian she just didn't feel ready.

Melissa Saunders had come on board at the veterinary clinic where Shay worked about a month and a half ago, and Jillian only had to hear Shay talk about her once to know she was ready.

"I'm so happy for you, Shayneese." Jillian covered Shay's hand with hers and squeezed.

"It's really nothing right now," Shay told her, packing up her things.

"We're just hanging out, moving *very* slowly. She had a bad breakup last year, so I know exactly what she's going through."

"Well, I'm still happy for you. Having somebody to hang with—besides me—is a good thing. When you're ready to introduce her, I'd love to meet her."

"You'll be the first. You know that." Shay stood, bent across the table and kissed Jillian on the forehead. "Catch you later, babe."

Jillian watched out the window as Shay walked to her car. She held her head up, a subtle smile decorating her face, and there was a little bounce in her step. It was slight, and somebody who hadn't known Shay for more than twenty years probably wouldn't have noticed it. But Jillian did, and it filled her with warmth and love for her friend. She took a deep breath and let it out slowly, then stood up and gathered her things. As she deposited her garbage in the garbage can, she glanced up at the counter.

Jen tossed her a last wink.

2005

Lonely No More

Twenty-Two

I feel like I'm drowning.

The thought came to Angie out of the blue as she drove back to the office after an appointment with a client. It was sudden, and it was frightening.

At work. At home. She couldn't keep her head above water. She was going under. It was just a matter of when.

She thought about work, how it was the same shit, only worse and worse each day. Mr. Guelli had retired last year; Jeremy was running the show.

"Little bastard," she muttered as she braked for a light.

As if a twenty-five-year-old being handed a thriving business wasn't enough to make Angie grind her teeth with envy, Jeremy had decided a bunch of new requirements and procedures should be put into place. Some made sense to Angie—hell, they should do, they were her ideas—like regular, weekly sales meetings and more visits by suppliers. Others were making everybody cranky and irritated. Weekly quotas were his newest baby, and in many sales companies, they were perfectly practical. But in this business, sales came and went with the seasons. It didn't matter if you wrote only a few orders in October because in November and December—when companies were buying holiday gifts for employees and customers—you were going to crush it. Jeremy didn't seem to get that. He chalked up the complaints of his veteran salespeople to general laziness and his uncle letting them "get away with too much for too long."

He was also requesting quote sheets. Any time a salesperson quoted a price to a client, they had to write up the details and e-mail

169

them to Jeremy so he could keep track of what was being closed and offer his help as needed. That part made Angie roll her eyes. Offer his help? He was a baby. "I've been in sales since Peach Fuzz was in grade school," Hope had spat angrily when she read the memo over Angie's shoulder. "Peach Fuzz" was the current nickname she had for Jeremy. It was much less colorful than her previous ones. "That little egomaniac had better stop insulting us."

Angie wasn't really in any danger. She'd been at the game long enough to know how to hedge her bets. She could finagle things if she had to in order to keep Jeremy happy—and not looking too closely at her. She saved orders from last week and included them on this week's quota report. She wrote up quotes after she actually closed the orders.

"I can play that little game," she said to the dashboard.

But she could also manage the sales staff so much better than he could. She knew it, but there was nothing she could do about it. So she went along, playing the good employee to Jeremy, playing sounding board to her fellow employees. Keith was spitting nails. He'd been at his job for ages and he was the most successful salesperson in the company. Everybody knew it. Common knowledge. Keith brought in more sales than Angie, Hope, and anybody else in the office, combined. The smart thing for Jeremy to do would be to leave Keith alone, let him do his thing, and reap the rewards.

"Dad always said if it ain't broke, don't fix it," she said as she turned into the parking lot of Logo Promo.

Unfortunately for Jeremy, he had the tendency to let his power go to his head on occasion. Not all the time. He wasn't a bad kid. Angie actually kind of liked him, would like him a lot more if not for the fact that he had ripped the job she had her heart set on right out of her grasp without her ever seeing it coming. But every once in a while, he'd do something stupid, something that jeopardized the good of the overall business.

Saddling Keith Muldoon with meaningless paperwork that pissed him off was jsut one case. Which planted a seed of an idea in her head that she decided to let germinate. She grabbed her briefcase from the back seat and headed inside.

In the meantime, Angie was torn between requesting a meeting with Jeremy to give him an 'annual report' that was really a tactful assessment of how he'd been handling things over the past year, maybe offering up some advice on how to handle certain people and/or situations, and sitting back, crossing her arms, and watching the whole thing crumble. Not that that's what would happen. More likely, the old-timers like Keith would move on to another company, Jeremy would bring in fresh blood, and Logo Promo would think it was just fine without them ... though it wouldn't be half the business it was before.

She reached her office, dropped her briefcase, and flopped back into her chair, suddenly exhausted. "Christ, I'm forty. I am too old for this shit."

At home, she was just as frustrated. Jillian seemed to always be just a little bit annoyed with her. She never remembered her partner being demanding, but lately, that's how it seemed. Hell, they'd been together for sixteen years; it seemed kind of late for a new personality trait to rear its head, but that's how it felt. Angie couldn't do anything right. She worked too much. She drank too much. She didn't do enough around the house (she'd been scolded last night for leaving dirty dishes in the sink ... again). She never wanted to talk. She wasn't interested in sex. She'd become boring.

None of it was true. Well, okay, maybe the working part was true. And the drinking had been an ongoing issue, but she couldn't help the fact that she was totally stressed out by her job. Coming home to somebody who did nothing but bitch at her didn't help. Who wouldn't want a beer or a glass of wine to calm her nerves? Jesus. She didn't do much around the house lately; that wasn't a total lie. But she was so damn tired all the time. That's also why she wasn't talking as much. She was on the phone all day at work. The last thing she wanted to do in her spare time was blather on and on. Not that Jillian blathered, but god, could she give Angie fifteen minutes to gain some equilibrium at home before launching into discussion?

As for the sex ...

Angie sighed. She was tired. She was irritable. She was forty. Those were her excuses. Was her sex drive gone? *Of course not.* Was it the same as it had been when she was twenty-five? Of course not! That only made sense. Jillian had always had a higher drive, or more intense desire. But lately, she was making a connection between their lack of sex and Angie's attraction to her, and there simply was no such link. Jillian was still the most beautiful, sexiest woman she'd ever met. Age had only improved her appearance, as far as Angie was concerned. The laugh lines around her eyes had become a bit more prominent and Angie loved them. Her tummy was a little less flat and Angie loved it. Her eyes were wiser, her voice was softer, her smile was gentler (except these days when she seemed irritable). Angie was drawn to all of those things. Nothing had changed but the urgency, and in Angie's eyes, that was normal.

Jillian didn't agree. Angie was fairly certain of that. Jillian could tell her exactly how many days/weeks/months it had been since they'd last had sex, and sometimes she would. It drove Angie mad. Jillian also told Angie that she felt old. She felt fat. She thought she was no longer attractive, and no matter what Angie said, Jillian didn't seem to hear her. She seemed tense. Annoyed. And worst of all: unhappy.

I've been naïve.

It was a thought that had crossed Angie's mind often lately. Was it common to assume your own relationship was the exception to the rule? That others may preach about how much work a partnership is, how many bumps there are that you don't expect, but doesn't everybody at one time or another think that's rubbish? Doesn't everybody, at some point during their own bliss, think, "That will never happen to us" or "We're not like that"? Angie knew she was guilty of thinking such things. Yes, she and Jillian had an amazing relationship, had always had an amazing relationship, but she was a fool if she thought there were no problems. Her wife was unhappy.

That thought simultaneously angered Angie and scared the bejesus out of her, mostly because she had no idea how to fix things. And god forbid Jillian should actually talk to her about how she was feeling. Jillian kept everything inside, festering, until it exploded out of her. That impending explosion was something Angie dreaded.

Advice. She needed advice. But from whom? A number of people crossed her mind: her mother, Hope, Dom, Shay. The idea of talking in depth about her relationship—and more terrifyingly, her sex life—with even close friends made her feel jumpy. This stuff was private. Shouldn't she be able to figure it out on her own without subjecting herself to embarrassment in front of somebody she cared about?

Her computer let out a ding, telling her she'd received an e-mail, but she ignored it. Her mind was anywhere but on work, even though that's where it should have been. A lot of things were on her plate, a lot that needed her attention, but she couldn't get past the niggling sensation in her brain telling her she was failing as a partner, as a wife. Jillian's face from that morning filled her head now, the expression of disappointment and worse, resignation.

Was Jillian still in love with her?

The thought came unbidden, out of nowhere, and it jerked Angie upright in her chair. She sat ramrod straight, her palms flat on her desk. It was the first time those words had entered her thoughts; she'd never doubted Jillian's love, never, not once.

Okay, this is ridiculous, she thought. I'm panicking for no reason. I need to get my shit together and stop this. Right now. Before I drive myself nuts.

They just needed to talk. That was all. Simple. She'd have to bring it up, of course, because Jillian never would. But Angie could do that. They'd talk, they'd get it all out on the table, and things would be fine. There.

With a curt nod to the empty air in her office, Angie turned to her computer and proceeded to throw herself into her work.

It was what she did best.

Twenty-Three

Jillian sighed as she completed some paperwork at her desk. The kids had been gone for about thirty minutes, and she had a staff meeting in twenty. All she really wanted to do was go home. She felt tired. Run-down.

Old.

Holding her right hand up in front of her face, she studied it. The skin was looser than it used to be. Not wrinkled (thank god), not yet, but not tight, the blue veins more prominent than she remembered them being. For the first time, she realized she had her mother's hands, no longer the strong, pretty hands of a young woman. Instead, hands that had seen better days. Hands that had a lot of miles on them, had done a lot of work.

Hands of a middle-aged woman.

Sliding open a desk drawer, she pulled out a makeup mirror and studied her face with the same scrutiny. It was true that everything started to go south as you aged. It seemed the outer corners of her eyes pulled down ever so slightly, the color not as bright as it used to be, crow's feet frighteningly obvious. Her smile lines no longer disappeared when she stopped smiling; they were there all the time and they horrified her. *When did that happen?* She still had the dimples, of course, and for that she was happy, but even the texture of her skin seemed to have changed, freckles and blemishes much more apparent than they used to be, her smooth, clear, creamy skin—also her mother's—a distant memory. Not for the first time, she wondered if her mother had had the same sense of worry, of near-panic when she realized she was no longer a young woman.

174

I wish I could ask her.

Jillian had never thought of herself as somebody who would dread aging, but as forty loomed just over the horizon, she had to fight the urge to turn and run, not that it would help. Angie had handled it with grace and a shrug, stating the simple fact that turning forty was "better than the alternative." Of course, she was still stunning, and could be well into her sixties. The only adjustment she'd made was coloring her hair. The gray had become a bit too clear in her mid-thirties, so Angie simply had it colored every five weeks. End of story. Other than that, she still looked completely delicious.

Jillian hated her just a little bit for that.

Staring into the little mirror, she shook her head back and forth. *My god, if I'm this much of a mess now, what will I be like when I hit menopause?*

A knock on her doorjamb saved her from the tears welling in her eyes. It was Marina. "Hey, you. Ready?"

Jillian nodded, wiping her face quickly, shoving the mirror back into its place.

"You okay?"

"Fine."

Marina studied her face as Jillian approached. "You sure?"

Jillian squeezed Marina's upper arm in gratitude. "I'm sure."

Clearly not convinced, Marina let it go. "I think the new gym teacher will be at the meeting."

"Phys ed teacher. I don't think you're supposed to call them gym teachers."

"Really? Why not?"

"I have no idea."

          🙐   🙐   🙐

Lindsey Page had soft brown eyes that were kind and a little bit smoldering. That was the first thing Jillian noticed about her when she was introduced at the staff meeting.

"Ms. Page comes to us from St. Augustine's and will be taking over for Mr. Taft, given his heart attack and unexpected retirement."

175

Carl Ritter was vice principal: scrawny, balding, thick glasses, the kind of man you just knew was picked on as a nerd when he was a student himself. Now he was able to get his revenge by bossing around a new generation of kids, and he often did so with relish.

"Please welcome Lindsey Page, our new physical education teacher."

Nods of welcome, along with hellos, went around the room as the meeting came to a close. Lindsey seemed to gravitate toward Jillian and Marina.

"Hi," she said, her voice surprisingly low, a slight gravelly edge to it. "Lindsey." She held out her hand to Marina, then to Jillian, as they introduced themselves.

"St. Augustine's, huh?" Marina asked. "Bit of a change coming from a Catholic school."

Lindsey chuckled. "Let's just say I didn't agree with some of their values." Jillian's gaydar immediately started clanging in her head, and she began to look for other clues as Marina and Lindsey shared Catholic school stories.

First things first: gym teacher. Always a check mark in the box. One corner of Jillian's mouth curved up into a half-grin. A definite athletic build, maybe 5'6", muscular and fit. *Yes, very fit.* Jillian swallowed, then chewed on the inside of her cheek as she wondered what sports Lindsey might play. Reddish brown hair pulled back into a casual ponytail. That threw Jillian a little bit until she reached up and wrapped a finger around the ends of her own long hair and admitted to herself that hair length meant nothing. Little if any makeup—not that she needed any with those big eyes and full lips. No nail polish, nails filed down neatly.

"And Jillian here teaches art," Marina said, interrupting Jillian's investigation.

"Guilty," Jillian replied.

Lindsey smiled at her, held her gaze for a bit longer than necessary. "I loved art in school." She pressed her palms together and pointed at Marina and Jillian. "Well," she said. "I should probably find my way back to my office and get my bearings so I'm ready for tomorrow." With a sheepish grin, she explained, "I've never had to go there from

176

here." Her encompassing wave indicated the conference room, which had cleared out, the three of them left alone.

"It's on the way to my room," Jillian said. "I can show you."

"Perfect." That smile again.

They said their goodbyes to Marina and headed down the hall. As they walked toward the gym, Jillian scrambled to make small talk. "I have always been jealous of the phys ed teachers I know because they have the most comfortable working wardrobes around." When Lindsey chuckled, Jillian asked, "How many pairs of sneakers do you own? Tell the truth."

"Six."

"Figures."

"So, how long have you been teaching here?"

Jillian furrowed her brow. "Fifteen years!"

"Wow. You don't look old enough."

A slight blush heated Jillian's cheeks. "I was hired right out of college."

"That makes you, what, thirty-seven?"

"Thirty-eight."

"Well, you don't look thirty-eight."

Jillian laughed. "Thanks. I think. And you're what? Twenty-five?"

Lindsey feigned being appalled, complete with a horrified gasp and a hand pressed to her chest. "I'll have you know I am twenty-nine, thank you very much."

"Baby."

Lindsey arched one eyebrow, and Jillian laughed. "Is that eyebrow supposed to intimidate me?"

"Isn't it? Damn it," Lindsey said, the arch still there. "I need to work on that." She looked up at the rooms. "I guess this is where I get off."

Jillian rolled her lips in, bit down on them. "Mm hmm."

"Thanks for walking with me."

"Any time. Welcome aboard. I think you'll like it here."

Lindsey held Jillian's gaze. "So do I."

What the hell was that? Jillian asked herself over and over as she drove home. Why had she been flirty with Lindsey? Not that she wasn't always flirty, but this had been intentional, very much so. Not good. Not good at all. Shaking her head to rid herself of the confusion that settled over her, she vowed to tread carefully around the new girl.

Jillian was not happy with her own state of mind recently, but she had no idea what to do about it. She growled with frustration as she unlocked the door and entered her house. As she tossed her keys on the kitchen counter, she briefly wondered—not for the first time—what it would be like to come home from work and have Angie already be there. She didn't bother dwelling, though. She'd gone that route in the past, and the only thing it had gotten her was depressed.

"Where's my girl?" she cooed as always, sifting through the mail, waiting for Boo to greet her. It took longer these days—her sweet dog was nearing fourteen, and she didn't get around like before. Glancing at the envelope from the gas and electric company, she tore it open and scoffed at the total due, remembering when they'd lived in their smaller house and owed half of what they did now.

When Boo didn't make an appearance, Jillian left the mail next to her keys and went looking. Boo's hearing wasn't what it used to be, and often she didn't even hear Jillian come home.

"Boo-Bear," she called as she entered the vaulted-ceilinged living room. Boo's round bed was tucked next to the couch, and Jillian could make out her white butt, less on the muscular side than in her younger days and more on the bony side. As Jillian approached, she could see Boo's chest rising and falling rapidly as she took quick, short breaths. She didn't get up, but her brown eyes rolled slightly in Jillian's direction.

"Oh, no." Jillian dropped to her knees and placed a gentle hand on Boo's side. The dog's nub of a tail wagged ever so slightly. "Hi, sweetie. How's my girl? You don't look like you're feeling very well." Jillian kept her voice steady, her tone light. Boo was emotionally in tune with her, always knew when she was in distress, and Jillian didn't want Boo worrying about her now.

Trying to ward off the dread and panic threatening to wash over her, Jillian found her cell phone in the kitchen and punched in number one to speed dial Angie. When it clicked to voicemail, she made a strangled sound and hung up, then returned to Boo.

Shay had prepared her for this as best she could. Boo was old. She'd been on medication for nearly a year, and at her age, her kidneys would most likely shut down on her at some point. She'd be lethargic, panting, but not in pain. So if certain measures had to be taken, Shay would drive right to the house. Jillian knew that the only way she'd have Boo put down was if she was in pain with no way to get better.

Jillian tried Angie again. A quick glance at the clock told her it was almost five. When she got no answer, she dialed the reception desk and was told she'd missed Angie by about fifteen minutes.

"You should try her cell," the receptionist suggested helpfully.

"Wow. What a great idea." Jillian was pretty sure her sarcasm was lost on the girl.

Hoping Angie was on her way home, Jillian went back into the living room. Boo hadn't moved, her breathing still shallow. Jillian stretched out next to her, lying down so she could look at Boo's face, into her brown eyes. She'd always felt such a connection to her dog, and this moment was no different. She knew exactly how this was going to go.

"Hey there, beautiful. How're you doing?" Boo's pink tongue lolled out the side of her mouth. Her breath was awful. Jillian didn't care. She kissed her right on her black nose, which was alarmingly dry. Boo's nub of a tail wagged gently.

"You're getting ready to leave me, aren't you, sweetie?" The crack in her voice was beyond Jillian's control, and her eyes filled. "It's okay," she said softly. "It's okay, baby girl. I know you're tired. I'd keep you here with me forever if I could, but I know you've got someplace you have to be." Her tears spilled over, rolling freely down her face as she told her dog everything that was in her heart. "You have been the best dog any girl could ever ask for. I want you to know that. You've taken such good care of me, and I will love you forever." She stroked Boo's

179

head, her velvety ears, her strong neck. Boo kept her gentle eyes on Jillian's and Jillian held Boo's gaze, watching closely for any sign that she was in pain. "I'm right here, Boo-Bear. I'm right here."

From her spot on the floor, she stretched for her cell and dialed Angie's number again.

ॐ   ॐ   ॐ

I can't do it right now.

That was the first thought that ran through Angie's head when she saw Jillian's number come up on her phone. She hit the button to mute the ringtone and motioned to the bartender as she dropped the phone into the inside breast pocket of her blazer.

Hope peered over enough to see who was calling. "Do you think it's smart to ignore the phone call of your significant other?"

"No." Angie took a too-large slug of her beer. "But I'm sure she's calling to ask where I am or what time I'm getting home, and she'll have that *tone.* That *attitude* that makes me feel like the worst partner in the world. And I just don't want to deal with it right now."

They sat on barstools at JAM—the latest incarnation of the local lesbian bar—for the Happy Hour specials. Dollar drafts, two-dollar well drinks from four to seven on Monday, Wednesday, and Thursday. What did knowing the Happy Hour prices and schedule by heart say about her? Angie ignored the thought.

Hope was gazing around the bar, probably noting the changes since she'd been there last with Angie. Gone was the upper class, polished-wood look. In its place were sharp angles, frustratingly low lighting, and house music. The clientele was decidedly younger, much less business-like.

"Christ," Hope muttered, "this place changes names more than I change my underwear."

"The curse of the lesbian bar," Angie replied. "Nobody can keep one open and make money. When will they learn? Bars are for boys. Lesbians don't go out much. Though I have to admit I love that I can breathe."

"And that you won't go home smelling like an ashtray."

"Amen to that." There'd been big controversy and many an uproar from bars and restaurants when New York state had passed a law banning smoking in public places, but Angie loved it. She abhorred the stench of cigarette smoke, hated how it clung to her clothes and hair so that even when she got away from it, she couldn't get away from it. "I remember ten years ago," she said. "You couldn't even walk into a bar for three minutes to look for somebody without having to throw all your clothes in the wash and take a shower."

Hope nodded her agreement. "I do feel a little sorry for the smokers, though, especially in the winter when they're all huddled outside around the ashtray like a bunch of outcasts."

"I don't. It's a filthy, dangerous habit, and this is a new era, for god's sake. They should all know better by now."

Hope hit her with a look. "Somebody took extra Harsh Pills this morning."

Angie blinked at her, then laughed. "I'm sorry." She shook her head. "I can't help it. I'm in total bitch mode lately. I hate everybody."

"Honey, I *invented* bitch mode." Hope held up her glass and they clinked.

"I don't know what's going on with me." Angie took a deep breath, let it out slowly. "Everything annoys me. Everybody bugs me. I just want to crawl in a hole."

"Who's bugging you?"

"Everybody."

"Not me," Hope said, her tone teasing.

One corner of Angie's mouth quirked up. "Not you."

"Jillian?"

"*Especially* Jillian."

"Work?"

"God, yes."

Propping her elbow on the bar and her chin in her hand, Hope groaned. "I know. Me too." They each sipped their beers. A few moments of silence went by. "I think a noncompete is coming," Hope stated.

Angie made a face. "You think Jeremy's got that up his sleeve too?"

"Guelli was too naïve to ever put one in place. Which was a dumb business move. Plus Keith probably wouldn't have signed one anyway. He'd want the freedom to take his customers with him if he decided to leave."

"I heard they don't stand up in court. I read a couple different articles. You can't keep somebody from making a living."

With a half shrug, Hope said, "I don't know. I suppose it's possible, but who wants to pay a lawyer to deal with all of it? Most people just sign and hope they never want to change jobs."

"No way Keith signs. He doesn't do anything he doesn't want to, and he brings in so much money, I doubt Jeremy could afford to fight with him about it. There's too much business to lose."

"Keith is the only one with that kind of clout."

Angie studied Hope's face. "Hopie, you bring in a nice chunk of sales. Don't sell yourself short. So to speak."

"I know. But I'm expendable. Aside from Keith, most of us are."

Angie wanted to argue, but knew Hope was right. They were all good salespeople, but Keith was the only one bringing in over seven figures in sales. Any of the rest of them could be let go, their clients divvied up among those that remained. Before she could offer any kind of defense, Hope shocked her.

"I'm thinking I may go before the noncompete is introduced."

"What?" Angie stared at her. "You're quitting?"

"I haven't told a soul, so I'm swearing you to secrecy."

Angie continued to stare.

"I'm serious, Angie. You can't say anything."

"You're going to leave me?" Angie's voice was small, almost childlike.

Hope held up a hand, palm out, as if stopping traffic. "Okay, cut that out. That is not something you're allowed to do. *That*, I cannot take."

"I can't believe it." Angie ran a hand through her hair. "I mean, I get it. But I can't believe you're thinking of leaving." It was true; she *did* get it. She totally got it. But the idea of being left at Logo Promo without her closest ally was a tough one to swallow. She drained her beer and signaled for another, making a face at the music, which suddenly seemed way too loud. "God, I hate this house shit," she muttered.

Hope's eyes were on her; she could feel the weight of them. Forcing herself to not be selfish, she asked Hope, "Where are you thinking of looking? Will you stay in ad specialties?"

With a grimace, Hope replied, "I've been doing this for more than twenty years. I don't know anything else." She ordered a refill and told Angie, "Steve over at Star Promotions offered me a job there. Higher commission cut. No noncompete."

Angie studied her for a moment before saying, "So, you're not *thinking* of leaving. You're leaving."

Hope nodded, looked away.

"Fuck, Hope. When?"

"I'll tell Jeremy at the end of the week."

"He'll want you to go immediately, you know. No time to collect any 'company secrets.'" Angie made air quotes. The idea of the ad specialty business having company secrets was ludicrous. Anything anybody wanted to know about their products or clients was readily available on the Internet or in the phone book.

"I know. I'm taking a week off. I'll start with Star in two weeks."

"God, this is moving fast." The bartender set an upside-down shot glass in front of Angie. "What's this?"

"From the woman at the end of the bar. Dark hair. Leather jacket." She left to attend to another customer.

"Somebody just bought me a drink. How cool is that?" Angie lifted her glass in salute to the woman and mouthed a thank you.

"How the hell does she know you're not with me?" Hope asked with annoyance. "That was ballsy. I'm insulted."

"Apparently, you're not taking very good care of me," Angie said, feeling just a bit lighter than before. Despite the facts that the woman was not at all her type, and also, crossing that bold of a line was not something she'd ever be capable of doing, it was nice to have somebody look at her with interest and a twinkle in her eye rather than irritation and disappointment.

"Well, Casanova," Hope teased. "I suggest you drink that up and get your ass home because your phone's been lighting up like a

Christmas tree the whole time we've been here. I can see it through your pocket when you lean forward."

Angie sighed, realizing with dismay that she did not want to go home.

Twenty-Four

The house was dark and quiet when Angie arrived home. Weirdly so. Maybe Jillian had gone somewhere and that's why she'd called so many times. Though she never left a message. Confusion clouded Angie's mind as she set her keys and bag down.

"Jill?" Her voice didn't echo, but it might as well have, the house felt so empty. Furrowing her brow, Angie moved through the house, glanced up the stairs and saw no lights. Maybe Jillian was working in her studio. When she took the first step, she caught something out of the corner of her eye in the living room, and changed direction.

Jillian was sitting on the floor in the dark, her back against the wall, Boo's head in her lap, the rest of her covered with an afghan. Angie squinted, but couldn't make sense of it all, so she bent to the lamp, clicked it on.

And she knew.

"Oh, god." Angie dropped to her knees.

Jillian's face was blotchy. Her eyes were red and swollen. Boo's eyes were lifeless, cloudy and glazed, her tongue protruding slightly.

"Jillian? Baby? Are you okay?" Angie touched Jillian's face, pushed her hair behind her ear. When Jillian finally turned her gaze to Angie, it was flat. Expressionless.

"Where were you?" Barely a whisper.

"I'm so sorry."

"Why didn't you answer my calls?"

"I—" A million excuses zipped through Angie's head. A million

185

lies. *My battery died. My phone was in my car. I had the ringer off.* I was in a meeting. Instead, all she could say was "I'm so sorry."

Jillian looked away, a fresh tear tracking down her cheek.

"I'll call Shay." Angie stood.

"I already did. I'm bringing her body in first thing in the morning."

"Oh, Boo." Angie felt her own eyes well, pressed her lips together, and bit down on them as she laid a hand on their dog. Silence hung in the air. Finally, Jillian spoke.

"Go on up. I'll be there in a bit." She didn't look at Angie.

Angie was torn. Part of her knew she should stay, but if there'd been an icy force field surrounding Jillian, it wouldn't have been much colder. It was painfully clear Jillian didn't want her around right now. Not that she could blame her. With a quiet sigh, she turned to the stairs.

It wasn't until she'd gone through her nightly routine—undressed, washed her face, brushed her teeth, ironed her clothes for the next day—and crawled beneath the covers that she allowed herself to grieve the loss of their dog. Flashes of Boo's entire life whizzed through her mind. That first day home, her too-big head and enormous feet making her look all out of proportion. That first night in the crate. The first day they took her swimming, only to discover that being in the water was the absolute last place she wanted to be. The time she was sprayed by a skunk, Angie and Jillian both in the tub with her, dousing her with tomato juice, laughing even as the smell made their eyes water. And always, *always,* Boo was by Jillian's side, her sweet brown eyes looking up at Jillian with such love and adoration. Angie had wanted to get Jillian a companion, a dog that would stick to her like glue. She'd succeeded. Boo had loved Jillian with perfect, unending intensity.

Jillian had to be devastated.

Alone in their bed, Angie cried as much for Jillian's loss as her own. Maybe more.

ॐ   ॐ   ॐ

When the clock radio clicked on, Kelly Clarkson was singing "Since U Been Gone."

"Shut up, Kelly," Angie muttered as she slapped at the snooze button.

She felt it before she looked, but a quick glance confirmed that Jillian had never come to bed. Rolling onto her back, Angie stared at the ceiling as memories of last night flooded her mind. She'd fucked up. In a big way. And she had no idea how she was going to make up for it. She had her reasons, and they were legitimate. She knew that. But Jillian had needed her last night, and Angie had made herself unavailable.

And Boo was gone.

She felt the dog's absence almost as keenly as she felt Jillian's. Tears welled and threatened to spill over. Crying first thing in the morning was not a favorite activity of Angie's, and she did her best to fight it off. The thought of going downstairs to the look of disappointment she knew would be on Jillian's face filled a pit of dread in her stomach, but she tossed off the covers and got herself out of bed.

Jillian looked terrible as she stood in the kitchen, her back against the counter, sipping her coffee.

"Hi," Angie said quietly as she pulled a mug from the cupboard and poured her own coffee.

"Hi." Jillian's voice was rough. Her blue eyes were bloodshot, the skin around them swollen. One side of her hair was matted against her head, and she wore the same clothes she had on the night before, now a wrinkled mess.

"Did you sleep down here all night?" Angie asked, though she knew the answer.

Jillian turned her gaze to the window. "I didn't want to leave her," she explained, in barely a whisper.

Angie set her coffee down and wrapped her arms around Jillian, who stiffened at first, but gave in and let herself be held. It took only a few moments before she succumbed to her emotions and began to quietly sob against Angie's shoulder. Angie started to cry then, and the two women stood for a long while, just holding each other and grieving their lost pet.

"I think there was part of me that really thought she'd live forever." Jillian's voice was muffled against Angie's shirt.

"I know. Me too."

"She's barely been gone a day and I miss her like crazy already. My heart hurts."

Angie squeezed her tighter, held her closer. She wanted to apologize again for last night, but was afraid of stopping Jillian's release. It seemed they had had so few close times like this lately, she didn't want to cut it short too quickly.

"I need to take her to Shay's clinic," Jillian explained, pulling back slightly and wiping her face. "They'll take care of the cremation."

"I'll go with you."

Jillian blinked at her. "You will?"

"Of course."

After studying her face, Jillian said, "Okay. Thank you." She stepped back, picked up her mug. "We can pick up her ashes in about a week." She cleared her throat, and Angie knew she was doing her best to keep her emotions in check.

"She was a good dog," Angie said, hoping to keep things positive.

Jillian gave a wan smile. "She was a great dog." Turning watery eyes to Angie, she added, "Best present I ever got."

After they'd showered and changed, they stood together in the living room. Boo's body was still on her round bed. Jillian had covered her with her favorite blanket, tucked it around her. Angie handed Jillian the keys to the car.

"Here. You go open the car and clear off the back seat. I'll bring her out."

"'kay."

Angie squatted next to the dog, slipped the blanket off her head, and just looked. "You were the best dog around," she whispered. "Thanks for being so good to us." She bent and kissed the white head one last time, the skin and short hair now startlingly cold against her lips. "We'll miss you, sweetie." With that, she replaced the blanket, scooped up the body, bed and all, and carried the whole load out to the car.

Jillian sat in the back with Boo.

Shay met them at the door, tears in her eyes, and she hugged each of them tightly. Jillian cried in her arms. "I'm so sorry." Her eyes met Angie's over Jillian's head, the feisty glare not lost on Angie. Shay must have known Jillian couldn't reach her last night. The guilt settled in once again, and Angie didn't try to fight it; she deserved it.

"Let me get one of my techs to help bring her in," Shay began.

"No, it's okay," Jillian interrupted. "We can do it." She looked to Angie, who nodded, and together they slid Boo's body out of the car and carried her through the back door of the clinic into an exam room.

The vet tech that met them was young, with green eyes filled with sympathy and understanding. She helped them settle Boo and her bed on the exam table. "Take as much time as you need," she said, her voice quiet and gentle. "I'll get the necessary paperwork. You can take her things with you—her collar and such—or we can get anything you leave back to you. Whatever is easiest for you." With a kind smile, she left them.

Jillian laid a hand on Boo's side. "She's so cold," she said.

Angie nodded, not trusting herself to speak around the grief. After a moment, she cleared her throat and said, "This is just her body, sweetie. She's gone now."

"To someplace awesome, I hope. Where she can run as far as she wants and eat as many carrots as she wants."

A chuckle spilled from Angie's lips at the mention of Boo's favorite snack. She reached for Jillian's hand; their fingers intertwined and held tight.

"This sucks," Jillian said.

"Yes, it does."

They stood for several moments. The tech tapped lightly on the door, then entered. Jillian signed a couple of papers, wiped her cheeks.

"We'll call you when you can pick up her ashes."

Angie nodded.

The tech told them again to take all the time they needed and quietly left them.

They stood some more, side by side.

Jillian took a deep breath, let it out slowly, then reached forward and unclipped Boo's red-and-black plaid collar. She grasped it tightly to her chest, bent over, and kissed Boo's head. "Bye, baby," she whispered, then turned and left the room.

It took Angie several more moments to pull herself together and follow.

Twenty-Five

Jillian ended the call and set her cell down on her desk. A quick glance at the clock—as well as the quiet emanating from the hall—told her it was late, well past time for her to go home. But going home was still hard. It had been only a week, and walking through the door was excruciating, knowing Boo wouldn't come bounding to meet her. The house seemed so quiet and still; she had a hard time being there alone. Angie had gently suggested they look into getting another dog, and Jillian wasn't against the idea, but she wasn't ready. It would feel too much like she was trying to replace Boo.

Instead of going home, Jillian found other things to do to take up her time. Her father was the biggest beneficiary, as she ended up at his house more often than not, sharing dinner with him or just drinks. She popped in on her brother at the real estate office, sat across from his desk and chatted with him between his phone calls. Even her mother reaped the rewards of her desire not to go home: Jillian had stopped by the cemetery three times this week. The groundskeeper shot her a look of worry yesterday.

She was going to have to face it. She had to go home, get back to her regular life. Maybe she needed to spend more time in her studio. Sketching always helped her to clear her mind, to think straight. Maybe that was a good, logical step.

The heels of her hands pressed into her eyes, she set her elbows on her desk and sighed heavily.

"Bad day?"

The voice startled her, jerking her muscles. Blinking the blurriness from her eyes revealed Lindsey standing in her doorway, hand out in apology.

"I didn't mean to scare you," she said, stepping into the room. They'd become friends in the weeks since Lindsey had begun working at the school, and one often popped in on the other to say hi.

Jillian waved it off. "It's no problem." Truth be told, she was happy to see a friendly face.

"Are you okay? You look pale."

"I'm fine. Tired. And the vet's office just called to tell me I can pick up Boo's ashes." Annoyed at the tears that filled her eyes, Jillian swiped at them with the back of her hand.

Lindsey perched her butt on the corner of Jillian's desk, her expression sympathetic. "I can see why you'd be upset. That's a tough one." She smelled good, Jillian noticed, musky and exotic. Her hair was pulled back in her usual no-nonsense ponytail, and her brown eyes were gentle.

"I guess if I get this over with, all the hard stuff will be done and I can start moving on." With a shrug, she added, "I don't know why this has been so hard. She was just a dog."

"Hey." Lindsey's eyebrows met just above her nose. "That's enough of that. Don't minimize your grief. Boo was a big part of your life. Mourning her does not make you weak."

Jillian gave a curt nod, not trusting herself to speak.

"Do you want me to go with you?" Lindsey's suggestion surprised Jillian, and she looked up at her with watery eyes.

"Would you?"

"Of course. Maybe having a friend with you will make it easier."

"Maybe it will." Jillian offered up a smile, then began gathering her things.

"Let me grab my stuff and close up my office. Meet you in the parking lot?"

Jillian watched her go, trying to ignore the fact that the navy blue running pants hugged Lindsey's ass in a rather pleasing way. Shaking her head, she pushed the thought out of her mind.

෨ ෨ ෨

"And?" Lindsey sat forward on the edge of the picnic bench. "Was I right?"

Jillian couldn't help but grin at the childlike anticipation of her friend. Dipping her head in assent, she said, "I do believe you were." Giving the cone a spin with her wrist, she licked what few little chocolate candies remained into her mouth.

The sight of her beloved dog reduced to a bag of ashes that fit into a box the size of an index card had threatened to pummel Jillian into a quivering mess of emotion, but Lindsey's quiet support kept her upright and to the car. There they sat, Lindsey keeping a warm hand on her shoulder, squeezing and rubbing until she'd pulled herself together. When Jillian turned red-rimmed, apologetic eyes to her, Lindsey had shifted the car into gear and drove. No words were spoken until Lindsey hit her turn signal to pull into the Abbott's parking lot.

"What are we doing here?" Jillian had asked.

"Life Lesson Number Seventeen: no problem is so big that it can't be made at least a little bit better by eating an ice cream cone with sprinkles."

Now they sat on a picnic table in very—surprisingly—comfortable silence, eating ice cream and people-watching. It wasn't until Jillian had chewed and swallowed her last bite that she looked Lindsey in the eye.

"What?" Lindsey asked, squirming in her seat when Jillian didn't speak.

"I just . . ." Jillian looked down at her hands, back up again, cleared her throat. "I needed a friend today. If not for you, I'd probably still be in the parking lot at the vet's bawling my eyes out."

"Well, I'm glad you're not. Ice cream is way better than tears, don't you think?"

"*Way* better. Thanks, Lindsey."

"You're welcome, Jillian."

It was another ninety minutes before Jillian made it home. Eventually, Lindsey took Jillian back to the school to pick up her car. There, an awkward hug goodbye, each of them acting as if they were coated with a noxious powder they didn't want to transfer to the other. Not thinking about Lindsey—about her warm eyes, her full lips, her comforting sense of humor—proved easier said than done on Jillian's drive home.

Angie's car in the driveway surprised her.

Jillian still felt punched in the gut every time she walked in the door, to not be greeted by a bounding, excited projectile of dog so happy to see her it was as if she wanted to crawl inside and share her skin. The keys made a loud noise when she tossed them onto the counter, and Angie came right downstairs.

"Hey, you. I was wondering where you were."

Jillian tried not to feel guilty about the concern that darkened Angie's face.

"Everything okay?" Her gaze landed on the sleekly polished wooden box, and the darkness was replaced by clarity, by understanding, and by sadness. "Oh, babe. Why didn't you call me? I would have gone with you." She took Jillian in her arms and held her.

The embrace felt comfortable and familiar, while at the same time uncomfortable and stifling, and Jillian forced herself to relax. "You've been so busy at work. I didn't want to bother you. Lindsey went with me."

"Lindsey the phys ed teacher you're always talking about?"

"I'm not always talking about her," Jillian said, her hackles rising just a bit.

"You do, sometimes." Angie grinned to take any sting away. "It's fine. I'm glad you weren't alone." She reached for the box, rubbed her fingertips over it gently. "It's so small," she murmured.

"That's the first thing I thought, too."

"Should we scatter her ashes or keep them in the house?"

Jillian blew out a breath. "I don't know. I sort of want her here with us. At least for now."

"Agreed." Angie picked up the box and went into the living room, Jillian following her. Along the way, she snagged a framed photo of Boo as well as her plaid collar. At the fireplace, she arranged it all in a neat little setup that brought yet more tears to Jillian's eyes. "There. How's that? At least for now. If we decide later we want to do something different, we can." She wrapped an arm around Jillian's shoulders and squeezed her close. "Okay?"

"Okay."

They stood that way for a long time.

For the next couple of weeks, Jillian busied herself by spending extra time in her studio. When she missed Boo, sketching her seemed to help reduce the pain until it was just a dull ache. Nearly a dozen half-sketches littered the floor in the room now, failed efforts to reproduce her from memory. Jillian had never excelled at drawing living, breathing things. Human or animal, she had trouble getting the right detail, the right shading. She preferred to stick to inanimate objects. Fruit bowls. Landscapes. Vases of flowers.

Eyes were particularly hard for her. For many, it was hands. The details of the human hand are extremely precise and incredibly difficult to emulate. For Jillian, it was the eyes. Human or animal, she had trouble sketching them so they didn't look like the eyes of a cartoon character. Eyes showed depth, thought, emotion. The ones she drew seemed . . . just flat. Today was no exception. Shaking her head in disgust, she tore another sheet from her easel and let it drift to the floor so she could start again.

Gazing out into space, she stood still for a long while, then turned back to the paper and began to work without thinking about it. She'd finished the eyes, big and dark, and had almost completed work on the upturned nose before she stopped to look at what she was doing—and realized that she wasn't drawing Boo at all.

The sketch was good. The eyes weren't perfect, but they were some of the best eyes she'd ever remembered drawing. She stared and stared, uncomfortably aware that they were Lindsey's.

After a few moments, she sighed heavily, ripped the paper off the easel, crumpled it into as small a ball as she could, and tossed it into the wastebasket. With a growl, she focused on the apple sitting upon her desk, and began to draw that.

195

"I appreciate you coming by to help me, Angelina." Her mom stood on a step stool and handed her a gravy boat from high up in the cupboard. Angie wrapped it in a sheet of newspaper and set it in the box on the kitchen table.

"It's no problem," Angie said. "But why are we boxing up dishes?"

"I bought some new ones."

"Of course you did," Angie said with a knowing grin, pretending to dodge the mock glare she was tossed. Alice was notorious for changing her décor often and on a whim. Dishes were no exception. "Who's getting these?" The dishes they packed had been around for a while, even by Alice's standards, mostly because they were pretty. Simple cream with a very subtle baby rose pattern around the edges.

"Since you and Jillian got the last ones, these will go to Maria. She still has those cheapo Corelle ones I gave her when she first moved out."

Angie nodded. Jillian loved the thick stoneware set Alice had given them a couple years back, heavy and solid with a green stripe around each piece.

"Speaking of, how is Jillian? I feel like I never see that girl anymore."

Angie almost told her mother to join the club, but knew she'd come across as whiney and a little bit pathetic. Besides, she didn't want Alice to know. "She's hanging in there. It's been hard for both of us, but harder for her. Boo was her baby."

Alice clucked her tongue as she shook her head. "You poor girls. You tell Jillian I want to see her face soon."

"I will. She's been really busy."

Something in Angie's tone must have poked at her mother because Alice stopped what she was doing to look down at her daughter. "What's going on?" she asked in her usual blunt way. It was something both loved and hated by each member of the family. If Alice wanted to know something, she didn't sugarcoat the question.

The half-shrug Angie made did nothing to move things along as she pretended to fiddle with the arrangement of things in the box. When she looked up, Alice stood still, a hand on her hip, an expectant look on her face. The frustrated breath of a child unable to pull something over on her mother pushed from Angie's lungs.

"It's nothing. She just seems kind of, I don't know, distant lately."

With a nod of her head, Alice went back to work, fishing a matching creamer and sugar bowl out of the very back of the corner cupboard. "I forgot I even had these," she muttered to herself. "Don't you think that probably has to do with losing Boo? It's only been a few weeks."

"Yeah, that's probably it." Angie wrapped the creamer in newspaper, the tiny lid in another smaller piece.

"Everybody handles death differently, honey."

"I know." Angie watched her mother flexing the fingers of her right hand, a subtle wince etched across her features. "You okay, Mama?"

"Fine. Fine. Damn arthritis is acting up today."

"What can I do?"

"My pills are up on my nightstand. Can you grab them for me?"

"You got it."

Angie entered her parents' bedroom for the first time in as long as she could remember. It was their sanctuary, always had been. With four kids, they'd needed one. Angie and her siblings were rarely allowed in once they'd passed age five or six. Now, as she looked around, she took note of things she wouldn't normally see. Her father had a magnifying glass to help him see the print of the cookbooks and paperbacks on his nightstand. His slippers lay neatly on the floor, but they looked like grandpa slippers. His dresser still held his Old Spice cologne, but also a roll-on bottle of Absorbine Jr. for his aching muscles, as well as an Icy Hot pain patch.

Alice's dresser and nightstand told a similar tale, of a woman who was no longer young. Her reading glasses were folded neatly in their case next to a stack of magazines. The remote for the small TV was also there, and Angie knew that if she clicked it on, the volume would be set somewhere between "Way Too Loud" and "Stun". Lately, she and her siblings had been turning down the volume on their parents' electronics. Prescription bottles sat in a tidy row near the remote: blood pressure, cholesterol, restless leg syndrome. And arthritis; she picked up the bottle and shook two tablets into her hand.

As she turned, her mother's dresser caught her eyes. The hairbrush had collected more gray hair than brown, and on the corner of the dust-free surface sat a framed black and white photo from Alice and Joe's wedding day. Angie picked it up, ran her fingertips over the smiling faces of her parents, and wondered how it was possible that they seemed so very young then, and now so very old. Gazing at the photo, she thought about Jillian's mother, how young she'd been when she'd died, and how lucky Angie herself was to still have both parents—even if they weren't the vital, unbreakable people she had thought they were.

Her parents were getting old, and there wasn't a thing she could do to stop it. This wasn't exactly a news flash for her, but for some reason it felt like it.

And in that moment, Angie felt every one of her forty years.

Twenty-Six

The Green Apple was an adorable, little bistro not far from Jillian's school. The unspoken habit embraced by Jillian and Marina—that at least once every week or two, they went out for Happy Hour as soon as they could escape their classrooms—now included Lindsey. They occupied the same window table every time, and it was a short wait before two Cosmos and a Heineken were delivered to them.

The mouth-watering aromas of garlic and fresh-baked bread filled the air. Jillian's stomach rumbled loudly, making the other two look at her with raised eyebrows.

Jillian shrugged. "What? Lunch was a long time ago."

"To surviving a crazy freaking week," Marina said, raising her glass. Jillian raised hers, and they clinked with Lindsey's bottle.

"Amen to that," Jillian said.

They sipped.

"You know, I have always wanted to be a teacher." Lindsey scooped up a handful of mini-pretzels from the bowl in the center of the table. "Ever since I can remember. I used to ask for school stuff for Christmas and birthdays." The other two chuckled knowingly. "I got one of those big easel chalk boards one year. I thought I'd died and gone to heaven." She took another slug, then focused on her friends. "But college did *not* prepare me for the politics."

"Amen to that, too," Jillian said, tipping her glass in Lindsey's direction. Turning to Marina, she asked, "Didn't you and I say the same thing our first couple of years?"

"A few hundred times." Marina brushed a fuzz off her flowing cream-colored skirt, rearranged it around her legs. "It's the hardest thing to get used to, in my opinion."

"Mine, too."

"And don't even get me started on the parents," Marina said, taking a large gulp of her drink as she groaned.

"Well, Lindsey's quite a bit younger than we are," Jillian pointed out. "Her upbringing might have been different."

"Maybe. But I can tell you, my mother knew my teachers' names and she kept up on what I was doing in school, but that was the extent of it. I swear, if some of these parents today could actually do the work for their kids, they absolutely would. And the kids I teach are *little!* You couldn't pay me enough to teach high school."

"Really?" Lindsey asked, then turned to Jillian. "What about you?"

"I wanted to teach high school," Jillian responded.

"Yeah?"

"At first, yup. I wanted to teach art history and art appreciation. All that good stuff. But the small kids?" She gave a wistful smile. "They've kind of grown on me."

"Finger painting is more exciting than you thought, huh?" Lindsey winked.

"Something like that."

"I don't know." Lindsey signaled to Jake the bartender for another round. "I understand that there is such a thing as politics in schools, and I get that certain things have to be dealt with, but I just want to teach the kids. The endless meetings and reports and more meetings and more reports just seem like such a waste of my time." Her ponytail bounced gently as she shook her head.

"You get used to it," Jillian said.

"That's what I keep telling myself."

They chatted for another hour, ordered a sampling of appetizers to help soak up the alcohol, then all three switched to water. As usual, Marina was the first one to call it a night.

Once they'd said their goodbyes and Marina had left, Jillian made an expression that was a combination smile and grimace.

"What's that face?" Lindsey asked.

"I'm still not used to the fact that I don't have to get home to Boo to let her out and feed her. It's been over a month, but it still catches me off guard sometimes."

"Do you think you'll get another dog?"

"I don't know. At times, I think I want to. I miss having a furry thing that loves me unconditionally and is so excited when I come home that she wants to burst." By unspoken agreement, they didn't talk about their home lives. Jillian knew Lindsey was fresh out of a relationship, but they hadn't discussed the details. "Other times, when I think about another dog, I feel like I'd almost be cheating on Boo. I know that's ridiculous, but it's true. And honestly? I didn't realize how much work a dog is until I didn't have one. It's a little bit freeing." She made a face. "And I feel *awful* for saying that. *Awful.*"

Lindsey laid a warm hand over Jillian's. "Don't. Don't do that to yourself. You're not awful, and you know it."

Jillian took a deep breath. "You're right. I was a good mommy."

Lindsey grinned. "Yes, you were."

"Okay. Cheer me up. Talk to me about something fun."

The next ninety minutes seemed to go by in a matter of mere moments for Jillian. As always, she found Lindsey to be entertaining, charming, fun to be around. The two of them laughed so often, they garnered smiling looks from other patrons, and then playfully scolded one another to keep it down.

A quick glance at her watch told her it was well past time for her to get home.

Lindsey grabbed her wrist before she had a chance to stand, her hand soft but firm. "You still wear one of those?" she asked, a twinkle in her eye.

"Yes, smartass, I still wear one. It's called a watch. Not that a young whippersnapper like you would have any idea."

"'Whippersnapper,' huh? My grandpa uses that word."

"Funny," Jillian said as she playfully slapped at Lindsey's arm. She signaled Jake, who sent their bill right over. She added her own money to the cash Marina had left. When she looked up, Lindsey was gazing at her with an expression that Jillian easily read but forced herself to ignore, despite the pang of excitement that hit her low in her body.

"I have so much fun with you," Lindsey said, her voice quietly serious.

"I know. Me too." Bending at the waist, she gave Lindsey a quick hug, not allowing herself to hold on longer than a couple seconds. "I'll see you tomorrow."

She exited the bistro as fast as she could without actually running. Once in her car, she popped in her Gwen Stefani CD and turned it up as loud as her ears could stand. Anything to obliterate the thoughts racing through her mind. Anything to keep her from focusing on what could become a problem for her. Anything to prevent her from actually dealing with the situation head on.

Singing aloud with Gwen seemed to help.

෨   ෨   ෨

The downstairs was dark when Jillian arrived home, though Angie's car was in the driveway. She'd hardly thought about Angie that day, and aside from leaving her a voicemail telling her she was going out with the girls, they hadn't had any contact all day.

Jillian smelled bacon as soon as she entered the kitchen. Bacon and eggs were Angie's go-to dinner when she didn't feel like actually cooking, and a little stab of guilt hit Jillian when she realized Angie had not only been home for dinner but had eaten alone.

Her nights out with the girls didn't tend to run quite so late most of the time.

Upstairs, the bedroom light shone and Jillian smiled as she saw Angie reading *The Da Vinci Code* in bed.

"Hi," she said, hoping her smile wasn't too big.

Angie lowered her book. "Hey. I was beginning to wonder if you were ever coming home." There was no accusation in her tone, no anger. That only made Jillian feel worse.

"I'm sorry." Unbuttoning her blouse, Jillian stepped into the walk-in closet, hung up her work clothes as she took them off. "We got talking and laughing and we just lost track of time."

"No problem. I wasn't going to start worrying for another hour or two."

Jillian poked her head around the door to see if Angie was serious. Her smile said she wasn't. Jillian's relief was palpable, especially since she understood exactly what it felt like to sit up at home and not know when your partner will show up.

"How are the girls?"

"They're good." The thought of telling Angie she had spent most of the evening alone with Lindsey made her feel like she might break out in hives, so she left it at that.

In the bathroom, she washed her face, brushed her teeth, did all her nightly ablutions. Staring at herself in the mirror, she again noticed the crow's feet around her eyes, the smile lines that hugged her mouth like a set of parentheses, a few stray strands of gray hair nicely camouflaged by the lightness of the rest of it. *You're an adult*, she silently told her reflection. *Stop screwing around and act like one.*

In her panties and a tank top, she lifted the covers and crawled into bed next to Angie, who was still reading. She cuddled up, laying her head on Angie's shoulder, draping an arm across Angie's midsection.

"Good book?" she asked.

Angie nodded, kissed Jillian's forehead without taking her eyes from the page she was reading. Her body was warm, her skin soft, and she smelled like her usual exotic scent, which Jillian still adored. And tonight, all those things combined to poke at Jillian until she thought she'd crawl out of her own skin.

With a quick kiss to Angie's cheek, she turned onto her side, facing away, and closed her eyes, praying for sleep to bring her to a new day so she could take a deep breath and start fresh.

Twenty-Seven

It was a Wednesday afternoon a few weeks later. Kids trickled through the halls like the end of a stream, running to meet parents, playing roughly with each other, being just as loud as kids are prone to be. After a few minutes, the halls went quiet. Soon the lights would flicker off as one of the janitors hit the switch. Jillian liked this time of day in the school; the end of the day sometimes felt like relief, like she could take a breath and relax. The parking lot showed only a handful of cars left as she turned the little rod to close the blinds on her windows, preferring to spend the end of her day away from the prying eyes of any passersby who might glance into her classroom. She gathered up supplies and went to work cleaning up paints and washing brushes that had already been washed—poorly—by her students.

When the sounds from the hallway became muffled, Jillian looked up to see Lindsey closing her door. She cut a smile her way as she closed the blinds on the door's window, something Jillian usually did on her way out anyway.

"Hey there."

"Hi," Lindsey replied. "Whatcha doin'?" She stood with her back to the door, her hands clasping the doorknob behind her.

There was an audible click. Jillian gave her a quick and what she hoped was a subtle once-over. Sporting her usual ponytail, workout pants, and an emerald green T-shirt, she looked every inch a strong, athletic woman. Jillian, pulling her eyes away and turning back to the sink, said, "I am performing one of the more glamorous tasks of an elementary school art teacher—cleaning paint off of everything in this room. Aren't you impressed?"

"Terribly." Lindsey's voice was suddenly close.

Closer than Jillian had realized. The sound of the running water had masked her approach from across the room, and now she was standing mere inches away from Jillian's shoulder. Lindsey was only a couple inches taller than Jillian, but at this proximity, their size difference felt enormous.

"Feel free to pitch in," Jillian said, doing her best to keep the conversation light. Something about Lindsey's demeanor today was different, and Jillian swallowed hard. Suddenly something was lodged in her throat, and she couldn't rid herself of it.

"Love to." Lindsey sidled up so their shoulders were touching, and Jillian wanted to kick herself for leaving an opening like that. They shouldn't be this close. Not with the confusion Jillian had been feeling. Not with the wide pupils in Lindsey's eyes.

As if reading Jillian's mind, Lindsey spoke. "Is this too close?" Her voice was low with a slight edge to it.

"Depends on who you're asking," Jillian responded.

"I'm asking you."

"No."

Yes! her brain screamed, even as their hands touched as Lindsey ran some of the paint brushes under the warm water. Jillian tried to pull hers away without being obvious about it. Her heart was hammering in her chest, and something suddenly became frighteningly clear to her.

Lindsey wanted her.

In a big way.

It was so obvious right now, so blatant. Why hadn't she allowed herself to see it and take the proper precautions?

She'd brought it on herself with all her flirting and teasing; she knew that. She should've kept her distance, but she hadn't. Why not? The attention was nice. No, the attention was *awesome*. Jillian couldn't remember the last time Angie had looked at her with the same intensity of attraction that Lindsey did. When was the last time she'd looked at Angie and known—just *known*—that Angie wanted to rip her clothes off right then and there? Sometimes, Lindsey looked at her like that, her eyes heavy-lidded, her expression causing a twinge low in Jillian's belly, and it was all she could do to tear her gaze away. Jillian had tried not to let it go to her head. And failed miserably.

Her brain tossed her an image of Angie that morning. Beautiful, as always, but preoccupied with work, barely noticing Jillian lounging in bed a bit and hoping to be rejoined. Angie giving her a chaste peck on the cheek as she left for the office.

Why couldn't I just talk to her? Why is it so hard? We've been together for nearly two decades, for Christ's sake. Why can't I open my mouth and just say what's on my mind? Am I afraid of the response I might get?

Horrified by the tears that threatened to overtake her, Jillian cleared her throat and turned to Lindsey.

"Look, Lindsey, we need to—" It was all she got out before Lindsey's mouth closed over hers. Paintbrushes and cups clattered into the sink as the water continued to run and a battle waged inside Jillian—a battle between her heart and her body.

Lindsey's kiss was soft, but firm. Gentle, but clear about what she wanted, how she felt. Her wet hands came up and cupped Jillian's face. Jillian's hands were also wet as she grasped Lindsey's forearms, and the whole time, their mouths stayed fused together.

Oh, god, when was the last time she'd been kissed like this? It had been months—*months*—and she couldn't recall this amount of passion, this amount of intensity. A flash of a memory hit her, of her and Angie in bed together during one of the last times, and fighting the urge to grab Angie's head, look her in the eye, and command her to "Kiss me" through clenched teeth.

Lindsey knew how to kiss her. Lindsey kissed her the way she wanted Angie to kiss her. The way Angie *used* to kiss her. And Jillian hadn't felt so attractive, so wanted in a very, *very* long time.

Time seemed to stop. All sound faded away until there was nothing but Lindsey's mouth on hers. Lindsey's hands in her hair. Lindsey's body pinning hers to the sink. Lindsey's tongue pushing against her own. Blood rushed in her ears as Jillian allowed herself to just feel, to lose herself in nothing but sensation, and she kissed back. Hard. Lindsey trailed her fingers along Jillian's neck, down her throat, quickly flicked open three buttons on Jillian's blouse, and cupped her breast, squeezed the nipple through her bra.

Jillian gasped into Lindsey's mouth, but didn't pull away, not even when Lindsey's hand trailed lower. They kept kissing. Even when Lindsey unfastened the fly on the front of Jillian's pants, they kept kissing. And when Lindsey slipped her fingers into the front of Jillian's panties, slicked through the abundant wetness there, and sent Jillian's arousal through the roof, they kept kissing. Jillian didn't pull her mouth away from Lindsey's until she had to—to groan out her orgasm.

They stood together, breathing raggedly, foreheads pressed together as Jillian tried to catch her breath. When she finally pulled herself together, she stepped away, freeing herself from the trap of the sink and of Lindsey's warm body.

Not looking at Lindsey, Jillian fixed her pants, buttoned her shirt, then said in the most matter-of-fact tone she could muster. "This can't happen again."

"Why not?" Lindsey's voice was almost teasing.

Jillian gave her a look—a raise of her eyebrows, a slight exasperated tilt of her head. "You know why not."

Lindsey was undeterred. She stepped closer, wrapped a strand of Jillian's hair around her finger. "You feel the same way I do. I know you do." With her other hand, she caressed the side of Jillian's face, played with her ear.

Jillian's eyes drifted closed. "It's not that simple," she whispered.

"Sure it is." Lindsey kissed her again.

A small whimper escaped Jillian's throat, though whether it was a whimper of frustration or surrender, she wasn't sure, and she felt her own body betraying her again, go slack and melt against Lindsey's. It would be so easy to lose herself once more, to just give in, let go, let Lindsey direct this scene, to follow her lead. Lindsey's mouth was so soft, so warm, so wet. And what she was doing with her tongue . . .

Jillian pushed herself free. "No," she said, and this time her firmness surprised both of them as Lindsey stumbled back a step. "It is *not* that simple. It's not." She looked around the room, realizing for the first time exactly where they were and how much trouble they could be in if somebody caught them. "Oh, my god. I can't believe this."

"The door's locked," Lindsey said as if reading her mind. "Nobody was going to catch us. Jillian." Lindsey stepped closer, cupped Jillian's face in her hands. "Look at me."

Jillian grasped Lindsey's forearms again, a war raging inside her, a battle between wanting to free herself and flee and wanting to lean against this strong, young woman, wanting to give her body to her again, let Lindsey explore her some more with those long fingers, that hot mouth, just *let* her. She'd never felt so completely, utterly uncertain in her entire life, and she wanted to cry from the stress of it all.

"Look at me," Lindsey said again, her voice steely this time, but gently so. Jillian obeyed. When their eyes met, Lindsey's expression softened. She brushed hair from Jillian's face, kissed her forehead, and gave her a tender smile. "You are so beautiful. Everything's going to be okay." She brought their lips together a third time, the kiss almost chaste at first, then slowly deepening. Jillian's hands moved to Lindsey's waist, pulling her in as Lindsey stepped closer so the full length of their bodies touched.

Kissing Lindsey made Jillian's brain foggy. She knew this, even with Lindsey's tongue in her mouth; it was true. When Jillian's brain was foggy, she made stupid decisions. This was a solid enough fact, one she was aware of, even as pleasure and desire raced through her bloodstream, like a deadly virus. Using all her strength—and now her limbs had become like jelly—she pushed away from Lindsey one final time, wrenching their mouths apart. She backed several steps away, holding her hands up, palms out like a traffic cop.

"Stop. Just stop. Please."

Lindsey cocked her head. "Jillian," she said, using her name as if trying to persuade a small child into doing something naughty.

"No." Jillian kept her hands up. Uncertain how long she could stave off this woman that she wanted—badly—to give in to, she quickly moved to her desk and gathered up her things. To her credit, Lindsey stayed by the sink, her expression one of sadness and disappointment, but also with a slight tinge of amusement, something Jillian did not want to analyze just then. Jillian looked at her, but was unable to hold her gaze. "I'm sorry," she said, her voice much steelier than she felt. "This *cannot* happen again."

∾ ∾ ∾

If Jillian could have run to the parking lot in full sprint without drawing attention to herself, she would have.

The desire to sit in her parked car and simply focus on breathing was strong, but she worried that her privacy would be short-lived. Lindsey's SUV was parked only three spots away in the mostly empty lot, and avoiding her would be next to impossible, so she started the car and drove around aimlessly for nearly an hour.

She'd kissed somebody who was not Angie.

"Jesus, Jillian, you did more than kiss her," Jillian chastised herself aloud. "You had sex. You cheated. You're a cheater."

Guilt poured over Jillian like a load of fresh soil, stealing her breath, threatening to bury her alive. Her heart hammered in her chest, hammered much faster than could be healthy, and she pulled into the first parking lot she could find, jammed the car into park, clawed at the door handle, and spilled out of the driver's seat like she was made of liquid. She stumbled to the grass and stood with her hands on her knees, struggling to catch her breath.

Jillian knew a panic attack when she saw one. She'd had students who'd suffered from them. Now she knew what one felt like.

She willed herself to calm down, forced herself to breathe deliberately, slowly in, slowly out . . . slowly in, slowly out. It took her several minutes—minutes that felt like hours—to talk herself back to normal. When she finally blinked her eyes into focus and looked up, rows of weathered gray headstones looked back at her.

"Oh, that's just perfect," she muttered, realizing she'd pulled into a cemetery.

Once her heart rate had returned to normal, she lowered herself back into the driver's seat, lay her head back against the headrest, and blew out a long breath.

From the seat next to her, her cell phone beeped. She glanced at the pile she'd tossed there haphazardly in her rush to leave. Digging past her lunch bag and jacket, she rifled through her tote bag until she felt her cell phone, which blinked a light to indicate she had a text message.

She didn't like texting. She was new to it, tried to avoid it when she could; Angie was the one insisting that, sometimes, it was easier than calling. She flipped the phone open and saw the message telling her she had a text from Lindsey's number.

"Shit."

Her finger hovered over the button for a long moment before she pressed it and read.

We need to talk.

An ominous phrase, if ever there was one.

Jillian flipped the phone closed again and tossed it to the passenger seat.

Twenty-Eight

Angie had made a decision, and she firmly believed that's why her days seemed to run along more smoothly. Not a lot more smoothly, but a little, and that made for a much lighter mood. With Hope gone and Keith even more self-absorbed than usual, she didn't have many allies at the office in whom she could confide, but that was okay. With any luck, she wouldn't be there a whole lot longer. She just needed to set up some time to talk with Keith. Once he heard her pitch, she was pretty sure she'd be on the path to a new, better, more profitable and less stressful working environment.

She felt good.

Now, if she could get her life at home to be as balanced, things would be perfect.

She had yet to tell Jillian about her plans, mostly because it never felt like the right time. The last thing Angie wanted to do was cheerfully suggest, "Hey, let's talk about me!" It felt like it'd been weeks since she'd even seen Jillian smile. She knew avoidance wasn't the best way to deal with the issue, but she wasn't good with conflict, and when Jillian was like this, flying under the radar just seemed best.

It was coming up on the anniversary of Jillian's mother's death. She was pretty sure that was what was bothering her. Every year at this time, Jillian got a little quieter, a little more pensive. The ornery part was new, but Angie tried to shrug it off.

Maybe she'd leave the whole new job thing as a surprise. Maybe she wouldn't say anything to Jillian until she knew it was all going to work. Plus, if Keith didn't go for it and everything fell through, Hope said getting her an interview at Star would be a piece of cake. So either way, she was making a change, getting out of Logo Promo. Any way she sliced it, things would be better. That would make Jillian happy.

"Honey, I'm home," she called out as she walked into the house. It was still so quiet without Boo. Angie wondered if it was time to suggest doing something about that. Jillian's keys were on the counter and the top of her blonde head was visible out the kitchen window. Angie followed the scent of her perfume and found her partner sitting on the deck in the fresh air, a glass of white wine in her hand.

"Hi." Jillian's greeting sounded normal, but her blue eyes registered a very subtle sadness that Angie was sure nobody else would catch. "You're home early."

Angie shrugged. "I'm turning over a new leaf."

"I've heard that before," Jillian said with a gentle scoff.

"I know. Can I join you?"

"Sure."

After kicking off her work shoes and pouring herself a glass of wine, Angie joined Jillian on the deck, taking the wicker chair next to her. "How was your day?" she asked, then took a sip.

Jillian took a deep breath, as if answering the question was going to take a lot of effort on her part. "Fine. Yours?"

"Not bad." She went on to tell Jillian all about the orders she'd written, closed, or delivered. She talked about Jeremy's newest rules and Keith's latest hundred thousand-dollar order. Mostly, she talked to fill the silence because she knew if she let the silence be, she'd feel the need to deal with it, and she just wasn't sure she was up for that.

Coward, the voice in her head accused. *Just ask her what's wrong.*

It bothered Angie to no end that she'd become filled with trepidation about her own relationship. She'd spent many sleepless nights trying to pinpoint exactly when she'd become hesitant to talk openly with her wife. She kept coming back to Boo and the day she died. Not only had she failed to be there for Jillian during a traumatic time, but she knew she'd failed. Since then, she'd been treading carefully, hoping to skate along until things improved. It was taking much longer than she expected.

"I'm going to go take a bath," Jillian said, pulling Angie out of her head. "My period's due any day now and my back is killing me."

"Okay." Angie forced a smile. "A good, hot soak should help. Need anything?"

"Nope. I got it."

"Did you eat?"

"I'm not really hungry. There's some leftover chicken in the fridge if you want that." She left Angie sitting alone on the deck.

Angie looked out onto their backyard for a long while. The songbirds in the evergreens at the edge of the yard chirped and tweeted to one another. A dog barked in the distance. All these things should have served to relax her, but instead, she just felt tense, like a jungle cat ready to spring.

With a sigh, she went into the kitchen to refill her wine glass. The cheerfully musical ringtone of Jillian's cell phone caused Angie to pull her head out of the fridge, where she was looking for food. A glance at the screen told her it was her mother.

"Hey, Mama."

There was a pause, and Angie smiled as she pictured her mother checking the phone in her hand to make sure she dialed the correct number. "Angie?"

"Yup. Jillian's in the tub, so I grabbed her phone. What's up?"

"Well, if I'd wanted to talk to you, I would have dialed *your* number, don't you think?"

"Looking for birthday ideas, are you?" Angie was sure her smug face came through in her voice.

"None of your business. Jillian and I have other things to talk about besides your birthday. Have her call me when she's done."

"Something expensive," Angie said loudly into the phone as her mother hung up. As she went to set it down, a beep sounded indicating a text message.

❧　❧　❧

Jillian tried to be soothed by the hot water but she still felt tense, like all of her muscles were rubber bands stretched to the limit. She closed her eyes, willed herself to just breathe, but the tension wouldn't go away.

A light knock on the door had her opening her eyes again. Angie peered around the door with a smile.

"My mom just called your phone."

"Did you answer it?"

"Yeah, I saw her number, so I picked it up. I'm sure she wants to know what to get me for my birthday. I told her you'd call her back." She handed the phone to Jillian. "You also got a text."

Jillian's heart started to pound. "From who?"

Angie gave an offhand shrug. "No idea. I didn't check." She closed the door as she left, and Jillian tried to be quiet about the breath she released. Quickly pushing some buttons, she called up the most recent text. It was from Lindsey.

I'm worried about you.

Another had come a minute later.

We need to talk about what happened.

Jillian typed quickly. *No. We don't.* She hit the volume button so the beep of the incoming text could not be heard, but it came in a matter of seconds.

Jillian. Please talk to me.

Jillian squeezed her eyes shut.

Hello?

Jillian sent another message. Stop texting me.

Lindsey's response took a bit longer this time. *I need you to talk to me. And you need it too. I know you felt the same way that I did.*

Jillian's thumbs moved over the tiny keyboard. *We made a mistake. It never should have happened. Please. Just leave it alone.*

Without waiting for a response this time, she deleted the entire conversation and then shut the phone off completely.

৵   ৵   ৵

It happened again three days later.

This time, things became hot and heavy before Jillian even had time to think. She'd wandered down to Lindsey's office after hours with every intention of talking to her about a student. Since she'd been avoiding the phys ed teacher for two days, she'd decided she at least owed her a conversation. She had an entire speech prepared, one that listed all the reasons why what they'd done was wrong and wouldn't happen again. With a deep breath to fill her lungs, she knocked on the doorjamb. Lindsey looked so happy to see her, it was almost pathetic.

Lindsey invited her in to her tiny, windowless office, shut and locked the door behind her, and the next thing Jillian knew, she was sitting on Lindsey's desk, Lindsey's tongue was in her mouth, Lindsey's hand was under her skirt, and Jillian was holding on for dear life as she buried her face in Lindsey's sweatshirt to muffle her groans of pleasure.

When they were finished, Jillian quickly straightened her clothes.

"I like the skirt," Lindsey commented, looking far too pleased with herself.

"Thanks." Jillian finger-combed her hair, reached for the doorknob.

"Want to go get something to eat?" Lindsey asked.

Jillian blinked at her for a moment before saying simply, "No. I don't think so. Thank you." She pulled the door open and left.

ॐ   ॐ   ॐ

They say the third time's the charm.

Such was the case for Jillian.

It was once again after hours. They were in her room, door shut and locked, blinds all closed tightly. Lindsey had wasted no time making her move, and Jillian found herself yet again seated on a desk with Lindsey standing snugly tucked between Jillian's knees. They were kissing deeply, but Jillian's thoughts were screaming so loudly in her head, she was surprised Lindsey couldn't hear them.

Stop it. Why are you doing this? Why do you continue to do this?

Jillian had no answer.

You don't even touch her. You have no desire to touch her. Does that mean nothing to you?

Again, no answer was forthcoming, but Jillian's attention was caught this time. It was true. This was the third time in as many weeks that Jillian had caved in to Lindsey's physical persuasion, but it was the first time it occurred to her how alarmingly one-sided things were.

As Lindsey's deft fingers slipped beneath the hem of Jillian's shirt and touched the bare skin of her belly, Jillian wrenched their mouths apart.

"Wait," she said, her breath ragged.

Lindsey was persistent, moving from Jillian's mouth to the side of her neck. "Wait for what?" she murmured.

Jillian craned her neck away and pushed gently at Lindsey's shoulders. "Just wait. Stop."

Lindsey pulled back, her hands gripping Jillian's waist, and blinked a few times to clear the haze of arousal from her eyes. She looked expectantly at Jillian.

"Lindsey," Jillian began, then paused to clear her throat and swallow. "This isn't right."

Lindsey scoffed. "No kidding. If you'd just come home with me, we could do it in an actual bed."

"No. No, that's not what I mean." She held Lindsey's gaze, knew exactly when Lindsey got what she was saying.

"But . . ." Lindsey looked down, the first sign of emotion Jillian had seen from her passing across her face. "We're good together."

Jillian took a deep breath. "You are amazing," she said, and she meant it. "And I am . . . so flattered that you feel the way you do."

"Flattered, huh?" Lindsey grimaced. "That's rarely a word you want to hear from the woman you've been making love to."

"I love Angie," Jillian said quietly, and for the first time in months, realized it was the absolute truth. "I love Angie, and I can't keep doing this."

"How would she feel if she found out?" Lindsey said sharply, challenging her.

But Jillian knew the threat was halfhearted. She looked at her until Lindsey's expression turned to one of guilt, and she looked away.

"I'm not going to tell her," Lindsey said grudgingly.

"I know. I'm going to."

Lindsey's gaze snapped back to her. "You are?"

"I have to. It's killing me. I can't sleep. I can't eat. I've lost weight—which isn't necessarily a bad thing—but she's been looking at me with concern, and it just crushes me. She knows something's wrong, but I think she's afraid to talk to me. So it's up to me."

"Jesus."

"Yeah, tell me about it."

They were quiet for a long moment. Jillian looked up at Lindsey, tucked a loose strand of hair behind her ear. "You're pretty wonderful, you know that?"

"Not wonderful enough, though."

Jillian smiled sadly. "You'll be okay."

Lindsey nodded. "I will. I hope this works out the way you want."

Jillian swallowed hard. "So do I."

      ά   ά   ά

"Can we talk?"

That's how it started. Angie actually looked relieved, which was ridiculous, since it wasn't a question that was usually followed by good news. But she sat down at the kitchen table across from Jillian, who'd already begun to crinkle a napkin in her hand.

They sat quietly as Jillian tried to think of the right way to begin.

"Are you leaving me?" Angie asked softly.

Jillian's eyes snapped up. "What? No. No, of course not. But . . ."

"But?" Angie's eyebrows raised and her brown eyes widened slightly as her face creased with worry.

"I . . . did something." Jillian tried to swallow, but it didn't seem to help. Her stomach was churning, and she realized with horror that throwing up was a distinct possibility.

Angie shook her head, confused. "You did something. What does that mean?"

"I . . . did something. Something stupid."

Angie continued to stare, but the tinge of dread was there in her eyes.

"I made a mistake." *God, just say it, Jillian,* her head screamed. But her tongue continued to stumble over words that weren't saying what needed to be said.

"What kind of mistake?" Angie's voice was just above a whisper, and Jillian was suddenly clear on the old adage: *The wife always knows.* Angie knew what she was going to say, but was waiting for her to say it. Jillian's fingers worked of their own accord, shredding

217

the napkin to tiny little bits of paper, even as her voice box decided to stop working.

"Are you having an affair?" Angie asked quietly.

Jillian had no idea five simple words could hold so much pain. She looked up, wished she hadn't when she saw the anguish on Angie's face.

"No." Adamantly, she shook her head. "No. It's over."

"So, you *did* have an affair."

Did three times constitute an affair? She asked herself the question mentally before closing her eyes at the absurdity of it. Yes. Any extramarital sex constituted an affair. She nodded her head slowly.

"With who?" Angie's voice had gone steely. The anger was setting in. Why shouldn't it?

Jillian was hesitant to answer, though she didn't know why. Turned out, she didn't have to.

"It's that gym teacher, isn't it? The one you spend so much time with? God, I'm so stupid. How did I not see that coming?"

Jillian gnawed on the inside of her cheek, no idea what to say. Angie's beautiful face had flushed red, and her hands were shaking. But it was the tears in her eyes that made Jillian's heart twist. "I'm so sorry," she said, her voice a strangled whisper.

"How long? How long has it been going on?"

Jillian shook her head. "Not long. A couple weeks. And it's over."

"Oh, good." The sarcasm was thick and heavy. "I'm so glad you spread your legs for somebody else for not very long and now it's over."

"Angie—"

Angie held up her hand, cutting Jillian off as she looked away. The tears spilled down her cheeks. When she looked back, the pain etched across her face was almost too much for Jillian to bear. Angie asked simply, "Why?"

Jillian's eyes welled too as she looked away. Her throat closed, making words next to impossible.

"Why, Jillian? I don't understand."

There wasn't a good way to explain it. Jillian could barely explain it to herself. How was she supposed to make Angie see what she'd been feeling for months now, years even?

"God damn it, I deserve an explanation, don't I?" Angie slapped the table, making Jillian jump.

A tear cleared Jillian's bottom eyelid and left a wet trail down her face.

"Don't I give you enough?" Angie stood suddenly and started pacing in the small room. "Haven't I given you everything I can? Haven't I? I work my ass off, Jill. For you. For us. I work constantly."

"That's not fair."

"What's not fair?"

"You throwing your work in my face. I have a job, too, you know. I work hard too, just like you." This was not the direction the conversation should be taking, and Jillian knew it, but she couldn't stop.

"Do you think I want to not be here for you? Do you think I *like* working eighty hours a week?"

"I don't know, Angie. Don't you? You're not responsible for supporting me, but you act like you are, like I'm some kept housewife who needs your paycheck to survive. That's your view, not mine. I don't need you to take care of me. This is supposed to be a partnership."

"I'm not the one fucking somebody else!"

Jillian flinched at the crude words. "It just happened." She wanted to put all the blame on Lindsey, but knew she couldn't, that she'd be lying.

"Well, that makes me feel so much better."

"I didn't mean for it to. I swear. It just happened."

"How? How does that 'just happen'?" Angie sneered, her anger ratcheting up, her eyes narrowing. "Did you trip and fall into her vagina? Did you walk into her by mistake and your tongue just happened to slip into her mouth? How does something like that 'just happen'?"

There was no explaining. She knew it. Angie was too angry—rightfully so—and Jillian didn't know what to say.

"It 'just happened.' Please. Give me a break. That line is such a load of bullshit." Angie was still doing a weird form of pacing while she muttered in disgust. "I can't believe this. I can't believe you'd be so reckless." She stopped moving then and threw her hands up. "Christ, I can't believe you're that easy."

Jillian's head snapped up then. Angie had a right to be angry, she knew. But insulting?

219

"And she's practically a kid. Isn't she, like, ten years younger than you? Were you sucked in by that? Her youth? What was it?"

Jillian rubbed at her forehead.

"Was it her hot little bod? Was that it? Couldn't resist the gym teacher? Were you playing out some old schoolgirl fantasy?"

Jillian clenched her jaw.

"I don't get it, Jillian. Seriously. I don't get it. What did she do for you?"

Jillian snapped. "She *noticed* me, Angie! She *noticed* me. She *wanted* me. She *really wanted* me, and she let me know it. *When was the last time you did?*"

Angie stood perfectly still.

Jillian closed her eyes, knowing a line had been crossed. A truthful one, but a line just the same. When she opened her eyes again, Angie was gone from the room. She could hear her stomp up the stairs, drawers slamming in the bedroom. More stomping around, and then Angie was down the stairs and out the door before Jillian could even bring herself to stand up. Instead, she stayed sitting, and sobbed like she'd just lost her best friend.

Because she was pretty sure she had.

Twenty-Nine

Angie could feel her mother's eyes on her as she pushed her eggs
around her plate with a fork. She'd been sleeping in her parents' guest
room for three nights—though she'd gotten very little sleep. Giving
no explanation, she had showed up on their doorstep and asked if she
could stay for a while. Of course they said yes and, god love them,
they didn't pry. They knew Angie would come to them when she was
ready, as she'd done since she was a child.

"You know," her mother said over the rim of her coffee cup, "just
because you're pushing your food around, that doesn't mean I don't
notice that you're eating none of it. I'm a mom. Nothing escapes
my attention."

Angie smiled in spite of her mood. "Don't I know it."

Alice sipped her coffee.

And Angie knew it was time to tell her.

The story poured out of her like water, along with all the things
she'd put together after learning the details. Jillian's nights out with
"the girls," which Angie now wondered if it was more like "the girl,"
her distance and silence lately, the haunted look in her eyes, the weight
loss, their fight, the cruel things they said to each other. All of it. Her
eyes welled up a couple of times, but she managed to hold it together
in front of her mom, even though the combination of remembering,
her stress, and the fact that she hadn't eaten more than a bite of food in
the past three days threatened to push her over the edge. She kept a
grip on her emotions and took a large gulp of coffee when she finished,
wincing as the hot acidity hit her empty stomach.

Alice took it all in, nodding at times, cocking her head at others, but never interrupting. When Angie was finished, silence ruled the kitchen for several long moments as Alice absorbed her daughter's words. Angie knew she was rolling all the information around in her head. It was how her mother dealt with things. She ingested all the material presented to her, took time to examine it from all angles, and then gave her carefully structured opinion. This was why it was better to talk to Alice than Joe about such matters. Joe was all emotion. He'd have started cursing Jillian after Angie's second sentence, and that's not what she needed. Not yet, anyway.

Angie could tell when Alice was ready to talk because she set her coffee down and folded her hands on the table in front of her.

"Have you talked to Jillian since you've been here?" she asked.

Angie shook her head. "She's called my cell and texted about a hundred times. I told her I needed some time."

"She's called here a couple times, but always hung up. Her number's been on the caller ID."

"You didn't tell me that."

"You didn't tell me anything," Alice countered, though gently. Angie grimaced. "I wanted all the information before I got involved in any way." Alice wet her lips. "It was just those couple weeks?"

Angie's head snapped up. "What do you mean 'just those couple weeks'? She slept with somebody else, Ma. I think it's a little more complicated than 'just those couple weeks.'"

"But she ended it pretty quickly, and then she told you about it."

"What?" Angie was incredulous.

Alice made a calming gesture with her hands. "Calm down, Angelina. I'm simply thinking out loud. All right?"

"Fine."

"Has anything like this happened before?"

Angie shook her head. "I don't think so. Though who knows? It's not like I saw this coming. I mean, I knew something was bothering her, but I never expected this." She swallowed hard, disguised her disgust by sipping her coffee.

"Do you think she's sorry?" Angie gave her a look and Alice raised her eyebrows in a gesture of *what?*.

Angie flashed to Jillian's face that last time. She had been in anguish.

Much as Angie wanted to not care, to say that it was the least she deserved for what she'd done, it was hard. She answered her mother honestly. "I think she's devastated by what she's done. And yes, I think she's sorry."

"Do you still love her?"

It was a question Angie had asked herself many, many times over the past seventy-two hours, and despite her hurt and her anger, she always came back to the same answer: yes. With all her stomped-upon, aching heart, yes. Angie nodded grudgingly.

"All right," Alice said, sitting up straight with determination. "Good. Then we need to figure out how you go about fixing things."

Angie stared at her, trying to keep her anger at bay. "Just like that? You think it's that simple?"

Alice's voice took on a stern tone, the tone she used when she was pulling rank and being Mom. "No, Angelina, I don't think it's simple at all. I think it's very, very complicated. And I am not happy with your partner at this point in time. Not happy at all. Now. You two have been together how long?"

"Sixteen years."

Alice blinked as if momentarily taken aback. "Has it been that long?" At Angie's nod, she added, "Wow. Time really does fly, doesn't it?" Pulling herself back to the conversation at hand, she continued. "All right. So, you've been together for sixteen years. Do you want to flush those sixteen years down the toilet?"

"Of course not, but I'm not the one who—"

Alice cut her off with an upheld hand. "No, we're not laying blame right now. We're answering questions. Important questions. Do you want to flush the past sixteen years down the toilet? Yes or no?"

"No."

"Good. Are you willing to listen to Jillian with an open mind?" At Angie's silence, she studied her daughter. "What?"

"She blames me. She says I didn't pay enough attention to her."

"Did you?"

Resentment began to bubble up. "Seriously, Ma? *I* am not the one who went looking for somebody else, and I can't believe you're

223

going to side with *her* and make her straying *my* fault. *She* made the mistake, not me."

"That's right." Alice slapped a hand on the table and leaned toward her daughter. "She made a mistake. *She made a mistake.* I'm not saying it was right. I am certainly not excusing her. But we all make mistakes, and if the person who loves us the most in the world won't give us a chance to explain—and hopefully forgive us—who will?"

Angie scoffed. "So I'm supposed to just go to her all 'Okay, so you took off your clothes for somebody besides me. No biggie. All is forgiven. Let's go out to eat'?"

Alice tilted her head and her expression showed just how ridiculous she thought her daughter was being. "No, that's not what I'm saying. What I'm saying is, if there's a reason that Jillian made her mistake, you'd better deal with it if you have any shot of moving forward together."

"So I take the blame?"

Alice sighed. "Did I say that?"

"You said maybe there's a reason Jillian made a mistake."

"Is there?"

Angie's eyes filled. "This is so unfair," she said softly. "I didn't do anything."

Reaching across the table, Alice closed her hand over her daughter's. "Oh, sweetie, I know. I know you didn't. My point is that people screw up. We do stupid things. We do things we immediately regret. And somebody like Jillian is going to beat herself up over it for years, mark my words. I know it, and you know it. So if *you* don't forgive her and *she* can't forgive herself, where's she going? Where are the two of you going together? That's the big question for you: can you forgive her?"

"I don't know," Angie whispered.

❧   ❧   ❧

This was extra stress that Jillian feared she was ill-equipped to handle, but she had no choice. She sat in Starbucks across the table from Shay and blinked at her as she ran possible responses to Shay's question through her brain in an attempt to come up with a good lie.

You look like death warmed over. What the hell is going on, Jill? Is everything okay? Are you okay?

She'd never lied to Shay. Their friendship was too important. She was always upfront with Shay, even when she didn't want to be; that's why she was sitting here instead of thinking of a little white lie that would've gotten her out of this meeting. At the same time, Jillian thought maybe it would be good to talk to somebody. She'd been rattling around the house alone for days. Maybe talking to somebody who knew her well would help. But this situation, this was not going to sit well with Shay. How could it possibly seem nearly as hard to tell her what had happened as it had been to tell Angie?

"Jillian." Shay's voice was firm, her eyes lined with concern. She reached across the small, round table and covered Jillian's hands with her own. "You're scaring me. Talk to me."

"I cheated on Angie." It just came blurting out of her mouth. Not the way she'd intended to present it, but there it was, and she was slightly relieved.

Shay stared at her, her mouth working, but no sound coming out. She let go of Jillian's hands and sat back in her chair as if all her energy had suddenly left her body. Slowly, she began to shake her head from side to side, disbelief, shock, and disappointment all clearly written on her face.

Jillian swallowed, wondered momentarily if she might get sick. "I know," she said. "I know."

"Wow." Jillian could see that Shay had more to say, but she just uttered that one word and continued to shake her head, as if doing so would change the words Jillian had said.

"It was a mistake," Jillian said. "It was a mistake. It didn't last long, and I told Angie about it right away. She's at her parents' for a little bit. I'm hoping . . ." She let her voice trail off, suddenly understanding that no explanation was going to remove that look from Shay's eyes. That look of judgment. That look of disillusionment. That look of disgust. "Shay, please."

"How could you?" Shay said, her voice low. "You saw what I went through. You *know* how awful it was. How could you do that to Angie?"

225

Jillian wet her lips, focused on the table top. "I was just…weak. She looked at me like I was gorgeous, Shay, and I was weak. It didn't mean anything; I never even touched her, it was always her touching me. I just…I melted. It had been so long since I felt like that. I couldn't help it. It just happened."

"Bullshit." Shay spat the word at her, interrupting her with a sneer. "That is a giant load of bullshit. Cheating doesn't 'happen.'" She made air quotes to stress her sarcasm. "It didn't 'happen,' Jillian. You did it. You. *You did it.* You are responsible. All the pain and anguish Angie is going through right now? *You* caused it."

Jillian swallowed, no response forthcoming. Really, what could she say? She didn't think she was making excuses for what had happened, it wasn't her intention, but maybe that's exactly what she was doing.

"I can't believe you'd do that to somebody you profess to love."

"I do love her." Jillian was feeling defensive, and she didn't want that, didn't feel she had the right to it. She'd expected disappointment from Shay, but not this kind of anger. It squeezed her heart. "I do."

"Right," Shay snorted. "I can see that." She stood suddenly. "You know what? I can't even look at you right now."

"Shay . . ." Jillian watched as Shay gathered her things and left the building, not looking back, not saying goodbye. Jillian's eyes filled with tears. Two best friends in one week: gone. It was no less than she deserved. Right?

She wanted to lay her head down on the table and cry.

                    ❧   ❧   ❧

For the past few evenings, Jillian had wandered the house looking at photos of family and souvenirs from trips she and Angie had taken. The hallway from the foyer was covered with framed pictures. Jillian's mother. Angie's parents. The four Righetti kids before they hit their teens. Dom, Pam, and their daughter Gia just weeks after her birth. The five Righetti nieces and nephews. When Jillian had met Angie, there were no nieces or nephews. Now Angie's brothers had five kids between them and Jillian's brother Brian had two. Seven new lives had come into being while Jillian and Angie were together. It amazed her. And the thought of losing some of them, of losing the entire Righetti clan, squeezed her heart painfully.

She sat down on the living room floor with the big glass jar of corks that Angie had been collecting since they first got together. Some of the events had completely slipped her mind, and when she read them off—moving days, promotions, births, finished projects, trips—she was both laughing and crying over the life they had together.

God, she was stupid. Worse: she was a walking cliché. How could she have just given in like that? When had she completely lost her mind? Lindsey had texted her a few times to see how things were going, but Jillian knew talking to her about it would be yet another mistake in the long line she'd made. She deleted every text and even erased Lindsey from her contacts. She didn't see any other option, and a part of her felt terrible about that. A bigger part of her was relieved beyond words.

The text from Angie late last night had come as a surprise.

I'm ready to talk. Are you?

Jillian was so thrilled to have any contact at all that she gave a happy little squeal, and sprang up out of bed as if yanked by invisible strings.

Yes! she typed back. *Can I call you?*

No. 2morrow. Starbucks on Jefferson at 9am.

Tamping down the disappointment and trying to look on the bright side, she answered. *I'll be there.*

OK.

After a minute or two went by with nothing further, Jillian couldn't help herself. *Angie, I'm so sorry. I just want you to know that. I was stupid and I'm so, so sorry. And I miss you.*

Jillian paced around the room as she waited for a response. The ticking of the clock in the hallway seemed inordinately loud as she waited for a text notification. Just when she was sure Angie wasn't going to answer, the phone beeped in her hand.

2morrow. We'll talk.

It had taken every ounce of strength she had not to call Angie.

She sat in Starbucks, at 8:40, nursing a Chai that churned and bubbled like sour milk in her very empty stomach. Eating had been next to impossible—when she made the attempt, she felt nauseous—and the irony was not lost on her that the only way she'd been able to lose any weight in her adult life was to have Angie move out on her. Jen, the cute barista, gave her the usual flirty wink when Jillian paid for her Chai, and the thought of Angie seeing anything even close to that filled Jillian with a sense of dread and worry that made her stomach give a sour churn. She took a seat at the table farthest from the counter, hoping to avoid Jen's gaze all together, and waited.

When she saw Angie walking across the parking lot, Jillian was immediately filled with a longing and a love so deep and intense it brought tears to her eyes. Those long legs that made for long, purposeful strides. All that dark hair blowing in the wind. The dark, soulful eyes—accented by shadowy half-circles underneath. Apparently, Angie was getting as little sleep as she was. Jillian wasn't sure if that made her feel better or worse.

Entering the store, Angie caught her eyes, then gestured to the counter, indicating she'd get her coffee and be right there. As Angie stood in line, Jillian's stomach increased its roiling speed, forcing her to set down her Chai and swallow down a small bit of bile that had worked its way up. She couldn't remember being quite so nervous ever before. She focused on breathing, just breathing, and waited.

Angie arrived with her latte and sat.

"Hi," Jillian said.

"Hey," Angie replied, and then looked away. She fiddled with her cup, the lid to her cup, the sleeve on her cup. She gazed out the window. Jillian watched, a mixture of sadness, guilt, and sympathy coursing through her.

Finally, Jillian cleared her throat and ventured a start to the conversation. "Are you okay?"

"I've been better," Angie said, edgy.

With a nod, Jillian said, "I know. I know, and I'm so sorry."

"Do you love her?"

The question was quiet, simple, and such a surprise that Jillian just blinked at Angie for several seconds. "What?"

"Lindsey. Are you in love with her?" Angie stared at her coffee as if she was afraid to look at Jillian when the answer came.

"No." Jillian didn't hesitate, and put as much strength, as much finality into that one word as she could. "Angie. Look at me." Angie hesitated, but finally looked up, her eyes filled with tears. "No," Jillian said again. "No, I am not in love with Lindsey. I do not love Lindsey. I never loved Lindsey. I love you."

With a scoff, Angie looked away, swiped at her eyes like an embarrassed twelve-year-old.

"Angie." Jillian waited until Angie looked at her again, then she repeated herself. "I. Love. You. Nobody else. You."

"You've got a funny way of showing it," Angie said quietly.

"I know. I know. I fucked up. I fucked up badly, and I'm so sorry about that. I will tell you every single day for the rest of my life how sorry I am if that's what it takes to get you to believe me. I swear to god."

Angie blew on her coffee, took a sip. Her brows furrowed as she rolled the words around in her head. Then she looked at Jillian and asked simply, "Why?"

"Why?" Jillian asked.

"Yeah. Why? Why did it happen? What pulled you so far away from me that you felt the need to sleep with somebody else?"

The question wasn't a surprise. It made perfect sense, plus she'd asked it already, that night before she left. She had been asking herself the same thing for the past seven days, since Angie had walked out. And the three weeks before that, since Lindsey had had sex with her in her own classroom, since she'd *let* Lindsey do that. And while she didn't have a definitive answer—mostly because there wasn't one— she had an idea.

Jillian inhaled deeply, exhaled slowly, wrapped her hands around her cup, and began to speak. "I don't think it was about you at all. Well, maybe a little bit, but mostly, I think it's about me." Holding up a hand quickly, she added, "And I know that sounds lame and it's not an excuse. Just a fact." She rolled her lips in and wet them while she looked for the right words. "I haven't been feeling great about myself lately."

"Lately?"

"Like, for the past couple of years."

Surprise was clear on Angie's face. "Seriously? Why?"

With a half-shrug, Jillian tried to explain. "I don't know. I'm starting to feel older. I'm starting to feel like I look older."

"Jill, you're only thirty-eight."

"I know. But I remember my mom telling me what a hard time she had when she was closing in on forty. I think I'm going through the same thing, and it's messed with my head." *God, I wish she was here,* Jillian thought.

"So . . . you needed to have a fling to make yourself feel younger?" The sarcasm in Angie's voice was not lost on her.

"No." Jillian let the barb go, knowing it was deserved. "But . . ." She sipped some of her Chai, chewed on the inside of her lip.

"But what?"

"But . . ." *Jesus,* she thought. This was not easy to say. She'd rehearsed it a hundred times last night and this morning, but it still sounded ridiculous in her head. She decided on a slightly different tack. "You know how I've always loved it when you tell me I'm beautiful or you think I'm pretty or sexy or whatever?"

Angie nodded.

"You stopped doing that."

Furrowing her brows, Angie just looked at her.

"A long time ago. You stopped. You started working so much. You stopped complimenting me. Our sex life practically disappeared altogether." Though the warning look on Angie's face made her pause, Jillian pushed on. "I know you don't want to hear that, but it's true. The combination of that and the crappy way I feel about myself was . . . not good."

"So because my work got hectic, and I stopped telling you you're pretty, you went and fucked somebody else? This is my fault?"

Fighting to stay calm in the face of Angie's anger, Jillian said quietly, "I didn't say that."

"You don't get enough attention or enough sex from me. That's what you're saying."

"Okay, that's not what I'm saying. And stop making me sound like an idiot. I do realize that there's more to a relationship than sex, Angie. I also realize that there's a difference between sex and intimacy—and lately, we've had neither."

Silence fell as they each absorbed what Jillian had said. The fact that Angie didn't get up and storm out was something, at least.

"Look," Jillian said, lowering her voice and choosing her words carefully. "None of this is an excuse. Like I said, I fucked up. I know that, and I will regret it for the rest of my life. I take responsibility for this mess. I am to blame. But you asked me why, and I'm giving you the best answer I can. It's vague, I know, because I honestly don't understand the whole of it." She reached across the table and grabbed Angie's hand, thrilled when she didn't pull away. "I do know that you and I are meant to be together. I am supposed to be with you. You are supposed to be with me. And my stupid mistake doesn't change that. I love you, Angelina. *I love you.* Tell me what I can do to fix this." Tears filled her eyes, and her throat tightened, but she choked through and continued. "I *need* to fix this. I'm a mess. You're a mess. And I miss you so much. The house isn't home without you there. Tell me what to do. Please. Tell me what to do."

Again, they sat quietly holding hands across the small table. Finally, Angie spoke up.

"You can't see her again. You can't be her friend."

Jillian nodded, not surprised. "Okay."

Angie looked up at her. "I mean it. You'll see her at work. That's bad enough. But you can't go out with her. Even if others are there."

Jillian nodded again. "Okay."

As if realizing her request might be overkill, she amended, "I mean, if there's a party or something, that's okay I guess."

"We can play it by ear," Jillian suggested, trying not to show too much joy over the fact that she might be getting a chance to have her life back. "I'll always let you know the situation, and you can decide what's okay."

With one nod, Angie said, "Okay."

They looked at each other, still holding hands. Jillian said, "So, will you come home?"

Angie swallowed hard, looked out the window at the traffic. When she looked back, she said, "It's not magically better, Jillian. You know that, right?"

"I know that. Believe me, I know that."

More silence.

"Okay," Angie said finally. "Then yes. I'll be home tonight."

Jillian wanted to laugh in delight and clap her hands together in happiness. She wanted to jump up and dance around the Starbucks. She wanted to grab Angie's face across the table and kiss her. Hard. She wanted to do all these things at once. But instead, she kept her cool, grinned, squeezed Angie's hand, and said simply, "Good."

～ ～ ～

Angie knocked softly on the doorjamb to Keith's office. When he looked up from his desk, she asked, "Can I talk to you for a minute?"

"Sure. Come on in. Have a seat."

She did so and closed the door behind her, which caused him to raise an eyebrow.

Keith Muldoon was a big man. At six feet tall with broad shoulders and the build of a defensive tackle, he had a personality to match: big. If you liked him, he was gregarious and commanded your attention. If you didn't like him, he could suck all the air out of the room. His suits were always impeccable, today's a black pinstripe. The jacket was hanging on a coat rack in the corner of his huge office, but his white dress shirt and red tie still looked freshly pressed, even at this late-afternoon hour. Angie had never really liked Muldoon, but over the years, her grudging respect for him had multiplied. The man could sell ice to Eskimos, he was that good. He had no college education, but he was better at his job and made more money at it than a large percentage of the college-educated people she knew, and that was cause for admiration.

Angie sat in one of the two wooden-armed chairs across from Muldoon's desk and placed a closed manila folder in front of her. He sset down his pen, folded his hands on the papers, and gave her his full attention. She took a deep, fortifying breath and plunged in.

"I don't think you're happy here since Jeremy took over."

Muldoon neither confirmed nor denied her statement. He simply waited for her to continue.

"Neither am I. I've been doing a lot of research and a lot of studying."

She told him about all the reading and exploration she'd done over the past months, poured it all out. She told him some of the ideas she'd had for the company, how she'd presented them to Guelli, only to have him turn them over to Jeremy, who'd pretty much taken them on as his own. She talked and talked for what felt like hours. Muldoon sat quietly, listened intently, never interrupting. "The bottom line here, Keith, is that you're the most amazing salesperson I know. We've been in this business for a long time; I don't know that either of us feels like we can change horses this late in the race. However." She stopped, leaned forward with her forearms on his desk, and looked him dead in the eye. "I think we'd make a great team."

Muldoon cocked his head, the first sign at all that his interest was piqued by her words. He looked at her for what felt like a very long while before he made a rolling motion with his hand and sat back more comfortably in his big leather chair. "Tell me more."

Trying to keep her grin tempered, she opened the manila folder and began to outline her idea.

2006

SexyBack

Thirty

Angie and Jillian had spent the last eighteen hours at the hospital while Angie's father underwent a series of tests to pinpoint what might be causing his weird symptoms—lethargy, confusion, slightly slurred speech. Of course, neither Angie nor any of her siblings knew of these symptoms until their mother called them from the emergency room where the doctor had sent them. Angie and her siblings—except for Tony, who was god-knows-where with god-knows-who—had all raced to the hospital from their jobs. Their spouses had all shown up over the next hour or two. The raised voices in the waiting room had stemmed more from worry than anger, though there was some of that too. They were asked to quiet down three times by the staff.

Bottom line: Joe'd had a mild stroke. A very mild stroke. So mild, in fact, that this type almost always went undetected. If it hadn't been for Alice's insistence that they talk to the doctor "just to humor me," as she'd put it, Joe's would also have remained undetected. As it was, no real treatment was forthcoming. Joe had to watch what he ate, keep track of his body, and stay vigilant. They were holding him for the rest of the night and sending him home tomorrow.

"Oh my god, I'm exhausted." Finally home, Angie tossed her keys to the counter and immediately bent into the fridge. "And starving."

"I told you to go with your brother to the cafeteria at the hospital," Jillian scolded, a gentle hand on Angie's back taking away anything sharp in her voice.

Angie stood up, a slice of American cheese in her hand. She tore through the plastic like she hadn't eaten in days. "I know," she said around the first bite.

237

Jillian shook her head with a grin and gestured to the table with her chin. "Sit down. I'll make grilled cheese sandwiches."

Angie did as she was told, then went so far as to make a pillow of her arms and lay her head down on them, watching Jillian as she worked. "Thanks," she said.

Jillian glanced at her, the same grin still on her face. "Welcome."

Angie squinted at the kitchen clock and had trouble registering the actual time.

Jillian slid a plate in front of her. She poured two glasses of milk, and sat down with her own plate.

"I'm so tired it feels like a Herculean effort just to lift this sandwich off the plate," Angie said. The sentence made her chuckle. The chuckle morphed into a weird half-giggle.

Jillian laughed, too. "You're punchy."

"I so am."

"We're going right up to bed as soon as we finish."

"Yes, ma'am."

They ate in silence for several more moments before Angie spoke again.

"It was weird today."

Jillian studied Angie's face, took note of her barely whispered voice. "Yeah? In what way?"

"It was the first time in a long time that I thought, 'Wow, my dad's getting old.' You know? I've never seen him look so small. So frail. My dad's always been this cinder block of a man, not tall, but solid. He could lift anything. Move anything. Fix anything. And today in that hospital bed, he just looked . . . old. Weak and frail and old." Her dark eyes filled with tears as Jillian closed her hand over Angie's.

"It's hard to watch your parents age," Jillian said. Her own father was still healthy, but weaker than he used to be.

"And it's just as hard not to, huh?" Angie added, thinking about Jillian's mother.

With a sad grimace, Jillian agreed. "Yup."

Feeling the need to change the subject, Angie said, "I'm sorry you missed your softball game."

Jillian shrugged. "I'm sure they got along just fine without me. I'd much rather be with you anyway."

Angie squeezed her hand. Pushing her empty plate away, she said, "Let's get some sleep."

𝔞 𝔞 𝔞

They barely stepped out of their clothes before falling into bed and sleeping for almost ten straight hours. When Jillian opened her eyes, sunlight was streaming cheerfully through the blinds and the clock radio said it was 12:45 p.m. A split-second of panic sliced through her before she relaxed. Thank god they'd both had the good sense to call in sick from the hospital today, before they'd had an idea of what was going on and how long they'd be. Instead of springing from the bed and bee-lining to the shower, she snuggled down into the soft bedding, pushed her backside into the solid warmth of Angie's body spooning her from behind, snuggled into the arm stretched out beneath her neck.

Her body ached from being in bed too long, but she was loath to get up, to leave the closeness of her partner.

Her partner.

That's what Angie was. In every way. Sometimes, when Jillian stopped to think how badly she'd messed up last year, how close she'd come to throwing it all away, she wanted to kick herself. But it turned out maybe that old saying was true: *everything happens for a reason.* She'd never believed it before, had always thought of the line as some sort of spiritual bunk that people used for situations they couldn't control or explain. You got laid off from your job of twenty years: everything happens for a reason. A drunk driver causes an accident that kills somebody else, but he walks away without a scratch: everything happens for a reason. The guilty murderer is found not guilty: everything happens for a reason. *Oh, please,* she always thought. *What a load of bullshit.*

The past year had caused her to look at things differently, though, and she realized that if she hadn't wandered down the wrong path when she did, if the mess with Lindsey had never happened, then she and Angie would never have talked about the state of their relationship, about what each of them was feeling, what each of them was missing, what each of them wanted. And things wouldn't have ended up the way they were now.

They were stronger. Solid. Sure.

It hadn't been easy. It had been a slow process that had taken months. They went to therapy, individually and together. Angie had been understandably reserved for a long time. She was gun-shy, and she didn't fully trust Jillian. Jillian knew that, understood it, but still found it almost unbearably hurtful. Angie had spent her first couple of weeks back home in the guest bed, not yet ready to share such close quarters with the person who'd sliced her so deeply. Again, Jillian understood. That didn't keep her from crying herself to sleep most nights.

Eating crow was exhausting.

Jillian smiled now as she thought about that. She'd been determined to eat as much as necessary to get her life back. Thank god Angie wasn't the kind of person who would enjoy torturing her. She didn't take pleasure in holding Jillian's mistake over her head. In fact, she seemed almost uncomfortable during those times when her lack of trust hung over them, especially since she told Jillian she accepted some of the blame for running their relationship off the rails. They dealt with those painful moments as best they could, and finally—unexpectedly—things changed. Angie came into the bedroom one night with a magazine and said simply, "I miss sleeping with you. Can I come in?"

Jillian had looked up from her book, blinked once, and thrown back the covers to let Angie in. Then they'd each gone back to reading, deliberately casual, Jillian trying not to let the enormous grin cover her entire face.

Another two months went by before they made love for the first time.

It was tentative at best, each of them exploring one another as if they'd never been together before. They started slowly with hesitant kisses that took long moments to deepen. They moved slowly, seemingly almost afraid to touch each other's bodies. But they paid attention to one another, actually *talked* as they moved, were surprised when they found their groove. With blessed release, Jillian's orgasm also brought an onslaught of tears, of apologies, of *I love you*s. Angie's eyes were not dry, and she held onto Jillian as if she'd never let go. And it was that grip, that embrace much more so than the climax itself that made Jillian certain they were going to be okay.

There's a difference between sex and intimacy, she remembered saying to Angie. But she understood that they were not mutually exclusive, either.

To Angie's credit, she made more effort, paid more attention to Jillian's sexual needs. It wasn't something they'd ever worried about in the past, but Jillian knew that was exactly why they'd ended up in the pickle they had. Angie's libido was not as strong as Jillian's. It never had been, and it never would be, and that was okay. They talked about it; that was the difference. Instead of making a move, getting rebuffed, and resenting it, Jillian actually *talked* to Angie. They set up date nights. They planned to have sex. No, it wasn't necessarily romantic, but it worked. It kept them connected in a way that they wouldn't be if they continued to neglect the sexual aspect of their relationship. And the open communication meant they enjoyed it more, which surprised them both.

Now Angie stirred behind her. Jillian felt her slowly wake up, gauged the change in her breathing. The arm draped over Jillian's side shifted as Angie's hand snaked up and closed gently over Jillian's bare breast, pulling her body back more tightly against Angie's. Warm lips moved across the side of her neck, nuzzled her ear as Angie's fingers toyed with a nipple.

Jillian's body went from zero to sixty in mere seconds, another strange side effect of their reconnection. It took almost nothing for Angie to turn her on. Not that she'd ever been difficult, but she felt like a teenager again. All Angie had to do was give her a certain look and Jillian's underwear dampened in anticipation. Now she moved to turn onto her back, but Angie held fast.

"No, stay," she whispered in Jillian's ear. "Just like this." She continued her mouth's assault on Jillian's neck, ear, shoulder. The arm under Jillian's neck shifted, and that hand took over with Jillian's breasts, kneading and pumping, while Angie's other hand slid slowly down her torso, over her stomach, and into the thatch of hair at the apex of Jillian's thighs.

Both women were already breathing raggedly, and Jillian was once again amazed at how quickly they were ready for one another. Without preamble, Angie's fingers slicked through Jillian's wetness, gently yet firmly, pressing and stroking in exactly the right way.

"You're so sexy," Angie said in her ear, causing Jillian to gasp a breath and do what she could to separate her legs and give Angie better access. "So sexy and so beautiful and so *mine*."

The possessiveness was also new, and hot, and it only served to push Jillian's arousal higher as she reached behind her to clamp her hand around the nape of Angie's neck. Then Jillian's climax overtook her and forced a strained groan from her throat, every muscle in her body seeming to pull taut like an overstretched rubber band. She gripped Angie's hair and rode out the orgasm, came down slowly, laid her hand over Angie's between her legs to stop her movements.

"Oh my god," she said softly a few moments later as they lay recovering, Angie placing tender kisses on Jillian's temple. "I think my bones have disappeared." Angie chuckled against her hair. Jillian turned her head to look into Angie's dark eyes. "I love you," she said.

"I love you, too."

They lay together for a long while, dozing. Angie checked her cell phone every so often, both of them figuring no news was good news, wanting to let Alice and Joe get home and settled before dropping by.

"Keith and I have decided on the first of the month."

Angie's voice sounded loud in the quiet of the bedroom. Jillian turned to see her face. She knew Angie'd been ready to leave Logo Promo for months now, and worried as she was about this new venture, she was also thrilled. Angie and Keith were going to start their own company, just the two of them. He would be the sales whiz, she would take care of the business end of things. They'd been ready to make the move for a long time, and Jillian was starting to worry the change was too daunting for Angie. After all, she'd been at the same company for nearly twenty years. This kind of a move wouldn't be easy for her.

"That's fantastic, honey. Really." She squeezed the hand she held. "I'm very proud of you."

"I think we'll be okay," Angie said, something she'd said over and over again. "I will take as many of my clients with me as I can, but

Jeremy will have his people fight me for them. Keith's people will most likely stay with him. I don't foresee a problem with that."

Jillian nodded dutifully. She'd heard all of this before, but knew for some reason that Angie needed to talk it all out, process it out loud.

"I probably won't make as much."

"But you'll be less stressed out," Jillian highlighted, just as she had the past three or four times they'd had this conversation. "You'll be home more. We'll be able to do more things together. You've wanted to manage for years now. This is your chance. You'll be happier."

At that last word, Angie looked at her. And smiled widely. "I'm already happier."

With joyous laughter, Jillian rolled on top of her, kissing her soundly. Pulling back, she looked Angie in the face and asked, "How do you suddenly know exactly the right thing to say?" As Angie searched for an answer, Jillian trailed her warm, wet tongue down Angie's neck, her chest, stopped to lavish attention on each breast before continuing south.

Any words she'd come up with had died on Angie's lips.

2011

Raise Your Glass

Thirty-One

Angie was wired.

It was going on 10 p.m., and she and Jillian were usually pretty close to fast asleep by now, given that they got up at 5:30 in the morning, but right now, sleep was the furthest thing from Angie's mind. She sat up in bed. The lights were off, as Jillian was on her side facing away from Angie, dozing. Tango, their two-year-old terrier mix, was curled up between Jillian's feet, and Angie was once again amazed by how animals gravitated to her. Tango loved Angie—and *loved* Jillian.

The TV was on, the volume low. Angie's laptop was in her lap as she toggled between Facebook, Twitter, and various news sites. Her smartphone was next to her hip, texts coming in regularly from different friends who were doing the same thing she was.

It was June 24. The nighttime summer air was warm and comfortable, the window near the bed wide open to let it in.

On the television, New York state senators took turns giving their opinions on the pros and cons of legalizing gay marriage.

Angie's heart was thumping in her chest. Her adrenaline felt like it was whipping through her veins. She was excited. She was nervous.

Never a person who was politically active, Angie was caught up in this particular debate. She very distinctly remembered watching the debate the last time it was up in the Senate. 2009. The middle of the day. Angie had been at work and tuned it in on her computer just to see how the process worked, not at all expecting the legislation to pass. She watched the impassioned pleas of the supporters, and they touched her. She listened to those against, and her stomach turned as

247

she felt belittled and insulted. And when the proposal was defeated, she sat in her office and cried, her tears taking her totally by surprise, as did her indignation, her anger, and her hurt.

This time felt different, though uncharacteristic superstition forced her not to be too optimistic.

It was a Friday night. Work had been wonderful—she'd hired a new salesperson in whom she had a boatload of confidence, and overall sales were up nearly fifty percent overall from this time last year. They now had three salespeople including Keith, who was so much happier than he had been that he'd actually turned into a really nice guy. He and his wife, Gina, invited Angie and Jillian over for dinner and drinks at least once a month. How weird it was to go from despising somebody to considering them a close friend. Life was strange.

Today had also been Jillian's last day of school before summer, and her entire week had been brutal. She was both excited and exhausted, thus her gentle snoring coming from the other side of the bed.

Many of Angie's friends were watching the Senate, too, many of them straight, and that warmed her from the inside. Hope kept texting her opinion on each of the senators.

Wow, how does Diaz sleep at night with all that hate inside?

A good question, to be sure.

Facebook was slow in refreshing, as it seemed everybody and their brother was on and posting. The comments were constant, and Angie felt a weird camaraderie with people she'd never met as she scrolled down the page on her laptop, knowing they were all watching with her. She noticed a comment from Shay. Keeping track through Facebook was about all the contact they'd had over the past few years, and Angie felt a familiar pang of sympathy for Jillian.

It had been a mistake telling Shay exactly what the two of them had been going through, and why. She had not taken it well. Not surprisingly, perhaps: She saw Jillian as a cheater, no better than Laura had been to her. And somehow she had never been able to get past it. Apparently, she preferred to give up more than two decades of friendship. On more than one occasion, Angie had wanted to talk to Shay about it—really, if Angie had forgiven Jillian, why couldn't Shay?—but Jillian had made her promise not to. Angie wondered if

Shay's anger stemmed from the fact that Angie and Jillian were still together while Laura had left without a backward glance—and was still with Kerry, the woman she'd left her for.

Jillian's pain at the loss of her friend was subtle, but obvious to Angie. Angie wanted to help alleviate it, but Jillian wouldn't allow it. Maybe it was one of the ways she chose to punish herself for having strayed. Angie left it alone.

Somebody's "OMG" on Facebook made her glance up at the TV. A Republican from Buffalo was talking, and Angie grabbed the remote and increased the volume so she could hear. As she listened, an "Oh my god" of her own slipped out. Jillian stirred next to her. Tango lifted his head.

"What's the matter?" Jillian asked, her voice rough with sleep. A smile touched her eyes as she took in Angie surrounded by her electronics. "You are so cute, you know that?"

"Babe, this might actually pass."

"Really?" Jillian glanced at the TV, not an easy feat from her flat position. "Who's that?" She pawed at the nightstand for her glasses—the newest accessory of her forties—and slipped them on.

Angie grinned at her. "Those things are so damn sexy."

Jillian's blush was visible even by only the television light, and she pushed playfully at Angie. "Seriously. Who is that?"

"That's Mark Grisanti. He's a Republican from Buffalo. He went into this against, but that's not what he's saying now."

They listened in astonishment as Senator Grisanti said that as a Catholic he was against redefining marriage, but that as a lawyer, he could not justify denying gay couples the rights to which they were entitled.

"Holy shit," Angie muttered, floored that somebody had actually followed the *you can't use your religion to make a law* rule. Grisanti had gone into this debate as a firm "no," but instead had voted "yes." The balance had shifted. The senators knew it, the gentle hum of the room picking up a notch. "This might actually pass," she said again.

With a nod, Jillian removed her glasses, rested her head back on her pillow and closed her eyes. She was beat, Angie knew, studying her face for a moment. Jillian hated being in her forties. Despised it.

But though her smooth skin did show some slight aging—crow's feet at the corners of her eyes, smile lines like parentheses surrounding her mouth—her face was every bit as beautiful as the day Angie had first seen her on that softball field so many years ago. Her blonde hair wasn't as shiny as it used to be, a bit of gray infiltrated here and there. The shape of her body had altered slightly; she hadn't put on weight, but things had shifted. She now had some extra belly that drove her absolutely insane. But Angie loved it. "It just means that our plans to grow old together are still in place," she told her over and over. Jillian continued to complain, but the ghost of a grin every time Angie used that line meant that it was worth it. Not a day went by now that Angie didn't tell Jillian she was beautiful or attractive or downright sexy. She'd learned that, petty as it might seem to some, Jillian was a person who needed that reassurance from the person who loved her most. It messed with her head if she was uncertain of her attraction. Rather than fight it or try to explain to her how silly her worry was, Angie had learned to accept it and do what it took to make Jillian happy.

It wasn't all that much to ask for, really. It was a ridiculously easy fix that Angie wished she'd started a long time ago.

They'd been together for twenty-two years.

Twenty-two years.

Angie could hardly believe it when she stopped to think about it. They'd faced bumps. Hell, they'd faced near-mountains—and scaled them. They'd loved. They'd lost. They'd fought. They'd hurt each other deeply. They'd pulled each other up from the depths of despair. And still, when all was said and done, there was nobody in the world Angie would rather have by her side, and there was no other thought in her head that was clearer than that one. Jillian was her destiny, and she was Jillian's. Their futures were inexorably entangled. They were *supposed* to be together. Jillian had said it back then in Starbucks when they did their best to bridge a rift that had seemed like a chasm, almost too big to fix—and she'd been right. They were supposed to be together. Always.

Was it corny?

Yeah, a little bit.

Did Angie believe it?

Yes.

With every fiber of her being, yes.

Her phone beeped. A text from Hope.

Here we go. Fingers crossed.

The senators were voting.

Another beep. This one from her sister, Maria. *I can't watch!*

Angie smiled, lost count of the votes, held her breath as goose bumps broke out across her skin. "This is it, babe," she said quietly, unsure if Jillian heard her.

The final count: 33 for, 29 against.

It had passed.

Angie blinked in disbelief.

It had passed. The Senate erupted in cheers and applause, as did the crowds outside the room. Deputy Governor Bob Duffy grinned widely. The Democratic senators hugged. The people outside the room screamed in joy. The newscasters could barely be heard over the celebration.

"It passed." Angie stared at the television, and unexpected tears filled her eyes. She said it again, louder. "It passed." She turned to Jillian, gave her a little shake. "Jill. Holy shit! It fucking *passed*!"

Jillian's eyes stayed closed, but her lips curled up in a smile. Tango stood up and looked from one of them to the other. Angie grabbed his furry face and planted kisses all over it, much to his annoyance.

Facebook exploded. Angie's smartphone began beeping nonstop, but before she responded to any of it, she threw back the covers and jumped off the bed. Tango followed, wondering what fun game they were playing. That got Jillian's attention enough to make her open her eyes and turn her head on the pillow.

"What are you doing?" she asked.

Angie dropped to her knees in her underwear and T-shirt. "Jillian Marie Clark, will you marry me?"

A beat passed. Jillian contemplated the ceiling. "Wow. Hmm. I don't know. This is all kind of sudden." Angie hit her in the face with a pillow, and Jillian burst into laughter.

Tango jumped back onto the bed, walked right up and stood on Jillian's chest. Jillian held his face and looked into his sweet brown eyes. When she spoke, it was a quiet whisper, as if it was just the two of them in the room sharing a secret that Angie couldn't hear. "Mommy has asked me to marry her. What should I say? What should I say?" Another beat. Jillian turned to Angie and grinned. "Tango thinks I should say yes."

"Smart dog. And what do you think?" Angie asked, still on her knees.

"I think there's nobody else in the world I'd rather spend another twenty-two years with. And then more. Yes. I would love to marry you."

Angie's heart felt as though it might burst from the emotion. She jumped back onto the bed and scooted next to the dog so they both peered down into Jillian's face. Angie looked deep into her eyes—which were wet—and they stayed that way. As a tear spilled over and dropped from Angie's cheek to Jillian's, she said simply, "I love you."

Jillian brushed Angie's hair away from her face, sifted the strands through her fingers. "I love you, too."

About the Author

Georgia Beers is a Lambda and Goldie award-winning author of lesbian fiction. Born and raised in Rochester, New York, she still lives there with her partner of twenty years, their two dogs and a cat. When not writing, she watches too much TV, reads voraciously, and invents new reasons not to work out. She is currently hard at work on her eleventh book. You can visit her and find out more at www.georgiabeers.com.

Acknowledgments

I'm not ashamed to admit that this was a tough one. Make no mistake, spanning nearly a quarter of a century with the same two characters is an exercise in patience and self-discipline, but I am very proud of the end result, and I couldn't have produced it without the help of some very important people.

My editors, Kelly, Caroline, and Jess. I have admittedly cursed each of you at one time or another, but ultimately, you had the book's best interest in mind, and your suggestions were logical and creative at the same time. Thanks for your hard work in making this a better story.

My writing support system, including my writing group at home in Rochester, as well as my writer and non-writer friends who are always a mere keystroke away. Writing is very solitary, and even people like me who enjoy solitude can find themselves in need of a little reassurance from others. When I was frustrated, angry, or all tapped out of creative energy and ready to pitch my computer out the window, I could send a note off to Steff or Rachel or Melissa or Nikki, and they were there for me. You guys kept me going, kept me positive, kept me writing. For that, I am eternally grateful.

My wonderful wife Bonnie. I would never have begun to even think I could write a story about a couple who's been together for over twenty years without having experienced it myself. 2014 marks our twentieth year together (!), and there is nobody on this earth I can imagine having by my side through the good and the bad, the bumps and the smooth sailing, the gains and the losses. You are my love, and I am incredibly lucky to have you. Heart (aka Boobs with a Hat On).

Lastly, my readers. For several years, I have received e-mails and requests from dozens and dozens of readers asking me when I would write a romance featuring a long-term couple. It was a unique idea, albeit a bit daunting, and I rolled it around for quite some time before an idea struck. You are holding in your hands the result of your wishes. Thank you so much for all of your encouragement and support. This one's for you.

Bywater Books

FINDING THE GRAIN

Wynn Malone

The tornado that ripped through Blue Riley's family farm tore her teenage life apart, killing her parents in her last month of high school, forcing her to abandon her home in Alabama and face an uncertain future.

But the support of her aunt, the excitement of college, and an unexpected love help her through her grief. Then disaster strikes again.

This time Blue casts herself adrift. For nearly twenty years she moves from town to town, job to job, woman to woman until at last she rediscovers the farming life that shaped her. Working with her hands reveals her true passion and finally Blue finds peace. Until the day her past walks through the door.

Wynn Malone paints a richly textured portrait of the South while Blue's search for love and meaning amid the ruins of her life reminds us of the hard choices we all have to make.

Print ISBN 978-1-61294-045-8
Ebook ISBN 978-1-61294-046-5

Bywater Books

LAST CHANCE AT THE LOST AND FOUND

Marcia Finical

In 1972 Bunny LaRue was young and beautiful. Days in the sun on the beach at Malibu and nights in the bars with the girls. Sex, drugs, and fun were everywhere and Bunny embraced it all.

After a photographer sees her on the beach Bunny finds herself making big money modeling for a lingerie catalog. Then she falls in love and life seems to be giving her everything she has ever wanted—until the day she loses it all.

As they years slip by life doesn't stay easy and Bunny must find the strength to confront her past and create a new future . . .

Last Chance at the Lost and Found is the compelling story of one woman's journey through twenty-five yeras of living as a lesbian and her determination to find love and happiness.

Print ISBN 978-1-932859-28-7
Ebook ISBN 978-1-932859-81-2

Bywater Books

UNDER THE WITNESS TREE

Marianne K. Martin

Civil War Secrets inspire a present day love story

An aunt she didn't know existed leaves Dhari Weston with a plantation she knows she doesn't want.

Dhari's life is complicated enough without an antebellum albatross around her neck. Complicated enough without the beautiful Erin Hughes and her passion for historical houses, without Nessie Tinker, whose family breathed the smoke of General Sherman's march and who knows the secrets hidden in the ancient walls—secrets that could pull Dhari into their sway and into Erin's arms.

But Dhari's complicated life already has a girlfriend she wants to commit to, a family who needs her to calm the chaos of her mother's turbulent moods and a job that takes the rest of her time.

The last thing she needs are Civil War secrets that won't lie easy and a woman with secrets of her own . . .

Tangled Roots, the prequel to *Under the Witness Tree*, will be available from October 2014.

Print ISBN 978-1-932859-00-3
Ebook ISBN 978-1-932859-94-2

Available at your local bookstore
or call 734-662-8815
or order online at www.bywaterbooks.com

At Bywater Books we love good books about lesbians just like you do, and we're committed to bringing the best of contemporary lesbian writing to our avid readers. Our editorial team is dedicated to finding and developing outstanding writers who create books you won't want to put down.

We sponsor the Bywater Prize for Fiction to help with this quest. Each prize winner receives $1,000 and publication of their novel. We have already discovered amazing writers like Jill Malone, Sally Bellerose, and Hilary Sloin through the Bywater Prize. Which exciting new writer will we find next?

For more information about Bywater Books and the annual Bywater Prize for Fiction, please visit our website.

www.bywaterbooks.com